Luke could see the wariness in Kathleen's eyes, and something else that pulled him nearer.

His fingers grazed her cheek. "You are the strongest woman I've ever met, Kate. Clancy is gone. He'll never hurt you again."

"Never again." She closed her eyes and nodded. She reached up and covered his hand with hers. "Thank you, Luke."

"You're welcome." He turned his hand over and captured hers. He'd never wanted to kiss anyone more, and it was all he could do to keep from pulling her into his arms. But the wariness lingered in her eyes and he leaned his forehead against hers. "If onlys" whirled through his mind… If only she could trust again. If only he could, too.

He cleared his throat. "We'd better go in before—"

"Someone wonders where we are?"

No. Before he threw caution to the wind, pulled her into his arms and kissed her.

Books by Janet Lee Barton

Love Inspired Historical

*Somewhere to Call Home
*A Place of Refuge

*Boardinghouse Betrothals

JANET LEE BARTON

was born in New Mexico and has lived all over the South, in Arkansas, Florida, Louisiana, Mississippi, Oklahoma and Texas. She loves researching and writing heartwarming stories about faith, family, friends and love. Janet loves being able to share her faith and love of the Lord through her writing. She's very happy that the kind of romances the Lord has called her to write can be read and shared with women of all ages.

Janet and her husband now live in Oklahoma, and are part of what they laughingly call their "Generational Living Experiment" with their daughter and her husband, two wonderful granddaughters and a shih tzu called Bella. The experiment has turned into quite an adventure and so far, they think it's working out just fine. When Janet isn't writing or reading, she loves to travel, cook, work in the garden and sew.

You can visit Janet at www.janetleebarton.com.

A Place of Refuge

JANET LEE BARTON

HARLEQUIN® LOVE INSPIRED® HISTORICAL

Recycling programs
for this product may
not exist in your area.

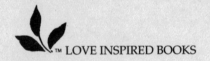

™ LOVE INSPIRED BOOKS

ISBN-13: 978-0-373-82982-8

A PLACE OF REFUGE

www.LoveInspiredBooks.com

Printed in U.S.A.

Cause me to hear thy loving kindness in the morning;
For in thee do I trust: Cause me to know the way
wherein I should walk; For I lift up my soul unto thee.
—*Psalms* 143:8

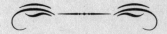

To the family I was born into,
and the one the Lord has given me,
for always giving me their love and support.
And most of all, to my Lord and Savior,
for showing me the way.

Chapter One

New York City
February 1896

A knock on the door this time of evening was never a good sign. Luke Patterson paused at the staircase and frowned, looking around for Mrs. Heaton, the owner of his boardinghouse. Neither she nor Gretchen, the maid, were anywhere to be seen and everyone else had scattered after dinner. The knock sounded once more and he took it on himself to answer the door.

"Sir, I've a young woman in my hack and was told to bring her to this address." The man at the door handed Luke a familiar-looking card. It was one of Mrs. Heaton's, embellished simply with only Heaton House, then the address and telephone number underneath. She often gave the cards to young women she thought might be in need of a safe place to come.

"What is it, Luke?" Mrs. Heaton asked as she hurried out of her study.

"This man has a young woman in his hack. He says

he was told to bring her here." He handed Mrs. Heaton her card.

"Well, tell her to come right in," Mrs. Heaton said.

"She's in bad shape, ma'am. She passed out on the way over. In fact I think she's more in need of the hospital right now than anythin'. My wife's a friend of her sister's and they told me to bring her here, and that's what I've done. They told me you'd given her the card."

Mrs. Heaton's brow furrowed. "I'm sure I did. Luke, please help this young woman in."

"Of course." Luke didn't bother putting a coat on against the cold February night air. He hurried out to the hack alongside the driver. The man grabbed a small carpetbag, helped him get the young woman out of the hack, up to the front door and into the house.

"I've got to get back to the family, sir. I hope she's all right." He dropped the bag on the floor and let go of the woman, leaving her to slump against Luke.

Luke immediately lifted her into his arms as the man hurried out the door. She was light as a feather and when she moaned, he shifted her in his arms, hoping to make her more comfortable.

"Where do you want me to take her, Mrs. Heaton?"

"Let's get her upstairs, so I can see what she needs, Luke. I've had Gretchen call the doctor and let the other women know a man will be in the upper hall."

Male boarders were normally not allowed on the upper floors, but there really wasn't any other way to get this young woman upstairs. She wasn't in any shape to maneuver the steps. As they passed under the light in the foyer, Luke cringed at what he saw. The woman in his arms looked as if she'd had a fist shoved in her face. Several times. And she had a cut on the side of her temple that oozed blood through a makeshift bandage. What had happened to her?

He followed Mrs. Heaton up the stairs to the landing and waited while she turned to go up to the third floor. Then she paused. "No, let's put her in Violet's old room. There's no need to jostle her any more than necessary. I'm sure she's in a lot of pain or she wouldn't have passed out, poor dear."

Mrs. Heaton hurried into the room and lit a lamp before turning back the cover on the bed. "Lay her down easy, Luke. The doctor should be here any moment now."

He did as told and then tried to step back to let Mrs. Heaton see to her. But the young woman held on to his hand and wouldn't let go.

"Pull up a chair, at least until the doctor gets here. For right now it appears she doesn't want you to go anywhere," Mrs. Heaton said.

Luke grasped the chair by the side table with his free hand and pulled it a little closer, sat down and clasped the young woman's hand with both of his. If he could convey that she was safe, he'd sit there all night. "Do you have any idea who she is?"

From the other side of the bed, Mrs. Heaton lowered the hood of the woman's cape and looked down on her. Luke could hear her sharp intake of breath. "It's hard to tell with her face so bruised and swollen, but with that red hair of hers, I do believe she's the young woman we met in the park last summer—the one you'd helped defend."

Luke leaned closer. The young woman's hair cascaded over the pillow and his heart gave a sharp twist at her moan. Its deep red color told him she might well be the woman in the park. Aside from the fresh bruising and swelling, he could see a fading bruise under her left eye—apparently she got beaten up on a regular basis. His fist clenched at the very thought of anyone treating a woman that way. And if she was the same woman from last summer, he had a good idea who did it.

Footsteps sounded on the stairs and Gretchen and another woman, whom he recognized as one who came to some of the benevolent committee meetings Mrs. Heaton often hosted, entered the room. She was probably a member of the Ladies' Aide Society as was Mrs. Heaton, but he wasn't certain.

"Clara! What brings you—"

"Kathleen's sister contacted me and let me know she'd sent her to you. I've been afraid something like this might happen."

"Kathleen? Is that her name? How do you know her?" Mrs. Heaton asked.

In what Luke thought was an effort not to disturb the injured woman, his landlady led Clara over to the windows. But in the quiet of the night, he could still hear what was being said.

The woman Mrs. Heaton had introduced as Clara Driscoll lowered her voice. "She works in my department at Tiffany Glass Company and yes, her name is Kathleen O'Bryan. Evidently her brother-in-law lost his job *again* and came home drunk today. When Kathleen got there, she found them in the middle of a fight and she tried to stop him from hitting her sister. That's when he came at her, hit her and knocked her down and hit her again. He left saying she'd better be gone when he came back."

White-hot anger surged through Luke as the young woman moaned. How dare the man touch her! He—

The doctor arrived just then and Mrs. Heaton turned to Luke. "Why don't you wait downstairs, Luke? I'll let you know what the doctor says and how Miss O'Bryan is doing in a little while. Thank you for helping me get her upstairs."

"You're welcome." Luke tried to slip his hand out of the young woman's, but she held on tighter. Her eyes fluttered open and she hoarsely whispered, "Thank you."

He leaned close and whispered, "You're welcome. And you're safe here. Doc and Mrs. Heaton are going to take care of you now."

Only then did she let go of his hand. He watched her eyelashes drift downward and turned to leave as the doctor took his place.

Luke cringed as he heard a louder moan this time and he fought the urge to rush back to her side. But the doc was the one who could make her feel better now. He'd only be in the way.

"Please do let me know how she is, Mrs. Heaton."

She gave a short nod. "I will."

Luke's heart twisted in his chest as he hurried down the stairs to the main floor and then down the next flight to the first floor where he and the other male boarders' rooms were. He'd try to get some work done—at least a scene or two on the book he was writing. Otherwise he'd only pace the floor waiting for Mrs. Heaton to let him know how Miss O'Bryan was.

He flipped through a few typewritten pages to get back into his writing, but in only moments Luke realized he wouldn't get any work done this far away from what was going on upstairs.

He gathered a tablet and pencil and went back upstairs and settled at Mrs. Heaton's desk. He knew she wouldn't mind; she'd offered to let him work in here before. Maybe he could at least make a few notes about his next chapter. Luke tried to concentrate on what he was writing but the connection to it and the woman upstairs was so apparent he couldn't concentrate on anything but her.

If not for meeting Miss O'Bryan that day in the park, he might not even be writing this book. Her name fit her well, or at least the woman he remembered from that day in the park last summer, when her brother-in-law was threatening both her and her sister.

She'd shown such dignity that day, but the look in her eyes told him how vulnerable she really was. Ever since that encounter, he hadn't been able to get her out of his mind and every time he caught a glimpse of hair the color of hers, he took a second look—at the park, on a trolley, in the tenements, when he'd gone on an assignment from his boss, Michael Heaton. Michael was Mrs. Heaton's son and owned his own detective agency. Until his marriage this past December, he'd lived here, too.

Michael felt he had reason to believe that his sister who'd been missing for several years might have wound up living in the tenements. He didn't want his mother to know of his fears, but he'd confided in Luke that he'd almost given up hope of finding her at all.

It was the traveling in and out of the tenements that had precipitated the change in his writing career. He liked writing the lighter dime novels that made him a living, along with occasional investigative work for Michael, but over the past few months, his goal had changed. He wanted to make a difference in people's lives with his writing. What he was working on now was a book that depicted life for those less fortunate in the city, and Luke hoped it would continue to call attention to their plight as Jacob Riis had done with his book, *How the Other Half Lives*.

Tonight he realized the woman upstairs had everything to do with the direction his writing had gone in— because of the way she and her sister had been treated that day in the park. The conditions he was afraid they lived in. And seeing her tonight—

"Luke?" Mrs. Heaton broke into his thoughts.

He jumped to his feet and came around the desk. "Yes, ma'am? How is she?"

"The doctor says Kathleen is going to be all right. But he said she's going to be in some pain for the next few days. He thinks she may have cracked a rib, too. Clara is giving her this week off and we're going to try to find out how best to help her. She'll be staying with us for now."

"That's good, I'm glad." Relief washed over him, knowing she'd be here. He couldn't explain the strange connection he felt for the young woman, but it was there and it was strong.

"Evidently her sister's husband has beaten Kathleen several times, probably because she comes to her sister's defense and keeps her from taking the beating," Mrs. Heaton continued. "Clara says Kathleen's sister, Colleen, is expecting a child. However, after tonight, she realized she had to get Kathleen out of there. Colleen was afraid that if she didn't, her husband might hurt Kathleen even worse."

Luke felt his lip curl in disdain for the man. "Kathleen will be safe here. I'll see that she is."

"I know you will. She's awake now and trying to remember what happened and why she's here. Things are slowly coming back to her. I'm going to take a food tray up to her and see if we can get her to eat something. I'll let her know you were asking about her and helped to get her upstairs."

"If you need me for anything at all—"

"Thank you, Luke. I know where to find you and I'm thankful you are here. We're going to take care of her."

Luke watched his landlady leave the room, thankful that she'd given Kathleen her card last summer. The pretty redhead might not know it, but she was in the best place she could be right now.

The vision of Kathleen's face, so lovely under all the swelling and bruising, came to him. He clenched his fist once more and went to look out of the window. He didn't know how long it would take, but he was going to find that no-good brother-in-law of hers. If the man were lucky, the cops would get to him before Luke did.

Kathleen opened one eye and then the other. A sliver of sunlight creeping through the slit in the draperies told her it was morning. The last thing she remembered from the night before was the nice lady... Kathleen closed her eyes and concentrated. Mrs. Heaton. Yes, the woman who'd given her a card last summer and who owned the home she'd been sent to...last night?

She took a deep breath. Why was she having such a hard time putting her thoughts together? Her face, her temple, her whole head ached, but nowhere near as bad as the night before—until she reached up to touch the bandage on her temple. The light contact was enough to make the throb feel like a pounding hammer.

She closed her eyes against the pain and held her breath until it eased off a bit. Then she lay as still as she could until she felt she could open her eyes once more.

Her mind flooded with unconnected memories. She remembered telling her coworkers good-night and leaving work. Money had been especially tight lately, so, though she was tired, Kathleen hadn't given in to the urge to take the trolley. Instead, she'd trudged over to Second Avenue and down to Eighth Street to the tenement building where she lived with her sister and her family. They seemed to have traded one pitiful existence for another since they'd left Ireland two years ago. Believing they'd have a better life in America, they'd pooled what little they had to make the trip, only to find life wasn't any easier here.

She didn't think the dreadful place could ever be home to her or her family. All the buildings in the area seemed the same to Kathleen. They were made of brick, with stoops in front. The six and seven stories housed scores of families, some even larger than hers, crowded in two- and three-room apartments. One had to know the number of the building and where it set on the street to be sure of where they were going.

But last night, as she'd neared their tenement and saw her nephews sitting on the stoop, her heart had dipped into her stomach and she'd felt a little sick. She'd known something wasn't right. Collin and Brody had looked at her with their big blue eyes and she could see they'd been crying. She'd bent and hugged them when they ran to her.

"What's wrong? What's happened?" she'd asked.

Collin had answered, "Papa came home early and started yelling and—"

"He was really loud." Brody wiped a hand across his eyes. "Mama started crying, and he yelled more."

"Mama sent us out."

Kathleen's heart constricted with dread. "Well, now, I'm sure things aren't as bad as you're thinkin'. Your papa does get worked up a bit at times. I'll go see what all the ruckus is about."

She hadn't wanted to take the boys, but—

A knock sounded on the door, bringing her out of her thoughts. The door opened just a crack and she heard a whisper. "Kathleen? It's Mrs. Heaton. Are you awake, dear?"

"Yes, ma'am."

"May I come in?"

"Of course." This was Mrs. Heaton's home after all and she'd opened it to her, a total stranger except for that chance meeting in Central Park last summer.

Mrs. Heaton entered the room and hurried over to her. "Are you still in pain?"

"Some." Kathleen tried to scoot up in bed and grimaced.

"I think a little more than that. Let me give you some of the medicine Doctor Reynolds left for you. Then we'll see if you feel like a cup of tea and maybe some toast."

"Yes, thank you." She opened her mouth as Mrs. Heaton brought a spoonful of medicine to her lips.

Kathleen swallowed the liquid and prayed it would work quickly to ease the pounding in her head.

"You were out again when I brought a tray up last night and I didn't want to wake you. I did check on you several times throughout the night and you seemed to be sleeping."

Mrs. Heaton talked as she straightened Kathleen's covers and pulled back the draperies on one of the windows—just enough to let a bit of light in, but not so much that it bothered Kathleen's eyes.

"Let me look at you." The compassion in the woman's eyes touched Kathleen's heart. She'd been nothing but kind to her. She sighed now and shook her head. "Doc said your bruising might look worse before it gets better. I'm afraid he was right. But don't you worry, you'll be back to your lovely self before you know it."

"Thank you for taking me in and for being so kind."

"You're welcome. I'm glad you kept my card and were brought here. Try not to worry about your sister. Mrs. Driscoll said she would check on her and get word to you on how she and your nephews are."

Kathleen let herself relax a little at Mrs. Heaton's words. Tears sprung to her eyes just thinking about the only family she had left. She tried to remember...why was she here? "I have so many questions about what happened, and I just can't seem to remember. Everything is just so disconnected and yet I feel I've been here before."

"You were. But only for one night last spring."

"I was?" Kathleen tried to remember but couldn't.

"Don't struggle with it, dear."

Kathleen tried not to show how much pain she felt leaning forward while Mrs. Heaton plumped her pillow and added another to prop her up. She bit her bottom lip as the woman eased her back onto the pillows.

"Doctor Reynolds said you might not remember everything right away but he thinks your memories will all come back to you in time. He said it was a good sign that you knew your name and Mrs. Driscoll's, and where you work."

"Work. I…" Kathleen furrowed her brow and looked at Mrs. Heaton.

"Mrs. Driscoll said not to worry about coming in today. She gave you the rest of the week off and said she would be back today to see how you are."

Kathleen released a relieved sigh. *Thank you, Lord.*

Another knock came on the door and Mrs. Heaton went to answer it. "It's Gretchen, I'm sure. I asked her to bring a tray up."

A woman dressed in a maid's uniform came into the room. She appeared to be around Kathleen's age of twenty-four. Her hair was blond and curly and her eyes were light blue.

"Put the tray on the dresser, please, Gretchen."

"Yes, ma'am." She turned to Kathleen and said, "I hope you feel better today, miss."

"Thank you," Kathleen said.

"If you need anything more just let me know, Mrs. Heaton."

"Thank you, Gretchen." The maid left the room quietly and Mrs. Heaton turned to Kathleen.

"Perhaps, after you've had some tea and toast, Gretchen and I can help you to the bathroom so you can freshen up. That might make you feel better."

The thought sounded wonderful to Kathleen. "That would be nice."

"Well, then, lets get some tea in you. One or two teaspoons of sugar?"

"Two, please." The pain medication seemed to be working, for the pounding in her head had eased to a lesser throb. Mrs. Heaton placed the tray in front of her and Kathleen picked up the teacup and took a sip.

"By the time you finish, Gretchen and I will be back to help you—"

"Mrs. Heaton, I don't know how to thank you for everything."

"You've already thanked me, dear. Just let yourself heal and know that you are safe here."

Kathleen managed a small nod.

"Are you up to a little more light, dear?"

"I believe so."

Mrs. Heaton opened the draperies fully on both windows and sunlight flooded the room, but it didn't bother Kathleen's eyes. She liked the way the light filtered through the lace panels behind the drapes.

"I'll be back in a bit," Mrs. Heaton said. She hurried off and Kathleen took another sip of her tea.

Only then did she really see the room she was in. It was huge—and more than just a bedroom. Decorated with lavender-and-yellow wallpaper and bed coverings of the same colors, the room was beautiful.

There was a comfortable-looking chair in the corner between the bed and a window. And there was even a small sofa in front of a fireplace. An armoire that matched the headboard of the bed was on the other side of the room. She'd never seen anything this nice in her life and wished Colleen could see it.

Tears gathered in her eyes once more at the thought of her sister and nephews. *Dear Lord, please keep them safe. And please help me to remember all that happened to bring me here. In Jesus's name, I pray. Amen.*

Kathleen couldn't remember when she'd eaten last, and even though she didn't feel hungry, her rumbling stomach told her she was. She picked up a piece of toast and took a bite. By the time Mrs. Heaton returned, she'd managed one slice and had finished her tea.

"Oh, good. I'm glad you got something down. Gretchen is coming, and we're going to help you to the bathroom. You'll be sharing it with Elizabeth. She's at work now, but you'll meet her this evening."

Kathleen wasn't sure she was ready to meet anyone else, but she didn't have the inclination or the energy to argue with this woman who'd done so much for her.

Gretchen came in just then and the two women helped her into a bathroom that was just off her room. She couldn't believe the size of it. She and her sister's family had to share a bathroom with the other tenants on their floor. This was so clean and large compared to that one—and she was to share it with only one other person? A room almost as large as their apartment and a bathroom connected to it? Such luxury was too much to take in.

By the time Mrs. Heaton and Gretchen had helped her into a fresh gown and back to bed, she was quite drowsy.

"I can't believe I'm sleepy again," Kathleen said as Mrs. Heaton plumped her pillow once more.

"I'm afraid I tired you out with all my talking earlier, dear."

"Oh, no. I'm sure it's the medicine."

"Could be. But the doctor said rest was the best for

you right now. You let yourself sleep whenever you can. I'll go let Luke know how you are doing today."

"Luke?"

"Luke Patterson. He helped me get you upstairs last night. He's the young man who came to your defense that day in the park last summer."

Memories crept in. Of strong arms picking her up and holding her close, of not wanting to let go of his hand. They came to her now, as did that day in the park when the handsome man had tried to help her and Colleen. They were one and the same? "He lives here?"

"Yes, he does. And I know he was quite worried about you last night. You wouldn't let go of his hand for the longest time. I must let him know you are on the mend. I'll be back with some lunch a little later. You get some rest now." Mrs. Heaton slipped out the bedroom door.

Kathleen leaned back against the pillows and released a pent-up breath. The hammering she had felt no longer pounded in her head, but in her chest. Luke Patterson. The man who'd become her hero in one brief encounter and whom she'd dreamed about several times since then had a name. And he lived here.

Kathleen's memories were so jumbled in with her dreams and nightmares of the night before, she wasn't sure what was real and what wasn't. But evidently, hearing that deep, husky voice she'd become familiar with in her dreams and the comforting feeling of being lifted and carried gently in a pair of strong arms hadn't been a dream at all.

"Man in the hall," Mrs. Heaton called as she led Luke up the stairs. She'd finally given in to his wish to see how Kathleen was doing for himself, although it'd taken a lot of persuasion to get her to agree.

Luke heard several doors slam as they reached the landing and he was sure the women weren't thrilled with his invasion into their domain. He looked straight ahead as he followed Mrs. Heaton to the room she'd given Miss O'Bryan.

He waited as his landlady knocked on the door. "Kathleen, dear, it's Mrs. Heaton. May I come in? I've brought you supper."

"Yes, ma'am. Of course you may," Kathleen answered.

Luke opened the door for his landlady and stood to the side while she entered. She turned to him. "You stay right here until I see if she's up to seeing you."

"Yes, ma'am." Luke hoped that she was, for he wouldn't barge in on his own, but he felt the need to see her, to hear her voice, to make sure she was all right.

It was but a few minutes before Mrs. Heaton returned. "You may see Miss O'Bryan, but not for long. She's still recovering, you know."

Luke nodded and entered the room with Mrs. Heaton right behind him as decorum demanded. Kathleen was propped up against a pile of pillows, covers pulled up to her neck. As he got closer he could see the bruising was still evident, maybe even worse than the night before, but her coloring seemed much better.

"This is Luke Patterson, Kathleen. He's not let me rest until I finally said he could come see for himself that you are improving. He's the young man we talked about earlier."

"Yes, I remember."

She looked up at him and for a moment Luke felt he might drown in the deep ocean blue-green of her eyes.

"Thank you so much for coming to my aid that day in the park and again last night."

"You're more than welcome, Miss O'Bryan. You look… I…" Luke was at a loss for words. He couldn't say she looked wonderful, for she still looked battered and bruised. "Ah, better."

"It's all right, Mr. Patterson. I know how I look. But rest assured, I'll recover and be the stronger for it all."

The lilting sound of her Irish accent made him smile. "I can see that by the glint in your eyes and I'm glad for your attitude. You were brought to the right place. Mrs. Heaton is going to take good care of you."

"She already has been," Miss O'Bryan said.

Luke nodded. "I can see that. I'm sure she'll have you joining us for dinner in no time."

"That's what Mrs. Heaton keeps telling me."

"You'll find that she is rarely wrong. I look forward to seeing you downstairs soon."

"Thank you."

"She'll be joining us soon," Mrs. Heaton said with a smile. "But it's time for you to go, Luke. The girls will be wanting to go down to dinner soon."

"Yes, ma'am." Luke smiled at Miss O'Bryan and gave a little nod. "Good night."

"Good night. Thank you for checking on me."

"You're welcome. Hopefully, you'll feel even better tomorrow." He turned to Mrs. Heaton. "Thank you for letting me see for myself that she is on the mend."

"You're welcome, Luke. Please tell the other men dinner will be served soon."

"Yes, ma'am." He resisted the urge to look at Kathleen once more and headed out the door, releasing a sigh as he headed down the stairs. She was going to be all right. And he was going to see she stayed that way.

Chapter Two

Kathleen leaned a little closer to the mirror. After almost a week her bruises were fading, but not fast enough. Mrs. Heaton had assured her that she only looked as if she'd been sick recently, but was on the mend. Kathleen hoped she was right because she'd agreed to have dinner downstairs with the other boarders tonight. If she was going to stay here, she figured she might as well get to know them.

She picked up the letter from her sister that'd been delivered the day before. While it did give her comfort to have word from Colleen, her heart twisted at the realization that she didn't know when she would be seeing her sister or her nephews again.

Kathleen sighed and reread the words once more.

Dear Kathleen,
Mrs. Driscoll has told me that you are healing and in the safest place you could be in this city. It relieves my heart to know that. I don't want you to worry about the boys and me. We are all right. Clancy knows how upset I am about what

he did to you and is trying to make it up to me.
He's found a job, but he is insistent that you not
come back and I feel you are better off away from
here. We can keep in touch through Mrs. Walsh.
Just use her address next door and she'll get your
letter to me. I'll send mine through her, too.
The boys and I miss you, but one day we'll find a
way to get together again, even if just for a short
while. Until then, take care of yourself and know
that I love you.
Your sister,
Colleen.

Kathleen willed herself not to cry. At least they could keep in touch with letters. That would have to suffice for now.

A light knock sounded on the door of the bathroom and she knew it was Elizabeth Anderson, the young woman with whom she shared the bathroom. Mrs. Heaton had introduced them the second night she was there and Kathleen really liked her.

"Come in."

Elizabeth peeked around the door. "Do you need any help getting ready? It's about time to go down."

"I only need your assurance that I look all right." Her fears diminished when Elizabeth came in wearing a brown skirt and tan shirtwaist, similar to what she had on, only her skirt was blue and her shirtwaist white.

"You look just fine. We don't dress for dinner here except on the weekends. Mrs. Heaton says we work hard and are tired at the end of the day, and she's not going to make us dress up just to eat dinner every night.

And then, when we do dress on the weekends and holidays, dinner feels special."

"I'm afraid I don't have anything any dressier than what I have on now."

"Don't worry. I have a couple of outfits I think will fit you. We're about the same size. Writing for *The Delineator,* I see all the newest styles and sometimes I buy on a whim. But the colors don't always look good on me and I haven't known what to do with them. I think they'll look beautiful on you and I'll be glad to let you have them."

"Oh, Elizabeth—"

"Now, don't try to say no. You'll be doing me a favor. As long as they're taking up room in my closet, I don't feel I can go buy anything new."

Kathleen knew Elizabeth would have made the offer even if the clothing fit her and she loved it all. She'd been so kind from the very beginning; Kathleen felt she had found a real friend in her. "All right. I'll accept and I thank you for your offer."

"I'm glad. I'll get them to you later."

"I'm nervous, Elizabeth. I've never even been in a home as nice as this, let alone had dinner in one. I'm not sure I'll know which fork to use or—"

"Just watch me and do what I do. You'll be fine."

"I really don't belong here."

"You belong here as much as any of us do—perhaps more," Elizabeth said. "Although there are some male boarders living on the first floor, Mrs. Heaton started her boardinghouse primarily for young women, after her daughter, Rebecca, went missing several years ago. And one of her priorities is to open her home to those who have a real need for a safe haven, sometimes for a short while, sometimes as a regular boarder."

"She's been wonderful to me. I'm so sorry to hear about her daughter." Her heart hurt for Mrs. Heaton. She knew what it felt like to be separated from loved ones and not know how they were.

Oh, Mrs. Driscoll had been very good to let her know that she'd checked on Colleen and the boys and that they were all right. But that held true only for that moment and there was no way of knowing what might have happened since the last report.

"It's been very difficult for her, but she carries on and takes care of all she can. I'm glad you kept the card she gave you that day in the park."

"You were there? I don't remember—"

"There's no reason you should. You had your hands full that day. But yes, I was there and so were some of the others. So quit worrying about how they will react to you. They'll be as glad as I am that you kept Mrs. Heaton's card."

She gave Kathleen a quick hug. "Come on, now. I could smell the roast chicken as soon as I came home from work today. You're in for a treat."

They headed out the door to the landing and were met there by another woman.

"Kathleen, this is Julia Olson. She works at Ellis Island and is a good friend."

"I'm pleased to meet you, Kathleen," Julia said. "Mrs. Heaton told us there was a new boarder, and we've been hoping you'd be able to join us for dinner soon."

"Thank you, Julia. It's nice to meet you, too."

Kathleen followed the two girls downstairs, trying

to calm her jittery nerves. Julia had been very nice and if her attitude was any indication of the kind of boarders Mrs. Heaton had, everyone else would be, too. She hoped so, for part of her wanted to run right back to her room and hide, while the other part desperately needed a diversion from worry about her sister and nephews.

Elizabeth led them to what Kathleen thought was the parlor, only it was much grander than any she'd ever seen. She tried not to show how out of place she felt as she took in the fine furnishings. The parlor suites were covered in a burgundy silk, along with several chairs upholstered in a gold-and-burgundy-striped fabric. The draperies were made of the same striped material, making the room look inviting.

There were several very comfortable-looking chairs clustered around a round table in another conversation area in one corner of the room. A piano sat in the opposite corner.

"It's beautiful," Kathleen said.

"It's very comfortable," Elizabeth said. "It's a great place to gather after dinner and we do so quite often."

Kathleen walked around the room looking at the various photographs here and there. There was one of a pretty young woman who reminded her of someone, but try as she might, she couldn't place her.

Male voices were heard in the foyer and Kathleen turned to see three gentlemen enter the parlor.

"Ben, John, come meet Kathleen O'Bryan. Luke, you've met her already," Elizabeth said.

At the mention of Luke's name, Kathleen looked past the two men headed her way and caught her breath as the man who'd come to her rescue walked toward her. He was as handsome as she remembered—if not more so. He hadn't been smiling that day in the park. But now his lips turned up in a smile that had her heart hammering in her chest to each step he took toward her.

"Kathleen, this is Benjamin Roth, a teacher, whom we call just Ben," Elizabeth said, pulling Kathleen's attention to the men standing in front of her. "Ben, this is Kathleen O'Bryan."

"Pleased to meet you, Miss O'Bryan." He had blond hair and blue eyes.

"And this is John Talbot. He's a reporter for the *New-York Tribune*."

"I'm glad you could join us this evening, Miss O'Bryan," the man with hair the color of rust said. His eyes were a cool blue-green.

"I'm pleased to meet you both."

Suddenly Luke appeared behind them, taller and broader than either man, and they seemed to move to the side to make way for him.

"And I believe you've met Luke Patterson," Elizabeth said.

"I have. Good evening, Mr. Patterson," Kathleen said.

Luke held out his hand and Kathleen found herself slipping her own into it. "It's good to see you are finally able to join us for dinner."

His voice was husky and deep just as she remembered and her heart warmed at the sound of it. The others had moved away, giving them a chance to speak in private.

"Mrs. Heaton has refused to let me come up to see you again, but she's been good to let me know you were getting better each day. Still, it's not quite like seeing for myself," he said. "I'm glad you're healing."

But when he reached out and touched her chin, it took her by surprise and she flinched. Instead of this man, she saw Clancy coming at her for the second time that night he'd beaten her and her hand went up to protect herself.

"I'm sorry, Miss O'Bryan," he said. "I should have known—"

His words brought her back to the present and she shook her head. "No. I'm sorry, Mr. Patterson. I just… remembered Clancy coming at me with his fist raised and—"

"I shouldn't have—"

"No, it's all right. Thank you for your concern, Mr. Patterson. And thank you for helping me the other night and—"

"Oh, good, it looks as if you've all met Kathleen. I'm glad," Mrs. Heaton said, coming into the room. "I came to let you all know that dinner is ready. Luke, will you escort Kathleen into the dining room? And Ben, would you escort me?"

"I'd be delighted to," Ben said.

"Miss O'Bryan?" Luke crooked his elbow and looked down at Kathleen.

She wasn't used to gentlemanly actions and wasn't totally sure what she should do, until she saw Mrs. Heaton glide her arm through Ben's arm. Kathleen mimicked what the older woman did, slipping her hand through Luke's crooked arm and resting it on his forearm.

They followed Mrs. Heaton and Ben and left John Talbot to escort both Elizabeth and Julia to the table. Once Luke had seated her and taken the seat to her left, she breathed a sigh of relief that she'd managed not to embarrass herself.

She was glad Elizabeth was sitting across from her so that she could see what fork and spoon to use. Why anyone would need so many utensils to eat one meal was beyond her. At home they only used what was needed, a spoon for soup or porridge, a fork for everything else and a knife only when needed.

"John, will you say the blessing, please?" Mrs. Heaton asked as soon as everyone was seated.

"Certainly." He bowed his head and Kathleen bowed hers along with the others.

"Dear Lord, we thank You for this day, we thank You that Miss O'Bryan is well enough to join us and we thank You for the food we are about to eat. Please help us to do Your will. Amen."

Kathleen was touched that he'd included her in his prayer and her heart filled with thanksgiving that she'd wound up in this home.

Gretchen and Maida, her twin sister who'd greatly confused Kathleen the first few days when they would come into her room, began to serve the meal of roast chicken, creamed potatoes, peas with baby onions and piping-hot rolls.

Kathleen thought this kind of meal was served only in fancy restaurants, the kind she could never afford. For a moment she wondered what Colleen and the boys were eating and swallowed hard. It didn't seem right that she should be treated so well when her sister was stuck in such horrible circumstances.

"Miss O'Bryan? Are you feeling all right?" Luke asked.

"I— Oh, I'm sorry. I'm fine. I was just thinking

about my family and wondering…" She shook her head. "I'm fine, really."

She glanced over to see that Elizabeth had used the large fork, and picked up her own. She took a bite of potatoes and tried not to embarrass herself as she gave her attention to the meal.

Elizabeth smiled across the table at her. "We've been thinking about going to the Metropolitan Museum of Art tomorrow. Would you like to go with us?"

"Oh, I don't know, I—"

"It will do you good to get out in the fresh air for a bit, Kathleen. If you are feeling up to it, that is," Mrs. Heaton said.

Kathleen had never been to the museum. Some of the girls she worked with had talked about going, but she'd never had the opportunity to go. She was curious to see all the museum held, and it would give her something to do. Her room was lovely but she was beginning to feel a bit confined. Now that her face was looking more normal she wouldn't feel self-conscious about being out in public. "You're right. It would do me good. I'd be glad to join you, Elizabeth. Thank you for inviting me."

"So we're all going?" Elizabeth asked.

"I'd like to," Luke said.

"Count me in," Julia said.

"John and I were the ones who first brought it up, so we're going," Ben added.

"Well, I'm going to visit Michael and Violet," Mrs. Heaton said. She looked at Kathleen. "Michael is my son and he and Violet Burton got married last December. They don't live far from here and you'll be meeting them on Sunday. They usually come to Sunday dinner."

"I look forward to meeting them." Kathleen was relieved to know the woman had a son who lived nearby. When she and her sister's family had come here to America, she'd dreamed of falling in love and having a home near her sister's.

But that had never happened. Instead it was all Clancy and her sister could do to pay the rent and feed their children—and that only with Kathleen's help. She wasn't sure Colleen and Clancy would be able to get along without what she'd contributed to their income and she vowed to send her sister what she could. It seemed that was all she could do. Kathleen needed to accept it and quit feeling guilty that life for her had changed for the better.

Apple pie was served for dessert—something that only happened on special occasions with Kathleen's family. She watched as Elizabeth picked up the smaller fork and did the same, praying that no one noticed that she had no idea what utensil to use.

Luke would have kicked himself if he could. He should have realized that Kathleen might be skittish about any man who entered into her space, touched her without being asked. He'd seen the fear in her eyes and known he never should have reached out to touch her.

He didn't understand it, nor did he particularly welcome it, but something about Kathleen O'Bryan called out his protective instincts in a way no other woman had ever done.

He didn't think she realized how lovely she was or how badly he wanted to get hold of her brother-in-law and teach him a lesson for what he'd done to Kathleen. She'd looked so vulnerable as he walked toward her in the parlor. And yet, there was a dignity about her that made his chest feel tight with an emotion he couldn't name.

Sitting beside her, Luke could tell she was unsure of what utensil to use by the way she kept watching Elizabeth. But why should Kathleen know which fork or spoon to use? He doubted her meals were anything like the ones he and the others had become accustomed to.

When the meal came to a close, he heard Kathleen release a small sigh and was almost as relieved as she sounded.

He quickly drew her chair out for her.

"Thank you, Mr. Patterson."

"My pleasure, Miss O'Bryan. Will you be joining us in the parlor?"

"Oh, I don't know. I—"

"Some of the boarders usually gather there for a bit after dinner and continue with whatever conversations they were having, or speak to someone else they didn't have a chance to speak with. It's a way for you to get to know the others," he added, hoping to persuade her to join them. The week had been overly long waiting for a glimpse of her just to know for sure that she was recovering.

"I suppose I should get to know everyone. It appears I might be here for a while."

"I'm glad to hear that," Luke said, a little unsure whether to offer his arm to her again. Everyone else headed toward the parlor singly and he didn't want her to feel awkward.

She saved him from making a decision as she began to walk unaccompanied. He fell into step beside her, feeling a bit awkward himself, but needing to ask. "How are you feeling?"

She stopped and turned to him. "Much better, thank you. I'll be going to work on Monday."

"That's good news." He was glad to know that she was getting better physically, but…he had to know. "How are you adjusting? I'm sure it's hard to be away from your sister and nephews."

Kathleen looked at him questioningly.

"They were there that day in the park." Luke remembered them pleading with their aunt not to send their papa to jail that day. How hard that must have been for her. The man should have been locked up. But she'd chosen to honor her nephews' pleas instead of assuring her and her sister of a few days of peace.

"Yes, they were." Her gaze met his and her eyes were bright with what he thought might be unshed tears. "I— Mr. Patterson, I never really had a chance to thank you that day. You saved my sister and me from his fists and I'd like to thank you now."

"I just happened to be in the right place at the right time. I only wish I could have saved you from this last episode." He nodded toward her face.

Her hand came up to touch her cheekbone and she smiled. "But you did save me from crumpling at Mrs. Heaton's feet."

"I'm glad I was here. Have you heard from your sister?"

"I have. I received a letter from her just yesterday and that's made me feel better. At least she and my nephews were all right when she wrote it. And we'll be keeping in contact through a neighbor. I still can't remember all of what actually happened that night. I only know what I've been told and the bits and pieces that come to me. I must admit, I'm relieved I won't be going back, but I don't know when I'll see my sister and the boys again."

They'd reached the parlor by then and Luke said quietly, "I'll be praying for them to stay safe and for you to be able to see them soon."

"Luke, Miss O'Bryan, come on in. We're going to play charades," Ben called.

"Charades?" Kathleen asked as they entered the room and took a seat on one of the sofas.

"Is it new to you?" Luke asked.

"I don't know. How do you play it?"

"It's a game where we guess a word or phrase from one's pantomime."

Kathleen shrugged and smiled. "I'm not sure. I'll watch tonight and perhaps play another time."

"All right. But once you catch on, feel free to join in," Elizabeth said.

For the next half hour, the others put on quite a show, trying to draw Kathleen into the game. But she held her ground and, while Luke was sure she'd caught on, she only watched and laughed at everyone's antics.

She had a light melodious laugh, one he would like to hear more often. Hopefully, he would. She'd be staying here, at least for the foreseeable future, and it relieved his mind to know that she wouldn't be living in the tenements. Never again would she live in those conditions, if he had anything to do with it.

Suddenly feeling exhausted, Kathleen said, "I think I'll go up now, if you'll all excuse me."

"Are you all right?" Luke asked in a quiet voice.

She nodded her head. "I'm just a bit tired."

"We're glad you joined us," Elizabeth said. "You are going with us tomorrow, aren't you?"

"I am. What time do I need to be ready?"

"I don't think we need to leave until after lunch, do you?" Elizabeth looked around the group for confirmation.

"That won't give us a lot of time," Ben said, "but perhaps for Kathleen's first outing, we shouldn't make it a long day."

"I don't want you changing your plans for me. I can go another time," Kathleen said.

"Oh, no. We want you to come along," Julia said. "We'll go back again."

"Then I'll be glad to go. Thank you all for making me feel so welcome tonight."

"It's nice to have a new boarder. With Michael and Violet married and gone, we've felt a bit…" Elizabeth's voice trailed off.

"Bored with each other, is what she's trying to say," Luke said. He grinned down at Kathleen.

"I did not mean that, Luke," Elizabeth said. "But now that you mention it, you might be right."

Everyone laughed, including Luke. Circumstances had always been serious when they were together and Kathleen had never heard him laugh. The sound was deep and husky like his voice, and it flooded her with warmth and seemed to brighten her mood. It was good to know there was laughter in this home.

"Good night," Kathleen said as she left the parlor. She went upstairs and readied herself for bed, thinking how nice all the boarders had been. Mrs. Heaton was right. They didn't ask questions she didn't want to answer, as she'd feared they might when she finally joined them for dinner tonight. Instead, everyone had gone out of their way to make her feel comfortable.

Kathleen thought it would be a while before she really felt at home here—at least until she learned to choose her eating utensils without checking to see what everyone else was using.

She pulled out her Bible and read *Psalms* 121:8 about the Lord preserving her going out and coming in from now on and for always. Peace stole over her. She was safe here. She prayed that Colleen and her boys would remain safe across town in a completely different world than the one she was in now. And she thanked the Lord for seeing her safely here. He had a plan. Kathleen knew He did. She only needed to trust that the Lord would reveal it in His time.

As she closed her eyes, her last waking thought was about Luke. There was something about his smile that put a hitch in her breath, and the concern in his eyes made her feel special in a way no one ever had. He made her feel a sense of safety she'd never known before. And yet, she warned herself that even Luke might not be the kind of man he seemed to be. From what she'd seen of men in the last few years…one never knew.

Chapter Three

Kathleen went down to breakfast for the first time the next morning to find Mrs. Heaton, Elizabeth and Ben already at the table.

"Good morning, Kathleen." Mrs. Heaton smiled from the head of the table. "I'm glad you felt like coming down this morning. As you can see, we all eat breakfast at different times. Just help yourself, dear." She motioned to the sideboard.

Kathleen was a bit disappointed that Luke wasn't there, but tried not to show it as she picked up a plate on the sideboard and chose some fluffy scrambled eggs, bacon and a biscuit. She was going to have to watch that she didn't gain weight living here, for the fare was much more than she was used to.

"Good morning. Have the others already had breakfast?" Kathleen took the seat she'd sat in the night before and was happy to see the utensil setting was one she could manage—one knife, one fork and a spoon.

"I'm not sure, but possibly," Elizabeth said. "I slept in today."

"Luke ate earlier. I ran into him on my way in," Ben

said. "He went down to get some writing done so he could go on the outing with us."

Kathleen was glad Luke was coming. She really didn't know him any better than the others, but she felt safe when he was around. "What does he write?"

"He writes dime novels," Mrs. Heaton said.

A writer? Somehow that surprised Kathleen.

"I'm glad you feel up to going to the museum, Kathleen," Mrs. Heaton continued. "Have you ever been before?"

Kathleen shook her head and swallowed the bite she'd just taken. "No, ma'am. But I've been told it's wonderful."

"It is. You'll love it," Elizabeth said. "Some of my friends have said that the Michelangelo collection is magnificent."

"Yes, I've heard that, too. Mrs. Driscoll has talked about it." She didn't mention that she really wasn't familiar with Michelangelo or his work as she'd never been to a museum of any kind. Hopefully she would be well acquainted with it by that evening.

"You can all tell me about it at dinner," Mrs. Heaton said, pushing back her chair. "You know, I don't believe you've seen all of this floor, Kathleen. Would you like a tour so that you know your way around?"

"Oh, yes, I would, please." She was finished eating and she pushed back her chair.

"Let's start with the kitchen," Mrs. Heaton said, leading her through the door on the other end of the dining room.

It was large and sunny and smelled wonderful. Gretchen turned from the sink to say, "Good morning, Miss Kathleen. It's good to see you this morning."

"It's good to see you as well, Gretchen."

Mrs. Heaton led her back to the hall and to a room across from the kitchen. "This is the back parlor where you may bring a guest. Gretchen and Maida are always happy to prepare refreshment for you and your company. It's a nice place to come to read or write letters or just a place to relax."

It was a very inviting room, smaller but just as beautiful as the larger parlor, and done in blues and greens with a homey feel to it. After that was a smaller room, very cozy with a wall of shelves filled with books.

"This is my study. You're welcome to borrow any book you'd like," Mrs. Heaton said.

"I do like to read, but haven't had much opportunity to in a while." Kathleen couldn't remember when she'd last had the time to read for pleasure.

"Feel free to help yourself anytime."

"Thank you, I will."

They walked out and Mrs. Heaton showed her where the telephone was in an area under the staircase. "Mrs. Driscoll has this number in case she needs to call you in. And I have hers if you should need to speak with her."

They were back to the foyer and Mrs. Heaton said, "That's about it for this floor—except there is a small garden out back. Downstairs is where the men's rooms are, and the next floor up from yours is where Maida's and Gretchen's rooms are, with a few other rooms that are used from time to time."

"It's beautiful, Mrs. Heaton."

The telephone in the cubby behind the staircase rang just then and Mrs. Heaton took it on herself to answer.

She put her hand over the receiver and whispered, "This is a call I need to take. I'm sorry, I—"

"Oh, no, please take your call. I'll see you later."

Kathleen gave a little wave and hurried upstairs to her room. A room she'd never thought to live in and wasn't sure she could afford to, until after she knew what Mrs. Heaton would be charging her. The woman had refused to discuss it until after Kathleen went back to work, telling her that she didn't owe a penny until then.

She'd hate to leave, but after seeing the rest of the house, she couldn't imagine that she could actually afford to stay. She might have to look into the YWCA. Kathleen made her bed—refusing to let Gretchen and Maida do it for her. They had enough work to do.

The bathroom was empty and she decided to wash her hair for the outing that afternoon. She toweled it dry as best she could and combed it out, knowing it would dry into near-uncontrollable curls.

When she entered her room, she noticed the door to her armoire was open slightly and went to close it. But color caught her eye and she opened it to find it full of clothing and a note attached to a gold dinner dress. At least that's what she thought it was from the magazines some of her coworkers had brought to work.

She unpinned the note and read, "Kathleen, these are the outfits I told you about. As you can see, the colors are much more suited to you than to me. This gold dress will work nicely for dinner tonight. I hope everything fits. If not, we can alter them. I took a sewing course from Violet Heaton last summer."

Kathleen hurried back into the bathroom and knocked on Elizabeth's door. When her new friend opened it with a smile, Kathleen threw her arms around her neck.

"I don't know what to say, except thank you, Elizabeth. I'm not sure I can accept your generosity though—it's too much."

"It is not too much, Kathleen. Aside from my buying on a whim, I have an aunt who buys clothes for me without taking into consideration the colors or styles I like. I wore them each once for her. I'll not be wearing them again. If you don't like them—" Elizabeth shrugged "—we'll just gather them up and I'll—"

"Oh, no. I do love them. And I'm sure they'll fit. Thank you."

"You are more than welcome. Come on, try them on and let's see if they need to be taken up anywhere."

They spent the rest of the morning with Kathleen trying on outfits, including a warm coat Elizabeth had assured her she didn't need.

"I have another newer one, Kathleen, and I like it better. This one is just going to hang in my closet or be given to someone else."

The coat fit perfectly, as did everything else, and all Kathleen could do was thank Elizabeth once more. As she tried on one outfit after another, Elizabeth ran back and forth between rooms to find the accessories that went with them. It was almost too much to take in.

By the time she and Elizabeth joined the others in the foyer to go to the museum, Kathleen felt as if she were the most blessed person on earth. Hard as it'd been for her to understand why things never seemed to get better for her sister's family, now she couldn't understand why things had changed so drastically, in the best possible way, for her. All she knew was that the Lord had blessed her beyond anything she'd ever imagined.

When Luke saw how happy Kathleen looked as she and Elizabeth came downstairs, he was very glad he'd written enough that he could take the afternoon off.

"Are you ready? Are your shoes comfortable?" he asked Kathleen.

"I'm ready and yes, my shoes are comfortable. Elizabeth gave them to me and she broke them in well."

"That was nice of her." Luke smiled and nodded at Elizabeth. He'd been sure the women at Heaton House would take care of any shortage in Kathleen's wardrobe. They seemed to have plenty and were always bringing in more from a shopping trip on Ladies' Mile.

"They look comfortable and that's good, because you're going to be walking a lot."

They all left the house and he fell into step beside Kathleen as the group headed for the trolley stop.

"This is a very nice neighborhood," she said. "I thought it would be, since Heaton House is so beautiful, but I haven't been out since the night I was brought here."

"Gramercy Park is a good neighborhood. It's an old one, but very well kept as you can see. The park is nice, too. We'll have to show it to you one day."

"There's a park?"

"Yes," Elizabeth said from behind her. "It's a small private one, open only for those living in the neighborhood. It really is a kind of oasis of sorts and you can't get to it without a key."

"It sounds lovely."

The trolley to the museum arrived and Luke made

sure to be right behind Kathleen as they stepped up into it. He had their fare paid before she could open her reticule.

"That's all right, miss. You're paid for," the driver said.

Luke wasn't sure how she would take him paying for her but it didn't take long to find out. He found empty seats for them and motioned for her to take the one by the window.

As soon as they both had sat down, she turned to him, her eyes flashing. "Thank you for getting my fare for me, Mr. Patterson. But I have a job and I don't expect you or anyone else to pay my way."

"Please don't be upset with me, Miss O'Bryan." He smiled down at her. "I know you haven't worked this week and I don't want you to go short until you get your next pay. Forgive me if I've insulted you."

Kathleen closed her eyes and gave a little shake to her head before releasing a sigh. "I'm sorry if I've insulted you after all you've done for me, Mr. Patterson. You and Mrs. Heaton know I didn't arrive with much and I realize you are only trying to help me. Please forgive me for being so prideful."

His heart twisted in his chest. This woman... "There is nothing to forgive you for, Kathleen. Not a thing. And if you want to pay me back, you can—after you get paid again."

Then she smiled at him and said, "Thank you."

"You're welcome." The tightness in his chest eased somewhat but he felt awful for injuring her pride. He'd have to be more careful from now on.

"Mrs. Heaton told me you write dime novels."

He was relieved that she'd changed the subject. "I do. Do you like to read?"

"Yes, although I haven't done much of it in a while. Where do you usually set your stories?"

"Oh, all over. Out West at first, but lately, I've been setting them closer to home."

"Does Mrs. Heaton have any copies in her library?"

"I believe I gave her some."

"Then I'll have to borrow one."

He wanted to tell her he could give her copies of her own, but he didn't want to upset her again. "Let me know what you think. Not everyone likes dime novels."

"I look forward to reading your work."

"I hope you enjoy it." Luke felt nervous—would she like his writing? He hoped so.

They'd arrived at the stop right outside the museum and he stepped into the aisle to let Kathleen out. Once out of the trolley, the group gathered to go inside. He hoped Kathleen liked the museum as much as he did.

As they toured the museum, Luke saw again why the Metropolitan was one of his favorite places. Though it was full of all kinds of art, the paintings interested him the most. With the special Michelangelo collection on exhibit, they spent most of their time looking at these works.

From the look on Kathleen's face, he was sure she was as enthralled with the paintings as he was.

He knew she was when she whispered, "I've never seen anything like this. The Lord certainly gave him a talent, didn't He?"

"He did. I think I could spend several days straight, right here, looking at his work."

"I'm so sorry we aren't going to see everything in

the museum today. Now I know why Ben wanted to get an earlier start."

"Oh, we'd never be able to see it all in a day, Kathleen," Elizabeth said from behind them.

"And I might not have been able to come if I hadn't had a chance to get some writing in. Besides, it gives us a reason to keep coming back."

"Oh, I would love to come back."

"You will." Luke smiled down at Kathleen. He'd certainly like to bring her again.

Hours later when they decided to call it a day, they went outside to find the weather had turned much cooler.

"Why don't we go to the nearest drugstore soda fountain and get some hot cocoa?" Ben asked. "It'll warm us up for the ride home."

Everyone agreed and before long they were all sitting at a round table sipping the sweet chocolaty drink. He watched as Kathleen interacted with the others. She seemed to be enjoying herself and so was Luke. He couldn't remember when he'd had such a good time on one of their outings.

Kathleen had never had an outing quite like the one that day, with men and women going together as a group. Everyone she knew was too tired to do much more on a weekend than get ready for the next work-week.

Which was what she proceeded to do when they got back to Heaton House. But she'd been surprised to find that her laundry had been done for her. She'd hurried downstairs in search of Mrs. Heaton. They hadn't discussed her rent yet, but Kathleen knew she couldn't afford to have someone do her laundry and she needed to let Mrs. Heaton know.

Kathleen found her in her study, sitting in front of the fireplace. "May I speak to you, Mrs. Heaton?"

"Of course you may. Come in, dear." She motioned for her to take the empty chair next to hers. "Did you have a nice time at the museum?"

Kathleen sat down. "Yes, ma'am, I did, thank you. But, Mrs. Heaton, I must speak to you about my laundry. I'm not sure I can afford to—"

"Kathleen, dear, don't worry. It's included in the rent."

"Yes, well, that's something we haven't talked about. I need to know what it is, please."

Mrs. Heaton quoted her a figure that seemed much too low. "Oh, Mrs. Heaton, that can't be right. I was paying my sister more than that for living with her and Clancy. I insist on paying you the regular amount."

"That is what I'm charging you, Kathleen, dear. I didn't start this boardinghouse to make money, but to help young women have a safe place to call home. And I set the rent accordingly." With that Mrs. Heaton put up a hand as if to end the conversation.

Kathleen didn't know what to say next.

Mrs. Heaton reached out and patted her on the hand. "If it makes you feel any better, there are those in need who spend a night or two here occasionally, just as you did that one time. I call them my temporaries and I don't charge them at all for the time they spend with me."

"But, Mrs. Heaton, I'm not a temporary now and I don't feel right paying so little, and then to have you feed me and do my laundry on top of it?" She shook her head.

"Kathleen, food and laundry are part of the board you pay."

"But you're barely charging enough for the room, Mrs. Heaton."

"Kathleen, this is my boardinghouse and I charge what I want. I want to help you, not make life harder for you. I know you worry about your sister and her boys. If you have enough left at the end of a week, send a bit to them."

"I don't know how to thank you."

"Oh, child, it gives me comfort to know that I'm providing a safe home for you and the others. That is all the thanks I want."

Remembering what Elizabeth had told her about Mrs. Heaton's daughter brought tears to her eyes and all Kathleen could do was hug the woman and hurry out of the room before she saw them.

She'd no more than made it to the hallway before she ran into Luke. Or she would have if he hadn't put out his hands to keep the near disaster from happening.

"Whoa there—are you all right, Miss O'Bryan?"

His hands were gentle on her arms but the moment she gasped, he immediately dropped them. "I'm sorry. I just didn't want you to—"

"I'm sorry. I wasn't watching where I was going." She brushed back the tears and looked up at him.

"Are you hurting? What's happened to make you cry?"

She'd never met anyone who seemed to notice so much about her. "I'm not hurting. It's just— Mrs. Heaton has been through so much heartache, and still she reaches out to others and—" She swallowed around the knot of tears and shook her head.

"She does do that. And I'm very glad she reached out to you." He pulled out a crisp white handkerchief and, knowing that the man intended no harm, Kathleen allowed him to dab at a lone tear that'd escaped and ran down her cheek.

"So am I." She was very thankful that she was here, thankful for Mrs. Heaton's support and for this man who stood there trying to help now.

He tucked his handkerchief in her hand. "You may keep it. If there is anything I can help you with, please don't hesitate to ask."

"Thank you. I'll wash it and get it back to you soon."

"There's no hurry. I have a lot of them."

Kathleen wasn't sure what to say next and was relieved when Luke spoke again.

"Are you going to join the others in the parlor before dinner?"

"Yes, but first I'm going to go up and freshen up."

"All right. I'll see you later, then."

"Yes. I'd better hurry before Mrs. Heaton calls us down." She hurried upstairs, aware of Luke's gaze on her as she did. He seemed too good to be true. She'd never met a man like Luke Patterson. And she liked him a lot.

But could she trust her instincts where he was concerned? That she didn't know. She'd seen too many men, abusive men like her brother-in-law, who treated their women badly. She thought it almost impossible to trust any of them. Still, believing it impossible didn't keep her from wishing it could be different.

Chapter Four

"Do you think that brother-in-law will come after Miss O'Bryan, Luke?" Michael Heaton asked. He'd asked for a few minutes with him while Sunday dinner was being put on the table and they'd gone to Mrs. Heaton's study.

"I don't know. But you can be sure I'll be on the lookout for him. I don't think Kathleen's sister will let him know where she is—she sent her here for her safety, after all."

Michael nodded. "I'm just concerned about Mother. And yet I'd never want to stop the good she does. But since I've moved out, I do worry about her. You can't be here all the time, but knowing you are around most of the time—actually more than I was before I married—and trusting in the Lord to watch over Heaton House…well, it gives me peace."

"I'm glad to know that."

"But I do remember that man from the park last year. He's a bad one."

"Yes, he is. I'm glad Kathleen—Miss O'Bryan got

out of there. But I believe she worries a great deal about her sister and nephews."

"I'm sure she does. Has she heard anything from her sister?"

Luke nodded. "They're corresponding through a neighbor. Still, I think she worries about the time in between letters."

"That's understandable," Michael said. "You know, she's quite pretty."

"Yes, she is." In Luke's opinion, *pretty* was an understatement. But then, Michael hadn't seen her come downstairs dressed in a gold dinner dress the night before. She'd looked beautiful. Her hair had been done up in what looked like a cloud of fire and he'd had a hard time keeping his eyes off her all evening.

She'd looked just as lovely today when she attended church with Mrs. Heaton, Luke and some of the other boarders. Michael and Violet were there when they arrived and Mrs. Heaton had introduced them to Kathleen before sliding into the pew to sit beside her daughter-in-law. She'd motioned for Kathleen to sit beside her and Luke had taken the seat on the other side of Kathleen. Ben, John and Julia slid in the pew behind them. Luke found he had to really concentrate to keep his mind on the sermon. It was from *Romans* 8, about how all things work together for the good of those who love God, those called according to His purpose. He sent up a prayer that all things were working for the good of Kathleen and her sister.

"Luke?"

"What?" Luke dragged his thoughts back to the present. "Did you say something?"

Michael laughed. "You must have been lost in your thoughts."

"I'm sorry. Apparently I was. What were you saying?"

"I said, one wonders why Miss O'Bryan isn't married with a family of her own."

Luke had wondered the same thing. "Her brother-in-law isn't the best example of a husband. Could be she doesn't want one. And if she had any suitors, he probably kept them away. If she married, he couldn't get part of her income to help out."

"True. I wonder what he's going to do now."

"I don't know. But it does weigh on my mind."

"Do you want me to assign a man to watch over Kathleen on her way back and forth to work?"

"No. I'll take on that job for now." Luke wasn't going to give over Kathleen's protection to anyone else.

Michael nodded. "All right. But if you need some help, let me know."

"I will."

A light rap sounded on the door just before it opened, and Violet, Michael's wife, peeked her head around it. "Dinner is ready, Michael."

"We're coming now, love." Michael quickly joined his wife and kissed her cheek.

Luke couldn't help but notice the smile Michael gave his wife and the look that passed between them. He'd known from the beginning that they were attracted to each other and gave himself some credit for getting them to admit it to each other. He was happy for them, but at the same time, seeing Michael and Violet together sometimes made him feel sorrow, too. It brought up memories of what could have been had his fiancée, Beth, not been killed in a bank robbery before he'd ever come to the city.

In fact he probably wouldn't be here if not for losing her. He couldn't stay in Texas after that. Instead he'd decided to go somewhere totally different and had ended up right here at Heaton House. He hadn't shared his sorrow with anyone—nor the guilt he felt that he hadn't shown up to see Beth home from work in time to do something—anything—to save her. It was only lately he'd begun to forgive himself.

Luke followed the couple to the dining room and watched as Michael put an arm around Violet's waist and leaned close to whisper something to her. She giggled and blushed.

Much as Luke liked being footloose to go where he needed to research his books and work for Michael, he had to admit that sometimes he longed for a relationship like theirs. Longed for someone to love again. But he'd vowed never to let himself fall in love with anyone else. He never wanted to chance going through that kind of heartache again—ever.

Everyone was already in the dining room when they got there, and he took his customary seat next to Kathleen. Michael took the seat at the opposite end of the table from his mother after seating his wife adjacent to him.

Everyone bowed as Michael asked a blessing over the food and then there was clatter and chatter around the table as everyone served themselves from the dishes Maida started around the table.

Luke held the dish of scalloped potatoes while Kathleen helped herself to a spoonful. Then he took a portion for himself and handed it off to Ben.

As conversation flowed around them, he leaned toward Kathleen and asked, "Are you sure you're ready to go back to work tomorrow? Did the doctor give his okay?"

"He did. I'm sure I'll be fine. And I must get back to work. Mrs. Driscoll was good to give me a week off, but I can't ask for more time."

"Are you worried that your brother-in-law might show up there?"

She gave a little shake to her head. "Not really, but the thought has crossed my mind from time to time."

It'd crossed Luke's and Michael's, too. "Well, just to be on the safe side, I'm going to accompany you to work and back, at least for a while."

"I can't be taking that much of your time, Mr. Patterson. You have your own work to do."

"You aren't taking it. I'm giving it. And don't you think it's time we call each other by our first names? Everyone else here does."

She looked around the table and nodded. "Yes, they do. I suppose we should…Luke."

Luke liked the way she said his name in her Irish accent. "And I agree, Kathleen." He also liked the way it felt to say her name out loud. He watched soft color flood her cheeks and wanted to say more, but before he could, Violet captured Kathleen's attention from across the table.

"What is it you actually do in Mrs. Driscoll's department at Tiffany Glass Company?" she asked. Her question got the attention of all the diners at the table.

"I help cut the glass at times and I work on foiling the pieces with sheets of copper."

"Oh, how interesting," Violet said. "And how do you go about that? Foiling the pieces of glass?"

"Bee's wax is applied to foil sheets, which are then cut into strips. Then the strips are wrapped around the pieces. Once we tamp down the edges and reassemble them, our work is done. Then the copper is soldered to the adjacent pieces of glass."

"It sounds as though it's very tedious work," Ben said.

Kathleen nodded. "Sometimes it is. And it's tiring. But seeing the finished product makes it worthwhile."

"Would you change workplaces if you found something else that might be easier on you?" Mrs. Heaton asked.

"If it were something I felt qualified for, possibly. Mrs. Driscoll hasn't said anything to any of us, but I've heard through some of the girls that she might be thinking of remarrying one day and they won't allow a married woman to work there."

"Not even the supervisor?" Julia asked.

"I don't think so," Kathleen said.

"So, if you got married, you wouldn't be able to work there?"

"Oh, no. That's why there's a lot of turnover in the department. Someone is always in training because it seems one of the girls is always getting married. But if Mrs. Driscoll does get married, I'm not sure I'd want to stay." She looked at Mrs. Heaton. "Has she said anything to you about leaving?"

"Not really. But Clara is very quiet about her private life. I know she cares a great deal about her 'Tiffany Girls,' though."

"She does, that. I'll be sad to see her go if she does."

"But you're bound to marry one day," Violet Heaton said. "You'd be leaving then, too."

For some reason the conversation had Luke wondering if there were some young man in Kathleen's life and he wanted to ask, but thought it'd be impertinent to do so...at least in front of so many people.

"And is there a young man in your life that we should have notified, Kathleen?" Julia asked as if she read his mind.

Her timing couldn't have been better and Luke was thankful for it as he listened for Kathleen's reply.

"No. I've had no time for young men," Kathleen said.

Luke told himself that it shouldn't matter to him whether Kathleen had a beau or not. He barely knew her. But somehow...it did matter. He let out a pent-up breath he didn't even realize he'd been holding.

After breakfast the next morning, Luke was ready and waiting to accompany Kathleen to work. He helped her on with the coat Elizabeth had given her.

"Luke, you really don't have to go with me. I ride part of the way with Elizabeth. I'll be fine."

"But you don't ride all the way with her. Besides, it does me good to get out first thing of a morning. I'll walk part of the way home and think about the next chapter I'm writing."

There was nothing to do but accept his offer as he walked to the trolley stop with her and Elizabeth. The two women sat together and he stood, holding on to the rope hanging from the ceiling. When Elizabeth got off at her stop, he took her seat.

He smiled down at Kathleen. "Did you get a chance to get to know Violet yesterday?"

Michael and his wife had stayed awhile until supper Sunday night and she and Mrs. Heaton had invited Kathleen to join them for tea in the back parlor that afternoon. Violet was easy to talk to and they'd discussed all manner of things. Kathleen liked her. "I did. She's very sweet and remembered Colleen and me from that day in the park. I think she was quite taken with my nephews Collin and Brody."

"Everyone who was there that day was concerned about you all."

"I'm thankful that Mrs. Heaton gave me her card for so many reasons. But one is that as much as it pains me to know everyone saw what kind of man my sister married, it is a relief not to have to explain it all to everyone. Besides, there is still so much I don't remember."

"Kathleen, his actions are no reflection on you. You could have been killed trying to protect your sister and—"

"But I wasn't, thanks to you, Luke."

"Anyone would have done the same thing."

"No. Not anyone. I—"

The driver called out her stop just then and Luke moved into the aisle to let her out, and then followed her out of the trolley. He walked the block to Tiffany Glass Company with her.

"What time do you get off work?"

"At five-thirty."

Luke nodded. "I'll be here."

Kathleen felt certain it would do no good to tell him not to come, so she thanked him instead.

Several of her coworkers came up just then and she

joined them to go inside. She turned back to see Luke standing by the curb. Evidently he was waiting until she got inside. She gave him a little wave and hurried through the door.

"Who is that, Kathleen? Do you have a beau?" a girl named Cindy said.

Kathleen's heart did a funny little twist at the very thought. "No. He's…just a good friend."

"That's too bad," another girl named Ruth said. "He's very handsome."

Kathleen was inclined to agree and yet she had no intention of giving her heart away to any man. Over the years, she'd seen Clancy change from the cocky young man her sister fell in love with to a hard-drinking, woman-beating, mean man. And no matter what her heart was doing at the thought of Luke being a beau, she was determined not to fall for any man. Not even the one who made her feel safe and cared for in a way she'd never experienced.

"I wouldn't mind having a friend like him," Cindy said. "If he's in the market for a wife and you don't want him, you can send him my way."

That thought didn't sit well with Kathleen at all.

She'd never had a man friend before. And deep down she knew that Luke was more than just a friend. He'd been there for her when she'd needed a defender the very most and he'd been there when she'd been brought to Heaton House. He made her feel protected and special. And she was not going to send him Cindy's way— or anyone else's for that matter.

As Kathleen stepped into the workroom, she put the thought of Luke paired with Cindy out of her mind.

"Kathleen, it's good to have you back with us," Mrs. Driscoll said. "I've got a new project all ready for you."

The rest of her coworkers welcomed her back and all of them seemed glad to see her. Thankfully, no one asked many questions about why she'd been gone— probably because some of them lived in the same kind of conditions that Kathleen and her family did. And besides, they'd seen her bruised before. She didn't feel the need to tell anyone she was no longer living in the tenement and she knew Mrs. Driscoll wouldn't have said anything about it.

It was still hard for Kathleen to believe that she'd begun a new life, and now that she was back at work she found it even more difficult not to feel guilty that her sister was stuck in her old life. It hurt to think of Colleen and the boys putting up with Clancy. She would so love to be able to get them out of the tenements. Much as she loved her work, she did wish she were able to help others.

"Here you go, Kathleen," Mrs. Driscoll said, bringing her the design and the cut-glass pieces she wanted Kathleen to start on. "It's ready for the copper foil."

"Oh, it's lovely, Mrs. Driscoll."

"Thank you. It's one I've been working on awhile now. I'm eager to see it finished." She patted Kathleen on the shoulder and lowered her voice. "Should you get tired, let me know. I can send you home early."

"I think I'll be fine. Mrs. Heaton has taken wonderful care of me."

"I'm very relieved that you kept her card and that your sister sent you to her."

"Thank you for coming to check on me."

"You're welcome."

Mrs. Driscoll went to check on another piece of work, and Kathleen concentrated on getting back to her job. She imagined she'd be tired by the end of the day, but it was good to be back at work. She carefully painted the outline of the brass design on what would become a Tiffany lamp, and smiled thinking about the weekend. It'd been the nicest one she'd had in a very long time—maybe ever. And never had she gone on an outing in mixed company, except with family.

She'd thoroughly enjoyed going to the museum and then singing around the piano after dinner that night. Then, yesterday, she'd enjoyed getting to know Mrs. Heaton's son and his wife.

After Sunday dinner, the men were talking about an upcoming sporting event at Madison Square Garden and the ladies had adjourned to the back parlor for afternoon tea. Well, she and Mrs. Heaton and her daughter-in-law had. Elizabeth was still at her aunt's and Julia had gone to visit a friend.

They'd just settled down with their tea when Violet turned to Kathleen. "You know, at Butterick, I didn't have to leave when Michael and I got married, but I know that it is that way with many businesses and it greatly disturbs me. I can't help but wonder... what about the married women who need to help support their families? Or the ones who are widowed with families?"

"It's very hard for them to find work, although many companies do hire married women," Kathleen had answered. "Colleen takes in ironing and such from time to time, but it's not anything she can really depend on. And if she worked outside, she'd have to count on a neighbor to watch the boys—at least until they are in school."

"What this city needs is someplace women could drop off their children while they worked. Somewhere they'd be safe and well cared for until she got off work," Violet said.

"Oh, that is a wonderful idea, Violet," Mrs. Heaton said. "It really is."

"Yes, but getting it implemented—"

"Might not be as hard as you think," Mrs. Heaton had said. "Let me give it some thought and contact a few people."

"If anyone could do it, you could, Mother Heaton," Violet had said affectionately.

Kathleen could see the two women cared a great deal about each other, and she greatly missed her mother who'd passed away when she was only fifteen—and she missed her sister.

Now she shook her head and tried to concentrate on foiling the glass pieces. Pushing an errant strand of hair out of her eyes, she sighed. Maybe she'd have a letter from Colleen today. She hoped so.

By the end of her shift she was more than a little exhausted. Her back was hurting and she was almost convinced that she did have a fractured rib. Maybe tonight she'd sleep in the corset Elizabeth had given her. It had seemed to help the night she'd tried it.

She headed out with the others and her heart did a little flip when she saw Luke waiting for her just outside the doors. She smiled at him and hurried over.

"You look exhausted," he said, lightly grasping her elbow. "Perhaps you should have waited a few days to return to work."

His concern touched her heart but she didn't want him worrying about her. "I'll be fine. Just need to get used to being on my feet again."

"Kathleen!" Cindy called as she and Ruth came running up to her and Luke. "It was good to have you back at work. We missed you!'

Then she turned to Luke. "I'm sorry. I don't believe we've met before. I'm Cindy White and this is Ruth—"

"Moore," Ruth said, batting her eyelashes at Luke.

My goodness, they were brazen. But it didn't seem to affect Luke. "I'm Luke Patterson, a friend of Kathleen's. It's nice to meet you ladies, but as you can see, Kathleen's first day at work was very tiring for her. If you'll excuse us, I want to get her on the trolley so she can get off her feet." He tipped his hat and propelled Kathleen away.

Kathleen looked over her shoulder to see the two girls standing there with their mouths wide open. She couldn't help but smile as she turned back around. This man…she was blessed to have him as a friend.

Chapter Five

Luke didn't like that Kathleen looked so tired. And the trolley, with all its stopping and starting, didn't help, he could tell from the look on Kathleen's face. He'd rent a hack tomorrow. It might not be any more comfortable, but it'd get them there faster. He wanted to put his arm around her and let her lean on him, but he didn't have that right and he didn't want to frighten her. Carrying her upstairs when she was beaten and bruised was one thing. Pulling her close in public was something all together different.

He saw her wince as the trolley came to a less than gentle stop. "Are you sure you're all right?"

"My side is hurting a bit," she admitted. "But I'll be fine. I guess I've gotten lazy this past week."

Luke had a feeling there was nothing lazy about this woman. "I don't believe that. You're still healing. Can't you sit down to work?"

"Actually, it's easier to stand most of the time. But I might try it tomorrow."

Elizabeth got on at the next trolley stop and even she could tell Kathleen was tired. "Long day?"

"A little." Kathleen smiled. "It will get easier."

Elizabeth gave Luke a questioning look. He shrugged. "That's what she says. But I think maybe her rib is giving her trouble."

"We'll wrap it when we get home. That should help a bit."

"I'm sure it will," Kathleen said.

But Luke could tell she wasn't feeling any better. He didn't know who was more relieved to get to their stop—Kathleen or him.

Once they got to Heaton House, she and Elizabeth quickly disappeared upstairs and he wondered if she'd be back down for dinner. He quickly called the nearest livery and made arrangements for a hack to be delivered the next morning. Kathleen wasn't going to ride the trolley again until she was much better.

Mrs. Heaton came out of her study just as he ended the call. "How did Kathleen do today?"

"I think it was hard on her. She seemed to be in some pain—her rib, I believe. Elizabeth was going to help her wrap it, I think."

"I'll go up and see if we need to telephone the doctor."

"Good." Luke felt better just knowing Mrs. Heaton would be checking on Kathleen.

"It's going to take a while for her to heal," she said as she pulled a letter out of her pocket. "But I have something that I'm sure will make her feel better. She got a letter from her sister today—well, I think it's from her sister. It has her neighbor's name on it but Kathleen said that's how they would correspond so her brother-in-law doesn't find out."

Luke watched her go upstairs and prayed she was

right. Hearing from her sister was bound to make Kathleen feel better. He went downstairs to wash up before dinner, and afterward he made a few notes on ideas that'd come to him for his next chapter. But his mind was on Kathleen and he couldn't concentrate. He dropped his pencil and sighed. It was time for dinner anyway. He'd work later. He joined the others in the parlor and was pleased that Kathleen and Elizabeth joined them only minutes later.

Mrs. Heaton announced that dinner was ready and he had only a moment to reach Kathleen's side and ask, "Are you feeling any better?"

"I am. Mrs. Heaton and Elizabeth wrapped my rib. I should have gone to work with it wrapped today. I'll be sure to tomorrow."

He escorted her to the dining room and pulled out her chair for her. John Talbot said the blessing and once Mrs. Heaton began passing dishes around and everyone began to talk, Luke turned to Kathleen again. She hadn't mentioned the letter so Luke took it upon himself to ask. "Mrs. Heaton said you received a letter. Is it from your sister? Is everything all right with her?"

Kathleen's smile told him it was good news—at least for now.

"She said Clancy is still working and the boys are doing well. They were happy to hear from me and said to tell me they love me."

Kathleen's eyes seemed to mist for a moment and she quickly blinked back whatever tears had begun to well there. "She said they aren't happy with their papa that I had to leave but they've accepted it."

"Perhaps you and your sister will be able to get together one day."

"I hope so. But it will be difficult. I don't dare show up at the apartment. And it's hard for Colleen to get away when Clancy is at home."

Luke wished he could find a safe way for Kathleen and her sister to get together. He'd have to give it some thought.

Once the meal was finished he pulled back Kathleen's chair. "Are you going to join the others in the parlor?"

She shook her head. "Not tonight. I really am tired and I think I'll go on up. Thank you for seeing me to work and home again, Luke. But please don't feel you have to keep doing it. I—"

"I don't feel I have to. But I will be seeing you in the morning. I hope you sleep well and feel better tomorrow."

"Thank you."

Luke watched as Kathleen made her way up the stairs to the landing. She was holding her side and he knew she wasn't feeling as well as she said she was.

He headed back down to get some work done, praying that Kathleen's rib would heal quickly and completely. He'd come to enjoy evenings in her company. Chatting with the others didn't hold the same appeal without her.

The week actually passed faster than Kathleen had thought it would. And she was getting used to being back at work. She'd taken to sleeping in a corset and her side was feeling much better by Friday.

She gave part of the credit to Luke's kindness in procuring a hack to take her to work and bring her home. She'd tried to tell him not to, but she was fast learning that the man had a mind of his own, and for the rest of the week she rode in relative comfort. The girls at work teased her constantly about Luke, insinuating that he was courting her, but she kept insisting he was a very good friend.

And he was. She'd never thought she'd have a man friend, but she felt more comfortable in Luke's company than any of the other boarders except for Elizabeth—and of course Mrs. Heaton.

But now, as she left work for the day and saw Luke waiting for her, her heart skipped a beat. She told herself it was only because she was glad the week was over.

Luke helped her in the hack and took a seat beside her as the driver moved out into the traffic. He grinned down at her. "You made it. A whole week. How are you feeling this afternoon?"

"Glad it's the weekend." She chuckled, knowing that wasn't what he meant, and quickly added, "My side feels much better."

"Good. But I'm glad it's the weekend, too. Do you think you might feel up to going to Michael and Violet's this evening?"

The couple had asked everyone over to their new home for dinner that night. "I do. I'm looking forward to seeing them again."

"Good. We're all looking forward to it. It's the first time they're entertaining and I think they're looking forward to having us as much as we're all looking forward to going."

Kathleen had found that traveling by hack was much quicker than by trolley and they were back at Heaton House in no time.

They parted ways inside, Kathleen to go upstairs to get ready for the dinner party and Luke downstairs to do the same. She felt excited to be going out for an evening. It wasn't something she'd ever done before.

Thankfully, Elizabeth had helped her choose what to wear and offered to do her hair. Kathleen still had trouble believing the life she was now living. Oh, she worked as usual, but the life she lived outside of work was so drastically different from where she'd been just weeks ago. She prayed that she wouldn't get so used to it that she couldn't go back, if she had to. But it wasn't easy. She wanted to see her sister and nephews, but she didn't want to go back to the tenements. She wanted her loved ones out of there!

She'd received another letter from Colleen telling her how glad she was that Kathleen was with such good people. Colleen only wanted what was best for Kathleen, but Kathleen wanted the same for her sister. Only she didn't know how to go about helping her to get it. At least, not now. All Kathleen could do was send what money she could—made possible only by Mrs. Heaton's generosity to her.

She was blessed. There was no other word for it. And whether it lasted or not, for now, Kathleen was determined to try not to feel guilty for it and to enjoy this new life the Lord had seen fit to give her—for however long it lasted.

Now she twisted and turned in front of the mirror, as much as her still-tender ribs would let her, and was pleased with what she saw. The dinner gown Elizabeth had given her fit perfectly and the emerald-green color complemented her coloring. Elizabeth had swept up her hair into a fashionable knot on top of her head and added a green feather to it.

"You look beautiful," Elizabeth said, coming out of the bathroom. "I did a good job on your hair, if I do say so myself."

"You made me look beautiful."

"Oh, Kathleen, one only has to look into those eyes of yours to see beauty. It shines out of you. You could wear a flour sack and look lovely."

Kathleen laughed. "You aren't of your right mind, are you? *You* look gorgeous in that color." Elizabeth was dressed in a rose-colored gown that looked wonderful on her. "And your hair looks great, too."

"Well, let's go see how Julia looks. She said she was wearing blue."

The three women met up in the hall and Julia did indeed look lovely in a deep blue gown. They hurried downstairs to join the others. Mrs. Heaton looked wonderful as always, dressed in an ivory silk. She, too, sported a matching feather in her hair and her eyes sparkled. It was easy to tell she was excited about her son's first dinner party.

The men all looked quite nice, and not at all uncomfortable in their evening dress.

Kathleen found Luke by her side to help her with her evening cape—another gift, this one from Julia, who'd said she had too many. As he held the cape for her to slip into, he whispered, "You look lovely, Kathleen."

"Thank you. You look very nice, too. It's fun to dress up, isn't it?"

"I don't mind once in a while," Luke said. "But I'm certainly glad Mrs. Heaton doesn't make us dress for dinner every night."

"So am I," Kathleen said.

Mrs. Heaton had ordered an omnibus to pick them all up and it was a high-spirited group that headed out into the still, cool night air. Kathleen was pleased that Luke took a seat next to her for the trip to Michael and Violet's home.

"I'm so glad you were all able to make it tonight," Mrs. Heaton said. "Michael and Violet are looking forward to seeing everyone. And a little nervous, too, I do believe."

"I can't wait to see their home now that Violet has it all decorated," Julia said.

"It's lovely. She has excellent taste," Mrs. Heaton said. "It's kept her very busy. But they did recently hire Gretchen and Maida's sister, Hilda, to work for them, although Violet does most of the cooking—with a little help from Michael."

Their home wasn't all that far from Mrs. Heaton's. One could actually walk there easily in warm weather, but Kathleen was glad for the warmth Luke provided sitting beside her.

"How fancy is this dinner?" she asked him in a whisper.

"Not much different than dinner at Mrs. Heaton's, I would imagine. Don't be nervous. You'll have a good time."

"It's those eating utensils I worry about," Kathleen surprised herself by admitting to him.

"Oh, that." Luke chuckled and leaned a little closer to whisper, "It can get quite confusing at times. I still watch what others are using."

"Yes, that's what Elizabeth has taught me."

"Well, even if we should pick up the wrong one, no one in this group would make fun of us."

Kathleen's heart warmed at the way Luke always made her feel better.

They were welcomed into a home smaller than Heaton House, but just as inviting. Michael opened the door to them and he and Violet ushered them in.

"Do we get a tour now that you have it decorated to your satisfaction?" Julia asked as they all shed their coats and hung them on a coatrack in the foyer. "Last time I was here, I was helping to move things over after your wedding. We saw the house, but not the home."

Violet laughed. "Of course you get a tour—right after dinner."

"And to that end, let's go to the dining room," Michael said. "I'm starving."

Violet had set place cards at each place setting and Kathleen's was adjacent to her host's end of the table and next to Luke. She appreciated the woman's effort to make her feel welcome and comfortable.

Once they were all seated, Michael said the blessing. "Dear Lord, we thank You for this day and for this gathering of family and friends to warm this home of ours. Please bless each one and keep us all Yours. Please bless the food we're about to partake together. In Jesus's name, Amen."

A woman—no doubt Hilda, who looked to be about Gretchen and Maida's age—began to serve bowls of soup. Kathleen wasn't sure what it was until Elizabeth said, "Oh, mock turtle soup. I haven't had this in a long time!"

Kathleen had never had it and watched to see which spoon to use. Once she took a taste, she was quite pleased. It hadn't sounded very good to her but it was surprisingly delicious. The rest of the meal was just as good—a salad of lettuce and tomatoes, fillets of beef with mushroom sauce, green peas and creamed potatoes.

As they ate, conversation flowed around the table. Kathleen had never been to a dinner party in her life. Having dinner at Heaton House had been the closest she'd ever come to it, and she found she quite liked sharing a meal with people who made dinner—or supper, as her family called it—an important part of the day. It was quite pleasant to have a meal with others who conversed with each other in a congenial way, instead of shoveling food in their mouths, complaining about their day and the meal. Or who left others at the table when one was through eating, as Clancy had always done. Much as she missed her sister and nephews, she did not miss anything else about living with her family. Only the three of them. And, oh, how she wished she could get them out of the tenements.

"Did you make all of this, Violet?" Elizabeth asked.

"Oh, no. Hilda is quite the cook and she did most of it. I did make the dessert, though," Violet said just as Hilda brought in a lemon pie piled high with a golden meringue.

"It's all wonderful," Kathleen said.

"Thank you," Violet said. "I'm glad you're recovered enough to be back at work and that you felt like coming this evening."

"So am I. Thank you so much for including me in your invitation."

"You're welcome here anytime, Kathleen. And you never need an invitation to stop by."

Violet's words touched Kathleen's heart, for she could tell the young bride meant them. She looked around the table and realized that she'd made friends of each person there. Michael had prayed God's blessing on each of them. But the Lord had already blessed her by bringing these people into her life.

True to her word, after dinner Violet showed them the rest of their home. The parlor was across the way as in Heaton House, and a bit smaller. Decorated in yellows and blues, it was quite inviting. There was no second parlor, but a small library connecting to the parlor.

"This is where Michael works and I read," Violet said. It was quite cozy with two chairs pulled near the fireplace.

They headed upstairs afterward and there were three nice-sized bedrooms, a bathroom and one smaller room attached to the master bedroom.

"This is perfect for a nursery," Elizabeth said.

"And will be used for just that one day," Michael said.

Kathleen couldn't miss Violet's blush as her husband looked at her. It was more than a little refreshing to see a couple so in love with each other. She remembered her parents' devotion to each other but she hadn't seen that kind of relationship in a very long time.

She'd often wondered if her sister's marriage had ever been a happy one. Was it the eventual struggle to get by that had made it an unhappy one?

Once in a while even in the tenements, she'd see couples happy and pulling together to make it. Still more often than not, she'd seen the total opposite—men mistreating their wives and children—so much so that she thought what her parents had shared was no longer possible. And yet, if what she saw between Violet and Michael was real, could it be possible for her?

"Your home is beautiful, Violet," Kathleen said as they all headed back downstairs.

"Thank you. We think so and of course, we love it. Up on the third floor are two other rooms and a bath. Hilda has one and, well, if Heaton House should ever be so full that Mother Heaton can't take in a temporary in need, as she calls them, we can offer a room."

It was obvious the Heatons put helping others at the top of their priority list and Kathleen was a grateful recipient of their generosity.

After playing charades for a while, they were served hot cocoa before going back out into the cool night.

"Spring is right around the corner," Michael said, "but it's been hard to tell the last few weeks."

"I'm looking forward to picnicking in Central Park," Julia said. "It won't be long before we can."

Kathleen glanced at Luke to find him gazing at her. She'd love to go to Central Park—and she'd love to run into her sister and the boys. But with them came Clancy and he was someone she never hoped to see again.

Once they were back in the omnibus, with Luke by her side once more, he turned to her and spoke quietly. "You know, when we can go to the park again, I don't want you to worry about running into your brother-in-law. He won't hurt you again, Kathleen. I won't leave your side—not for a moment. I promise you that."

"Thank you, Luke."

No wonder she felt safest around this man. Somehow he'd appointed himself her guardian and for that she could only be thankful.

Chapter Six

The next few weeks were some of the best Kathleen could ever remember as she settled in more at Heaton House. Her rib hurt less each day and she no longer came home from work totally exhausted.

Evenings were always enjoyable and she along with the other women had gone on several outings to Ladies' Mile, to browse and see what would be in fashion that spring. So far she'd never come home with anything, but she at least was learning how to accessorize the clothes Elizabeth, Julia and even Violet had given her. She particularly liked browsing at Macy's and Lord & Taylor.

She and the other girls from Heaton House enjoyed window-shopping as much as anything, watching the wealthy come out of stores with their servants trailing behind, carrying their purchases.

Kathleen had never really had good women friends except for her sister and she greatly enjoyed getting to know the women of Heaton House.

She'd learned that Violet and Michael had been neighbors back in Virginia where they both were from, but it wasn't until Violet came to the city to try to pay off the mortgage to her family home that they'd fallen in love.

"I'm so glad you've found true love, but I'm not sure I can ever give my heart to a man," Kathleen said one Saturday afternoon when they were having tea at a small café along Ladies' Mile.

"Oh, Kathleen, don't think that way. There are good men out there."

"But how does one know they'll remain good? My sister Colleen thought Clancy was a good man when she first met him. But it didn't take long after they married for her to find out otherwise. Only by then she loved him and thought she could change him." Kathleen shook her head. "She's been miserable ever since they married."

"I'm sorry about that, Kathleen. But you can't let yourself believe that all men are like your brother-in-law. They aren't. You already know that. Look at my Michael and then of course there's Luke."

Luke. He did seem to be the exception of—

"And there's John and Ben," Mrs. Heaton added. "They're all good Christian men, Kathleen."

"They seem to be." Kathleen sighed. "But how does one ever know if they'll change when they marry or if they are only on their best behavior during the courting stage? Living in the tenements, I've seen some good men who treat their wives right. But I've seen so much more of the opposite kind of men. I'm just not sure I'll ever be able to trust my heart to anyone."

"I'm going to pray you change your mind, dear," Mrs. Heaton said. "A loving man and a good marriage are a true blessing. Just let the Lord guide you—" her gaze took in Kathleen, Elizabeth and Julia "—all of you—in your choice of a husband. Listen to your heart and the Lord and you won't go wrong."

Her words gave Kathleen something to think about as they started back to Heaton House, but still she didn't see marriage in her future. It had to be easier not to depend on a man for either your livelihood or your happiness. It certainly hadn't been for her sister.

When they returned there was a letter waiting for her from Colleen and she hurried upstairs to read it in private. She settled down in the comfortable chair by the window and slit the letter open with the beautiful letter opener Mrs. Heaton had given her.

Dear Kathleen,
It is always so good to hear from you. I'm glad to know that you are recovering and beginning a new life out of this place. Thank you for the money you sent. It has come in very handy this week as Clancy lost yet another job. He's been in one of those moods and I'm glad you aren't here to see it.

The boys say to tell you they love you and thank you for the penny candy you provided through the money you sent. Of course you know that I love you, too. I'm so thankful that we can at least keep in touch by letter. I hope to report that Clancy has a new job next time. Pray for us, won't you?
Love always, your sister Colleen

Clancy without a job was not a good thing. Kathleen bowed her head and whispered a prayer. "Dear

Lord, please watch over Colleen and the boys, please keep them safe and keep Clancy from hurting any of them. Please let him find a job soon. In Jesus's name I pray, Amen."

She brushed at the tears just thinking of her nephews and her sister brought about. She wasn't there. She couldn't do anything other than leave it all in the Lord's hands—and trust that He'd watch over her loved ones.

Kathleen sighed and pushed herself out of the chair, her side giving a small twinge as she did. She freshened up and changed for dinner. She'd write Colleen tonight when she came back up and tell her she never stopped praying for them.

That evening, Michael and Violet joined them for dinner and everyone was in high spirits as they discussed going to the symphony the next week. Kathleen had never been before and was very excited about it.

Just as Kathleen and Violet were heading to the parlor with the others after dinner, a knock came on the door. Kathleen had learned that a visitor this time of evening was rare, and they stopped to see who was at the door Gretchen opened.

Kathleen felt a sliver of apprehension seeing one of the policemen who'd been at the park the day Luke had come to her defense.

"Evening, ma'am," he said to Gretchen. "I'm Officer O'Malley and I'd like to speak to Kathleen O'Bryan, if I may."

Dread flooded Kathleen's heart as she stepped forward. "I'm Kathleen O'Bryan, Officer. What do you need to talk to me about?"

She was barely aware that Luke stood by her, if for

nothing else but support, as did Violet and Michael who moved to stand on the other side of her.

"Miss O'Bryan, there is no easy way to say this. I'm sorry to report that your sister has been shot and is in the hospital, ma'am."

"No!" If not for Luke's quick grasp of her arm, Kathleen was sure she would have crumpled at his feet. "Is she—"

"The doctors say she will be all right. But she is asking for you."

"I must go to her." Trying to gather her thoughts, Kathleen turned away then back again. "Yes. I must go now. The children. Where are they?"

"They're with a neighbor. I believe her name is Mrs. Walsh."

"Good." Kathleen nodded and released a deep breath before asking, "And Clancy? Colleen's husband?"

"He is dead, ma'am."

Kathleen felt herself begin to slump for a moment but again Luke was there to hold her up. She pulled herself together, let out a deep breath and stood straight once more. "What hospital is my sister in, Officer?"

"Bellevue. We can take you—"

"I'll take her, Officer. I have a hack on the way now," Luke said.

Kathleen assumed that he'd had someone call for one and was proved right when Michael came back to say the cab would be right there.

"We'll be going with you," Michael stated.

"All right, then." The officer nodded. "As long as she's not by herself. The neighbor said not to worry about the children, ma'am. She'll take care of them until you can get there."

"Thank you, Officer."

"I'm sorry to bring such news. I'll see you at the hospital."

The hack arrived and Luke helped her out to it. The ride to the hospital was one of silence, no one knowing what to say. Kathleen did the only thing she knew would help. She prayed silently and continually.

When they arrived at the hospital, they were taken to a room on the second floor and led through a row of beds on each side of the room. They passed other patients, some moaning and groaning in pain, others just lying there staring out into the room, and still others curled up and seeming to be asleep.

They stopped about midway down the aisle and Kathleen could no longer keep her composure as she saw her sister, her face black and blue from what must have been a beating, but with a huge bandage over her shoulder and part of her chest. She couldn't hold back a deep sob.

A nurse was with her and she turned to Kathleen. "Are you her sister?"

Kathleen nodded, wiping at her eyes. "Is she...is she going to be all right?"

"Yes. But—" The nurse shook her head and leaned closer to whisper, "I am sorry to tell you that she lost the baby."

Kathleen closed her eyes, but the only sound that came out of her mouth was a small moan as the nurse continued, "She just drifted off, but she's been waiting for you. I'll see if I can find a doctor...and here comes Officer O'Malley. He can tell you what happened before she came here. Perhaps you'd like to talk in the hallway?"

Kathleen hesitated while the officer stood by her side.

"I promise she's going to be all right, but it will take time to heal and get over the sorrow," the nurse said.

With a short nod, Kathleen and the officer headed toward the hallway with Luke, Michael and Violet following behind.

Officer O'Malley led Kathleen to a bench and sat down beside her. "You may get more information from your sister when she can talk more easily, or from her neighbors, but this is what I know. About five o'clock, one of the neighbors alerted us that there was a huge ruckus going on in your sister's apartment. They'd heard her screaming and the children crying."

Violet brushed at the tears that seemed to flow of their own accord.

"When we got there, we had to break down the door. Your brother-in-law had a gun in his hand and from the looks of her face, that's what he beat her with," Officer O'Malley continued. "Soon as we yelled for him to stop, a shot when off and, well, that's when he shot your sister. He turned, we told him to drop the gun and he shot again. I don't know whose shot killed him but both my partner and I pulled our triggers about the same time."

Kathleen closed her eyes and began to rock to and fro. Violet quickly sat down on the other side of her and put an arm around her.

"I'm sorry, ma'am. I hate this part of my job." The look in the officer's eyes said he was telling the truth.

"Oh, no. Please..." Kathleen paused, shaking her head. "Thank you for saving my sister's life. If you hadn't been there, she might not be here right now."

From the corner of her eye Kathleen saw a youngish man come up to them. "Miss O'Bryan?"

"Yes." She turned to him.

"I'm Doctor Addison. I just wanted to let you know that your sister will be all right."

Kathleen sighed with relief and swallowed around the knot in her throat.

"She's very lucky. If that bullet had hit her a little lower, she'd be gone. As it is, she'll be very sore for a while and won't be able to lift much, but she'll recover. It may take longer for her to get over the losses she's suffered tonight, but in time, she will. She'll be here a few more days before she can be released, but she seems to be worried about her children and kept calling for you."

"I'll try to set her mind at ease," Kathleen said. "Is she awake yet?"

"Let's go see."

Kathleen stood and followed the doctor back to her sister's bed. She sat down and reached out for Colleen's hand. *Thank you, Lord, for bringing her through. Please heal her completely and quickly. Please help me to know how to help her now.*

"I have to get back to write up the report," Officer O'Malley said. "Please tell Miss O'Bryan that I'll be checking on her and that if she has any questions before then to contact me."

"We will," Luke said. "Thank you, Officer O'Malley."

The policeman inclined his head and headed down the hall.

Restless, Luke got up and went to the door of the hospital room. He watched as Kathleen pulled up a chair to sit by her sister. His heart broke as he saw the expression on her face when she reached over to take her sister's hand.

He sighed and pinched the bridge of his nose as he sent up a prayer asking for the Lord to heal Kathleen's sister and be with her and her family.

Michael came up behind him and nudged his arm as he looked at Kathleen once more. "Come on, Luke. It could be a while. Let's take a seat."

Luke nodded and the three of them sat on the bench Kathleen had vacated earlier. He turned to Michael and Violet. "I want to give her all the time she needs. You two can go on home. I'll get her to her nephews or wherever she wants to go when she's ready."

"We'll wait awhile. We probably should go with you. No telling what the apartment looks like. If there's blood—" Violet stopped and shuddered.

Michael put an arm around his wife and pulled her close. "At least she won't have to worry about that brother-in-law taking his rage out on her family or her anymore."

Or about me getting hold of him one day. Luke began to pace the floor. He wanted to be by her side, should she need him, but she hadn't asked him to go with her and he didn't have the right to impose himself on her at this time. He couldn't help but wonder what Kathleen would do now that her sister's husband was no longer a threat to her or her sister and nephews. Would she go back to live with them? He didn't want her to leave Heaton House.

Luke continued to pace for what seemed like hours. In reality it was probably less than one before Kathleen joined them again.

"She seems to be sleeping peacefully now. And I promised her I'd go home to the children. I'm sure they're quite frightened and I need to get to them and assure them their mama is all right."

Her eyes were bright with unshed tears and she shook her head. "I don't know what to tell them about their papa." She looked around. "Is Officer O'Malley still here? I'll get him to take me home."

"He had to go, but he said he'd be checking on you," Luke said. "I'm going to take you wherever you need to go."

"We're all going with you," Violet said.

"Violet, I'm not sure that's a good idea, you—"

"Kathleen, your sister's children need you now. I want to help." Violet put an arm around her friend. "Let's get you to them."

Kathleen looked at Luke and then Michael.

"But—"

Michael shook his head. "No sense in arguing with her, Kathleen. Violet has her mind made up. And she's right. You don't know what you're facing when you get there and we want to help."

Finally, she nodded. "All right. Let's go."

It didn't take as long as Luke feared to procure a hack to take them to Kathleen's sister's building. As the driver pulled up to the tenement, there was no little amount of curiosity about the arrival of a hired vehicle from those still on their stoops and the street outside.

Luke and Michael helped the women out of the hack and Kathleen led the way inside. Several people recognized her and asked about her sister. No one expressed condolences about her brother-in-law, which told Luke the man wouldn't have many mourning his demise.

He followed Kathleen up the stairs. The hall was dark and dingy, stuffy and smelling of everything imaginable, and Luke didn't want her to move back here. Ever.

Chapter Seven

Luke could tell that Kathleen was distressed that they were seeing where she'd lived by the way her back stiffened as he followed her up the narrow staircase. With each flight he tried to ignore the heat that rose with them, the aromas that assailed them. When they reached the fifth-floor landing they started down the dark hallway. Somewhere a baby needed a diaper change and someone else must have cooked cabbage. He could hear a couple arguing as they passed one door.

Kathleen seemed to hold her back even straighter as they continued on. Midway down the hall she stopped and knocked on a door. The door creaked open only an inch or so and a man peeked out. Luke recognized him as the man who'd brought her to Heaton House. Once he saw Kathleen, he opened it a bit wider. "Sorry about your sister, Kathleen. I'll get Rose."

He'd barely turned away before he called, "Rose! Kathleen is here for the kids."

A woman came to the door, wiping her hands on a dish towel. "Oh, Kathleen, how is Colleen?"

"They say she'll be fine, but she doesn't look it. She's

badly bruised, and you know she was shot, don't you? And…" Kathleen paused and swallowed hard. "She lost the baby."

"Oh, I'm so sorry." Rose reached out and put a hand on Kathleen's shoulder.

"She insisted I come see about the children and I knew she wouldn't have any peace until I did. Nor would I."

"I tried to get them to eat, but they only pushed their food around on their plates. They are welcome to stay here until you can make arrangements—"

"No, thank you, but I need to see them, please." Kathleen's voice broke and Luke could only imagine how she felt. It'd been a while since she'd seen the nephews she loved so much.

Rose nodded. "Let me get them for you."

"Thank you, Rose."

It was only a moment before two little boys came running. "Aunt Kathleen!"

Luke heard Kathleen's stifled sob as she dropped to the floor and gathered the two little boys into her arms. They began talking over each other, telling her about their mama and papa arguing and papa hitting mama and all the blood, sobbing as she gathered them closer and rocked them back and forth.

"I'm here now. And Mama's going to be all right in time. It's going to be all right."

They clung to each other and Luke looked away as his emotions threatened to get away from him. He saw Violet put a hand to her mouth and tears gather in her eyes as Michael pulled her closer to him. Evidently they were touched just as much.

Kathleen stood and looked at her neighbor. "Thank you, Rose. I—"

"No need, Kathleen. I'll keep them tomorrow while you go see about Colleen. Just bring them over when you get ready. And I'll help out when she gets home. A woman shouldn't be treated the way Clancy treated her. She'll be better off without him."

Kathleen only nodded. "Thank you. I'll see you tomorrow."

From there, they formed a little caravan, with Kathleen and her nephews in front, Luke behind her and Violet and Michael in the rear. She stopped at a corner apartment and unlocked the door. The children clung to her as Kathleen turned to him and Michael and Violet.

"Thank you for bringing me home. I appreciate it more than I can say, but we'll be all right. I'll arrange to get my things in a few days—"

Luke's chest tightened. She intended to stay here.

"Nonsense," Violet said. "We'll get your things to you and we aren't leaving now. I'm going to see if you need help in cleaning up…" She swallowed hard and pushed her way inside.

"Violet, I can do it." Kathleen followed her and Luke could hear the relief as it whooshed from her chest.

He looked around but there was no evidence of a gunfight in the room they were in. Someone, probably Rose, had cleaned up what must have been a horrid sight and Luke was thankful for all their sakes. "You do have some good neighbors, Kathleen."

She nodded as she looked around. "Even better than I thought. Thank you for seeing us home. Please, everyone, your evening has been taken up—"

"Kathleen, stop talking like that. You are our friend

and we care about you," Violet said. "Let's light a lamp or two. It will be better for the children."

Luke and Michael did as she suggested, quite certain that Violet was going nowhere until she was convinced Kathleen and the children would be all right.

"Do you think the children would eat if I make something?"

"Thank you, Violet, but I doubt it. I'll make them something if they get hungry later."

"I'd be glad to make you all something." She looked around and Luke could see the disgust she was trying to hide from Kathleen that anyone had to live in these conditions. There were only three very small rooms in the apartment and no bathroom. It appeared they had to share one down the hall, or maybe even on another floor. The kitchen, if it could be called that, was in a corner. It consisted of a small sink, a tiny range and a small icebox.

The blood might have been cleaned up, and it appeared that Kathleen's sister tried to keep the apartment clean best she could, but the overall squalor of the building and the neighborhood couldn't be fixed so easily.

"Kathleen, why don't you go back to Heaton House with us? You know the children would be welcome."

"No, Michael, but I thank you. I can't impose on your mother any more than I already have."

"Please come back with us, Kathleen," Luke said. "The boys can share my room."

Kathleen shook her head. "Thank you for the offer, Luke. But I can't. I'm not being stubborn. I'm doing what is best. If we were to go back to the boarding-house, that would show the children a side of life they can't live in forever and it would make it harder for them to come back here. We'll get out of here one day, but until then we must accept that this is our life. It won't be forever, I assure you."

"But it doesn't have to be now, either."

"Yes, Violet, it does. My sister will come home, Rose will help her and watch the children while I work and we'll get on our feet. It will be easier without—"

She looked down at the two boys who still clung to her skirts. "We will be all right. And I will be in touch. Don't worry."

Luke could only watch as Violet looked at the children and swallowed hard. She turned back to Kathleen. "All right. We'll get your things to you."

"Thank you." Kathleen reached out an arm to hug Violet. "Your friendship means more to me than I can say."

She turned to Michael. "As does yours and your mother's. Please tell her I will be in contact and thank her for all she's done for me. Now, please go so that I can explain things to the children and comfort them."

Luke saw the resolve in Kathleen's eyes. She needed them to leave. But he wasn't going just yet.

"You two go on. I'll be along shortly," Luke said in a quiet voice, looking Michael in the eye, trying to convey his need to talk to Kathleen alone.

"All right."

Even Violet seemed to be more at ease knowing Luke wasn't leaving just yet.

"We'll be checking on you."

Kathleen nodded and Luke had a feeling that she was just trying to appease Violet so that she would leave.

"Come, Violet. I'll bring you back," Michael said.

Violet nodded and followed him out the door.

Kathleen turned to him. "Thank you again for being with me once more in my time of need, Luke."

"Kathleen, let me help you get the boys to bed. And then I'll go. Please."

He thought she was going to turn him down, but she nodded instead. "This is Mr. Patterson, Collin and Brody. He's a friend of mine."

Collin nodded. "I 'member him. He helped you and Mama at the park that day."

Luke remembered the way they'd clung to their mother's skirts that day, hiding behind her in fear and yet begging Kathleen not to send their papa to jail.

He bent down to their level and looked the one called Collin in the eyes. "It's good to meet you again, Collin. I remember you, too."

Luke held out a hand and the young boy looked at him for a moment before slipping his smaller hand into Luke's. Luke gave it a shake and then turned to the younger boy. "And you're Brody?"

He nodded and sidled closer to Kathleen.

"I'm pleased to meet you, too. Your aunt has missed you very much."

Tears welled up in both boys' eyes.

"We missed her, too," Collin said.

"Well, you'll be seeing a lot more of her again now. Will you let me help Aunt Kathleen get you ready for bed?"

Brody stuck a finger in his mouth and nodded. Luke picked him up and looked at Kathleen. "Tell me what to do."

Brody put a hand on Luke's cheek and turned his

face to look at him. "Didn't your mama teach you how to wash for bed? Ya put water in a bowl, get a clean rag and scrub your face and hands and then yer feet."

Luke chuckled and even Kathleen joined in as they set about getting her nephews ready for bed.

Much as she'd wanted everyone to leave, Kathleen had to admit Luke was a great help and his presence comforted her.

But once the boys were ready to be tucked in, she turned to him. "Thank you for helping me, Luke. But it's getting late and I need to make sure they go to sleep assured their mama is coming home."

"I understand, but I still wish you'd take them back to Heaton House, Kathleen. It's not too late and we'll all help out with them."

"But, Luke, they can't stay there and it would be so much more difficult for them to have to come back here again." She knew firsthand how hard it would be.

Luke only nodded. "Go on and tuck them in, then. I'll be here when you get through. I know how to make myself a cup of tea."

"But you can't—"

"I'll only stay until you have them asleep and I know *you* are all right."

There was a glint in his eye that told her she might have won the battle over her staying here with the boys, but he wasn't going anywhere until he spoke to her again.

She gave a brief nod and headed to the room she'd shared with her nephews. They were both sitting on their pallets waiting for her.

She gathered them close and rocked back and forth,

thankful they were all right and she was with them again. But talking to them about their mama and papa was the hardest thing she'd ever done—after seeing Colleen in that hospital bed, her face black-and-blue, all bandaged up and knowing she'd lost the baby. She had to keep reminding herself that the doctor and nurse said she would be fine…eventually. But her sweet sister certainly didn't look like she'd be all back to normal anytime soon.

"Mama's going to be all right, Aunt Kathleen?" Collin asked as she'd cuddled them and tried to assure them. "She's not going to die, is she?"

"Oh, no, Collin, your mama isn't going to die. She'll have to stay in the hospital for a little while, but she's going to be all right. And you'll have to be good boys and help her some. But I know you'll do that."

"Oh, we will," Collin said, his eyes big and overly bright. She wasn't sure if he was going to cry or not. He looked at his little brother. "Won't we, Brody?"

Brody solemnly moved his head up and down and cuddled closer to Kathleen.

"But your papa won't be coming home." Kathleen held her breath waiting for them to ask why.

Instead, Collin only asked, "Never again?"

"Never again." Kathleen felt guilty for the surge of relief that washed over her at the realization that her brother-in-law would never be able to hurt her sister again. That he was gone for good and that he got what he deserved. *Lord, please forgive me. I know I should feel sad for him, but right now all I can feel is relief that he won't hurt anyone again. That I can be part of my family's life again.*

Whether the boys realized their papa was dead or

not, she didn't know. They didn't ask. Nor did they cry. Collin had only said, "He won't be able to hurt Mama or you again."

"He won't be able to hurt anyone." Kathleen didn't tell them about the baby, she'd let Colleen do that or at least ask her if she should when she saw her again. For now, the boys had heard enough bad news. She looked down on the innocent faces and thanked the Lord for answering her prayers and for letting Colleen be alive, for letting the boys be unharmed.

After saying their prayers with them and kissing them good-night, she slipped out of the room, leaving the door cracked so she could hear them if they needed her.

Then she went out to find Luke standing at the window, waiting for her. She joined him there.

"Are they asleep?" he asked.

"Not yet, but it's been a tiring day for them. I'm sure they will be soon."

"I can see why you've missed them so much."

Kathleen drew a ragged breath and nodded. She tried to blink back the tears that fought to be let loose.

Luke reached out to brush a tear and she flinched. His hand stilled. This was Luke, she reminded herself. Not Clancy. He only wanted to comfort her. At that knowledge she leaned her cheek into his hand and sighed.

Luke pulled her into his arms and for the first time in a very long time, Kathleen gave herself over to the emotion. Her breath released on a sob and she let the tears come. He rocked her back and forth and rubbed her back with one hand until her tears were spent. Then he raised her chin so that he could look into her eyes.

"I'm sorry. I've got your shirt all wet and—"

Luke stopped her words with his fingertips on her lips. "It will dry. You needed to cry it out."

She nodded but didn't know what to say next. She didn't want him to go and yet, she knew she must send him away.

"Thank you for being here. I—"

"And you need some rest. I don't want to leave you, but I'll check on you tomorrow. There is a telephone in this building somewhere, isn't there?"

She nodded. "The landlady on the first floor has one."

"If you need me for anything, you telephone me."

"I will."

"Promise?"

"I promise."

His arms were still wrapped loosely around her and he placed his forehead against hers. "I'm sorry about your sister, Kathleen. But I'm so glad you weren't here when it happened. You might have ended up in the hospital, too. Or worse. And I..." He pulled back slightly and raised her chin. He shook his head and sighed. "You lock up good. I won't leave until I hear all these locks click."

"All right."

"The kettle is hot. Make some tea and I'll see you tomorrow."

She nodded.

He went through the doorway and pulled the door shut behind him. "Lock up now."

Kathleen did as he said, turning the three locks.

"Good night," Luke said from the other side of the door.

"Good night." Kathleen heard his footsteps fade be-

fore she turned and then hurried to the window. She
pulled the thin curtain back and glanced down just as
Luke left the building and looked up. She didn't know if
he saw her or not but she waved, just in case. He waved
back and she touched the windowpane, as if she could
touch this man who'd begun to mean so much to her.

Once he was out of sight, she went to check on the
boys and found them fast asleep. She pulled the covers
up over them and kissed their cheeks.

She pulled the kettle from the back of the stove and
poured it over tea she'd placed in a small pot, then went
to look out the windows while she waited for it to steep.

The view was the same as it was when she left.
Buildings, just like the one they lived in, lined up
across and down the street. So many people living in
squalor. Such an extreme difference in the way she'd
been able to live these past weeks.

She'd been relieved when Violet and Michael left.
They were wonderful friends, but she hated for them
to see the conditions she'd lived in before she'd come
to Mrs. Heaton's home. Hated that they had to know
the ugliness that happened in the tenements at times.
Hated that they knew it had happened in her family.
And yet she knew they cared. They would treat her
and her family the same as they had from the day they
took her in and she would always be grateful to them.

Still, it had hurt to see Luke go, knowing that she
wasn't going back to Heaton House anytime soon, if
ever. At that thought her heart tightened as if it were
being squeezed by a vise and she swallowed around
the knot in her throat. She'd known it was too good
to be true.

Would she see her friends again? Or would they

go on about their lives? She certainly couldn't expect them to come here. And with Colleen in the shape she was, it'd be up to her to take care of her sister and the boys. They were all the family she had and she loved them. At least Clancy couldn't hurt any of them again.

But, oh, how she longed to be back at Heaton House, longed to have gone with Luke and taken the boys with her. Still, she had to do what was best for the boys.

She looked around the apartment and saw a mouse come out of hiding and skitter across the floor. It was a sight she'd seen often but it still sent a shiver down her back.

Living here was horrible, especially after living at Heaton House. But now she was more determined than ever to get her family out of the tenements and into something they could call home. And one day she would.

Chapter Eight

Luke let himself in Heaton House with a heavy heart. One of the hardest things he'd ever done was to leave Kathleen and her nephews in that apartment. And when he'd looked up to see her looking out her window, he'd almost rushed back in to insist she come with him.

But she had a stubborn streak and he couldn't really argue with her reasoning. It would be hard on those boys to live at Heaton House and then have to go back. They'd be dealing with enough in the weeks to come. And Kathleen—how hard must it be for her to have lived here and then have to return to that apartment?

"Luke? We're in the parlor," Mrs. Heaton called. "Please come join us."

Luke was a bit surprised to find Violet and Michael had come back there and were waiting for him to return. They were in the parlor with the others and had filled them in on what they knew of the evening.

"How are Kathleen and her nephews?" Mrs. Heaton asked. "I remember those little boys from that day in the park."

Luke smiled. "I'm sure they're better now that they

have their aunt Kathleen. I believe they were almost asleep when I left."

"And Kathleen? How is she?" Violet asked.

Luke swallowed hard, remembering her sobs. "It's been hard on her, but Kathleen will do whatever she needs to."

"We told Mother that we tried to get her to bring her nephews here, but that she said no," Michael said.

"Well, they aren't going to stay there for much longer, rest assured of that. Not if Violet, Elizabeth and I have anything to do with it," Mrs. Heaton declared. "We've been working on a project for a while now— even before Kathleen came to stay. And even harder once she did."

"What is it?" Luke asked. "What do you have planned?"

"It will take Kathleen and her sister both working, unless one of them marries and possibly even then, to afford a decent place to live," Mrs. Heaton said. "But they have no child care apart from depending on a neighbor and that isn't something they can depend on permanently. And it's not getting them out of the tenements.

"So, we are going to try to get some kind of child care started," his mother added. "Surely there are those who love children and would be thrilled to be paid to keep them while their mothers work. Or maybe it will be a chance for some mothers to work and have their children with them while they watch over other children, since not all employers want to hire married women—especially mothers—although some of them are the most in need of work."

"Are you hoping that some businesses or benefactors will see the need and provide the space?" If so, the idea made good sense to Luke.

"Yes. That's it, exactly." Violet seemed pleased that he was interested.

"It's a good idea," Michael said. "I'll run it by some people I know. If you can get a few started in different parts of the city, then it will be easier to get more people on board. What about our churches? If we could get them to sponsor or help to sponsor one or two children or the homes, that would help."

"That is a wonderful idea, son. Would you bring it up to the church elders?"

"Certainly I will. I must say, I'm quite proud of you all for coming up with this idea," Michael said.

"You know, I'd like to write an article about the need," John said. "I can't guarantee that it will get in the paper or, even if it does, that it won't be buried on the back pages, but it might generate some interest."

"Oh, John, that is a good idea," Elizabeth said. "I'll run it by my editors at *The Delineator*. Maybe they will ask to reprint your article or ask for another."

"Thank you, Elizabeth."

Luke hoped the plan worked. He wanted Kathleen and her family out of the tenements as soon as possible.

Everyone seemed very enthusiastic about the project and Luke could see that Mrs. Heaton, Elizabeth and Violet were quite determined to carry it through.

"For now," Mrs. Heaton said, "Clara has excused Kathleen from work, but she won't be able to do it indefinitely. And of course that doesn't fill their immediate need for food and all—"

"Why don't we take up a collection? I'm sure everyone here will chip in and maybe Mrs. Driscoll could collect from work," Elizabeth said.

"That's another great idea," Luke said. He'd been planning on sending something to Kathleen anonymously but he'd add his contribution to the rest. "How long do you think this plan will take to firm up?" Luke asked.

"We're hoping to be able to tell Kathleen and her sister about it in a few weeks," Mrs. Heaton said.

Luke nodded. That wasn't all that long. Not really. So why did it feel like forever?

Luke knew the tenements would look much worse in the daylight, but when he accompanied Mrs. Heaton and Elizabeth to take Kathleen's things to her the next afternoon after Sunday dinner, he was still taken aback by the utter hopelessness in the faces of some of the tenants.

He'd been in and out of areas like this one before, but never had someone he cared about lived in those conditions. Much as it bothered him before, having Kathleen move back there lit a fire inside him to complete his book.

Many of these people had come to this country to have a better life than where they'd come from, just as Kathleen's family had. But if this was better—and he didn't possibly know how it could be with people so crowded together—he hated to think of what it must have been like in their homelands.

From the look on Mrs. Heaton's and Elizabeth's faces, they were dealing with the same kinds of feelings. Luke lifted Kathleen's satchel out of the hack and

Mrs. Heaton and Elizabeth grabbed the bags of extras they'd brought.

If possible, the stairwells and halls were dingier in the daylight where what sunlight did find its way in caught up all the dust moats and illuminated the filth. The odors clung to the air and the yelling seemed even louder, although not quite as menacing as in the dark of the night before.

They didn't know if Kathleen would be home or not, but were hoping that she was as they made their way down the hall to her sister's apartment. Luke knocked on the door and waited. He thought he heard the murmur of voices, but couldn't be sure where it was coming from.

Just as he'd decided to check with the neighbor and see if Kathleen had left the boys with her and gone to the hospital, the door opened slightly. Kathleen peeked out and then opened the door a bit wider. She stood there with her two young nephews peeking out from behind her skirt.

"You didn't have to do this today," Kathleen said. "I would have come to collect my things."

"We wanted to check on you and your family," Mrs. Heaton said, smiling at the children. She brushed past Kathleen and into the apartment. "And your sister? How is she, do you know?"

"I haven't had a chance to go see her yet, but I'm praying that she is better."

"Well, let's take care of that," Mrs. Heaton said. "Luke can take you to the hospital and Elizabeth and I will stay with the children until you get back."

"Oh, no, Mrs. Heaton. I couldn't ask you to do that. Thank you so much, but this is no place for you. I'll leave them with the neighbor later on and go see about Colleen."

"No place for me? It's no place for you and your family, either. It is no place for anyone, Kathleen, dear. But if you insist on staying here for now, then you must expect to see us from time to time. You've become dear to me and to all of us, and we'll not let that connection be lost."

"I—"

"Please, Kathleen, let us help you," Elizabeth implored. "The children will be fine with us and we brought them a treat."

"Might as well say yes, Kathleen," Luke said. "We aren't leaving and you may as well let me take you to the hospital to find out how your sister is doing."

"I…" She looked around the room and then gave a shrug as if she didn't want them to see it, but as they were already inside, there was nothing she could do about it. "All right. Thank you."

She turned to the boys. "This is Mr. Patterson from last night. Do you remember him?"

Both boys nodded and Luke smiled at them.

"And this is Mrs. Heaton, the lady whose home I lived in while I was gone, and this is Elizabeth. She's a good friend, too. They are very nice people and they're going to watch you while I go see how your mama is doing. You behave yourselves, you hear?"

The boys nodded again, Brody with a thumb stuck in his mouth.

"I'll tell Mama that you miss her and want her home quickly." She kissed the tops of their heads and nodded to Luke. "Let's go."

The boys continued to hold on to her skirt, looking

first at Elizabeth and then Mrs. Heaton. Then the older boy—maybe five or six years old—whispered to his little brother. The little one nodded and smiled at the women. Still keeping one hand on Kathleen's skirt, he gave a half wave as if a little afraid to fully acknowledge seeing them before.

"It'll be fun. We brought you a treat," Mrs. Heaton said, looking at Kathleen and giving her a wink.

"Gretchen sent some of her molasses cookies and some other things she thought you could use," Elizabeth explained, digging into one of the bags and bringing out a smaller bag of cookies.

The boys looked to their aunt and at her nod, they immediately let go of her skirt and hurried over to Mrs. Heaton, who handed each of them a cookie.

"Thank you," Kathleen said as she and Luke walked out the door.

She walked ahead of him and Luke could tell by now that when she held herself so rigid, she was trying to hide her emotions.

But last night, just for a few minutes, she'd let her guard down and let him see a side of her he was sure not many did. And somehow that made him feel that she might be coming to trust him. Maybe, just a little. Only time would tell.

Kathleen let Luke help her into the hack he'd kept waiting outside. As they had last night, children and others had surrounded it—they didn't see many hired vehicles in this part of town.

But many of them asked about her sister and told her they'd say a prayer for her. Kathleen kept assuring herself that the hospital would have gotten word to her if Colleen had taken a turn for the worse, but she wouldn't rest until she saw her.

"Thank you for coming," she said, turning to Luke. "I was about to take the boys to Rose, but they were afraid to leave in case their mama came home today. I tried to tell them that she'd have to stay in the hospital a few days, but they don't really understand and I couldn't bring myself to tell them about the baby."

"That's understandable, Kathleen. It'd be difficult for any of us." He reached out for her hand and she slipped it into his, somehow needing his touch. Luke covered her hand with his larger one and gave it a light squeeze. "Maybe you'll have good news to share with them when we get back."

"I hope so. Right now my prayer is just for Colleen to get better."

"I'm praying the same, as I'm sure all the others at Heaton House are."

"Thank you, Luke. It does comfort me to know that."

They arrived at the hospital just then and Luke helped her out of the hack and then kept a hand on her elbow as they went inside and up to Colleen's room.

Kathleen turned to him at the door. "I'm not sure if you— She doesn't know you, other than what I've written in my letters and…"

"It's all right, Kathleen. You go on in. I'll wait over on that bench for you." He pointed to a bench right across from the doorway where he could see into the room. "If you need me, just wave."

Kathleen nodded. She really wished he could come with her. Colleen had looked so terrible last night, that even though the doctor said she'd recover, Kathleen wasn't so sure. She'd like some support when she saw her for the first time today. But she didn't know how Colleen would react to seeing Luke or anyone besides her and she didn't want to stress her any more than she already must be.

She made her way down the aisle to the last bed. Colleen's eyes were closed and Kathleen pulled a chair up to her side as quietly as she could. Her sister's color looked a little better than last night—at least where it wasn't bruised.

Kathleen bowed her head to pray and placed a hand over Colleen's. Her touch made her sister jerk awake.

"Ahh...Kathleen, 'tis you. How are my boys? Where are they?"

"Shh, don't get yourself all wound up. Collin and Brody are fine. I wouldn't have left them if they weren't. But they are anxious for news of you and I had to see how you are."

"I lost the baby.... Did they tell you?"

"They did. I'm so sorry, Colleen. But I'm thankful that you are still here with us. The boys and I need you."

"And I need to get out of here so I can take care of them."

"Colleen, you need to recover more before you even think of coming home. I'm taking care of the boys until you can."

"Where are they? Are they with Rose?"

Kathleen shook her head. "No, Luke—Mr. Patterson—came by to bring me to see you, and Mrs. Heaton and one of my friends are with the boys at your apartment."

Colleen looked around. "Luke—he's the man who helped us that day in the park? The one you've written me about?"

"Yes."

"Where is he now?"

"He's in the hall. I wasn't sure how you'd be or how you'd feel about seeing a stranger with me."

Her sister surprised her by saying, "Please ask him to come in. I'd like to meet him."

Kathleen stood and looked down the aisle to see Luke looking into the room from his bench. He hadn't grabbed a paper to read. Instead he seemed to be doing just as he said he'd do. Waiting to see if she needed him. She smiled and waved him in.

Luke smiled and nodded as he stood and made his way into the room.

"Here he comes now."

As Luke made it to her side, she turned to Colleen. "This is Mr. Luke Patterson, Colleen. Luke, this is my sister, Colleen Sullivan. She wanted to meet you."

"I'm pleased to meet you, Mrs. Sullivan. And I'm very sorry about your loss."

Kathleen saw the tears well up in her sister's eyes as she nodded. "Thank you, Mr. Patterson. And thank you for helping us that day in the park and for being there for my sister the night I sent her to Heaton House."

Luke smiled down at her sister, who looked so battered and bruised, much as she herself must have looked when she arrived at Heaton House. "You're welcome, but there is no need to thank me. I would hope any other man—"

"Oh, no. Not just any man would have come to our aid that day. But you did. And for that, Kathleen and I will be forever grateful."

Kathleen could tell Luke didn't know what to say and he seemed a bit uncomfortable, so she quickly changed the subject. "Do you know when your doctor will be in to see you?"

"You just missed him. He came in earlier and said that I might be able to go home tomorrow."

"That seems awfully early after all you've been through."

"I'll heal better at home than here. I want to be with my boys. And besides, look around, Kathleen. They don't have any empty beds in this ward."

Kathleen glanced around the ward and found her sister was right. Last night there'd been a couple of empty beds, but today it looked as if those were filled and a couple more brought in.

"Well, I'll be there to help you. I do have to let Mrs. Driscoll know why I didn't come in today."

"I would imagine that Mrs. Heaton has already done that. She mentioned that she'd telephoned her this morning," Luke informed her.

Kathleen saw her sister smile. "I'm so glad Mrs. Heaton gave you her card, Kathleen, and that you kept it. It appears I sent you to the right place."

"Oh, there is no doubt about that, Mrs. Sullivan," Luke said. "None at all. I'll be glad to help Kathleen get you back home tomorrow, if the doctor does release you."

"That would be nice of you, Mr. Patterson. Thank you."

Luke's offer didn't surprise Kathleen but it warmed her heart and gave her some peace. Her new friends—or family, as she'd come to think of most of them—weren't going to forget her just because she wouldn't be living at Heaton House. They'd already shown they'd be there for her and her family. She had much to be thankful for.

Chapter Nine

Colleen had been allowed to come home the next day. Luke had helped get her home, but she still seemed to be very fragile and he could tell Kathleen was afraid to leave her alone.

Once she was settled in her room, Kathleen came out and said, "Would you mind staying for a few minutes while I run and ask Rose if she can come over while I go to the grocers and the pharmacy?"

"I will, but there's no need to ask Mrs. Walsh. I can run any errands you need," Luke said. "I can take the boys with me and you can stay with Colleen."

"I don't want to impose on you." She shook her head.

"Kathleen, you aren't imposing on me." Luke rubbed the back of his neck and sighed. "I'm your friend—at least I hope you consider me one. Please let me help you."

"You have work to do, Luke. You can't keep taking off for me."

"I can write at night—one of the blessings of being a writer." He pushed an errant strand of her beautiful hair behind her ear. He'd love to pull her in his arms and tell her not to worry, that as she took care of her sister, others were trying to find a way to help them both. But he didn't want to say anything in case Mrs. Heaton and the others' plans fell through.

And just because she'd let him hold her once didn't mean it would ever happen again. He could see the wariness in her eyes and quickly lowered his hand. "Now, please give me a list. Your sister needs to nap and it will do the boys good to get out in the fresh air and quit worrying about their mama for a bit."

Collin and Brody had been overjoyed to see their mother and now they each sat on the bed beside her. But Colleen looked exhausted and they looked worried.

Kathleen nodded and began to write a short list. Then she handed him some bills and called to the boys. Luke stuffed the money in his pocket, knowing she'd never take it back.

"Want to go to the store with Mr. Patterson?" she asked the boys. "He's going to pick up a few things for us and you two know what items your mama uses and can help him, if he has any questions."

Both boys grinned and nodded, and Luke had a feeling they didn't get to go to the grocery very often. He'd be sure to pick them up some candy while they were out.

"You stay right with Mr. Patterson, do you hear?" Kathleen said as they headed out the door.

"Yes, Aunt Kate," Collin said.

Kate. Luke quite liked that name. He turned and said, "I'll make sure they do…Kate."

Her cheeks turned pink when he winked at her and shut the door behind him. Yes, he liked that name just as much as he liked Kathleen. Perhaps it was because he'd come to care for the woman—no matter what her name.

The air inside the halls hadn't freshened any at all and as he and the boys stepped outside, they all seemed to inhale deeply, even though the air outdoors wasn't all that fresh, either.

Both boys slipped a hand in each of his and looked up at him. His heart went out to them. Losing a father—even though the man hadn't deserved the family he had—then finding out they weren't going to have a baby brother or sister after all, and seeing their mother in such bad shape had to affect them. And yet they looked up at him trustingly, and a familiar protective feeling washed over Luke. He could easily come to care for Kathleen's family, almost as much as he cared for her. He wanted them all out of the tenements as soon as possible.

They picked up the boys' mother's medicine first and then headed for the grocer she used. Collin and Brody were very good in the store, helping him pick the things they were familiar with, pointing out which brands of canned goods his mother used, along with staples.

"Aunt Kate can fry the best potatoes," Collin said with a sigh.

They weren't on Kathleen's list, but he put a bag on the counter along with several other things he could tell the boys might like and that he thought Kathleen might need but not have the money to buy.

He made arrangements for the groceries to be delivered and then let the boys each pick out a stick candy. They grinned as the grocer handed them their choices.

"Thank you, Mr. Patterson!" they both said at the same time.

"You're welcome." Luke wondered how long it'd been since they'd had a piece of candy.

They took their time getting home and when they did, it was to find that the groceries had already been delivered. He thought Kathleen might be angry with him for adding to her list, and figured she'd tell him all about it when she sent the boys in to see their mother.

"She's awake and asking for you," she told the children.

They hurried into her room and Luke turned to Kathleen, ready for whatever it was she had to say.

But she surprised him. Hands on her hips, she looked at him and shook her head before advancing toward him. "Luke Patterson, you are a good, kind man. It appears the boys let you know of their fondness for fried potatoes."

"They say you make the best. I wouldn't mind trying them out." He grinned at her, relieved that she didn't appear mad.

He looked down at her as she stood in front of him, and he had the strongest urge yet to pull her into his arms and hold her. But his instincts told him that holding her in his arms the night everything happened had been an exception and she'd permitted it only because of the stress she was feeling at that moment. Kathleen still seemed skittish around him most of the time and he didn't want to damage the fragile friendship they appeared to be developing.

"Thank you." Kathleen made an abrupt turn and went back to putting the groceries up. "I'm sure you have things to do, but you may come back for supper, if you'd like."

"Oh, I'd like. Thank you. What time should I be here?"

"About six, if you can make it by then."

"I can."

"Did they thank you for the candy?"

"They did. They are very good boys, Kathleen. You have every reason to be proud of them."

"They're pretty special."

"They are that—just like their aunt Kate. Thank you for the invitation. I'll see you at six."

Rose had asked Kathleen to let the boys come play with her son later that afternoon while Colleen slept and Kathleen took that time to straighten up and wash a few of the boys' clothes. She was hanging them up on a makeshift line strung out the window when a knock came on the door.

She opened it to find Mrs. Heaton and Violet. It was so good to see them that she fought down the humiliation of having them in this neighborhood and this building, and opened the door wide.

"It's so good to see you, Kathleen, dear," Mrs. Heaton said. "We miss you a great deal."

"I miss you all, too." And she did. More each day.

"How is your sister, dear?" Mrs. Heaton asked.

"She's very weak, but I think being home will help her. The boys cheer her up."

"Where are they?"

"With a neighbor. She has a son Collin's age and she thought Colleen could rest better if they played with him for a while. They seem to keep wanting to check on her just to make sure she's here, I think."

"That's understandable."

"Let me make us some tea."

"We don't want to make more work for you."

Kathleen was already putting the kettle on. "It's not work and I'm ready for a cup. Please take a seat at the table."

"We'll join you, then," Mrs. Heaton said, sitting down at the table. Violet did the same. "We have something we'd like to tell you."

"Tell me?" Kathleen sat down. "What is it? Not bad news, is it?"

"Oh, no, dear. And we certainly wouldn't burden you with any more of that right now, even if it were."

"Then what?" Kathleen couldn't imagine what it was they wanted to tell her.

"Well, you know we love you at Heaton House." Mrs. Heaton smiled. "And if you didn't know, let me assure you we do. We and your coworkers have been very worried about you and your family, too. And, well, none of us want you to worry about money while you are helping out your sister." She pulled an envelope out of her parasol and placed it on the table. "We all want you to have this."

"Oh, Mrs. Heaton, I can't—"

"Kathleen, you *can.* It's for your family and we aren't going to take no for an answer."

Kathleen looked from one woman to the other.

"Mrs. Heaton is right. We aren't taking it back, so you might as well accept it and use it to help Colleen and the boys," Violet reiterated.

Kathleen swallowed around the clump of tears in her

throat. "I don't know what to say. I can't begin to thank you all for everything you've done for us."

"We just want you to feel free to help your sister, but know that we are already thinking about ways to help her, too."

"What do you mean?"

"Well, we can't tell you just yet. But, Kathleen, we aren't going to just let you and your sister fend for yourselves. I wish you'd bring them all to Heaton House."

Kathleen shook her head.

"I am trying to understand why you think it's best not to. We want you back at Heaton House."

"Oh, Mrs. Heaton, I'm not sure I'll be coming back. I—"

"You'll be back, dear." Mrs. Heaton reached over and patted her hand. "You'll be back, if for no other reason than to visit. Don't think for one moment we're not going to expect that."

Kathleen wasn't sure what to say. Wasn't sure of anything at that moment except that she loved these two women. They'd become family to her in the short while she'd known them and she couldn't wait for Colleen to meet them.

Mrs. Heaton pushed the envelope over to her. "Now take this for your family's sake, Kathleen. Please."

"Everyone wanted to contribute, Kathleen," Violet said. "This will make it easier for you until you can work again."

Kathleen had no idea when that would be. Colleen had to get much stronger before she could. "Thank you. Please thank everyone for me."

Overwhelmed with gratitude, Kathleen got up to pour boiling water over the tea leaves in the teapot that'd belonged to her mother and left it to steep before wiping her eyes and turning back to her guests.

"I hope there comes a day when I can repay you by helping others as you've all helped me and my family." Oh, yes, she'd been truly blessed the day she'd been taken to Heaton House.

She turned back to pull down cups and saucers for their tea and tried to get her composure. *Thank you, Lord. For all of those who've reached out to help, and especially for Mrs. Heaton and Elizabeth...and for Luke.*

Over the next few days, Luke spent his time going back and forth between Heaton House and Kathleen's sister's apartment. He'd enjoyed the fried potato supper she'd prepared on Monday and fought the urge to overstay his welcome when he left that night.

Colleen seemed to be improving each day, but still appeared quite fragile. But by the middle of the week she was up and around and had even told Kathleen that she thought she'd be all right if Kathleen needed to go back to work. Mrs. Walsh had offered to help her with the boys.

Now, Luke listened as Kathleen used him as a sounding board.

"I'm not sure what to do. I can't stay off work indefinitely, but I don't feel Colleen is well enough to be left alone yet." Kathleen added some seasonings and stirred the soup she'd put on earlier. "At least with the collection that Mrs. Heaton took up for us, I don't have to worry about rent for the next month and we can eat. But Mrs. Driscoll can hold my position for me for only so long."

"Don't be worrying about it right now. She gave you all of this week off. Take the time, Kathleen." Luke was afraid that after all she'd been through even before her sister's near murder, she could easily have a setback herself if she tried to do much more. "Your sister and the boys need you and by Monday you'll feel better about leaving your sister for the day."

"That's true, I will."

There'd been several meetings in the small parlor at Heaton House about Kathleen and her sister's situation and the plan for child care homes. Luke knew what was going on because Mrs. Heaton, Violet and Elizabeth had kept him and Michael apprised of the situation, but until they had everything firmed up, he'd promised not to say anything to Kathleen and her sister. And he didn't want to get their hopes up in case it all fell through. But he prayed daily that the plan would come together and Kathleen and her sister could move out of this neighborhood.

Colleen appeared in the doorway of her small room and Kathleen hurried over to help her to the kitchen table. "Mr. Patterson, it's good to see you. I believe I've been sleeping my life away these past few days. Kathleen tells me you've been keeping my boys in treats. Thank you."

"It's been my pleasure. You have good boys, Mrs. Sullivan."

"Please, call me Colleen. Mrs. Sullivan makes me feel old."

And probably reminded her of the husband who nearly killed her, he thought. "Colleen it is. And I'm Luke."

He didn't want anyone feeling he should be invited

to eat each night and thought that Kathleen's sister would feel more comfortable if he left. She did have better color now, but he could tell from the sorrow in her eyes and the way she wrapped her arms around her middle that she mourned the baby she'd lost, possibly the husband, too, and she still had pain from the gunshot wound. But these two sisters were made of tough stock and he prayed the Lord would ease their burdens.

"I'd best be on my way." Luke got up and headed toward the door. "I told Mrs. Heaton I'd be there for dinner tonight. I've imposed on you enough this week."

"You've done nothing of the sort. You've been a great help and the boys love having you around," Kathleen said, walking him to the door. "But we take up enough of your time."

"No, I believe it's the other way around. I know it goes against your grain to let me help, but you've been very gracious in letting me." He grinned and winked at her when he was sure Colleen wasn't looking. "I'll see you tomorrow."

"Luke, you don't have to—"

"I know. But I'll see you tomorrow anyway."

He finally won a smile.

"See you then. Good night."

"Good night, Kathleen."

He spoke to several people as he passed their apartments on his way to the stairs. And he'd gotten used to the stuffiness and the smells—well, maybe not totally. What he'd learned was not to breathe deeply until he reached the street, and found it helped a lot.

He walked outside amid people trying to escape both the heat and the odors, he supposed, and walked as fast as he could over to Third Avenue and toward

Gramercy Park, taking deep breaths of the fresh air. He hated leaving Kathleen and her family in the tenements more each time he had to.

Seeing them up close on a daily basis, even getting to know some of the tenants, had given him new insight and understanding of the struggles most of them faced. While he'd never use the names of Kathleen and her family, or those he was getting to know, their plight lent new energy to the writing of his book and he'd been staying up late into the night working on it.

But the days and early evenings, he saved for Kathleen and her family. He'd come to look forward to visiting with Collin and Brody, and Colleen, too, when she felt up to it. The hardest thing was leaving them and coming back to Heaton House.

Much as he loved living there, it felt lonely to him without Kathleen's presence and the few hours he spent with her and her family weren't the same as seeing her first thing in the morning at the breakfast table and again in the evening for dinner and then spending time in the parlor after dinner. He missed the outings they'd had and—

Luke sighed. Kathleen had to do what she could to help her family. He knew that and his esteem for her grew daily. She never complained, never whined about how her life had changed. And yet he was sure she wondered what the future held for her and her family.

He wondered the same. And he wanted to fix it all, only he didn't know how. And even once Mrs. Heaton's plan was put into place, he didn't know if Kathleen would be moving back to Heaton House or not.

He arrived home just in time for dinner and took his seat, trying not to think of Kathleen's empty one beside him. Nor did he want to compare the meal Mrs. Heaton served to the simple one Kathleen's family would be eating.

When Elizabeth asked about Kathleen and her family he was more than glad to talk about them.

"The boys seem to be doing all right and Kathleen's sister was up when I left there. But I hope your plan comes together soon, Mrs. Heaton. I'd surely like to see them get out of there."

"That may be sooner than you think, Luke," Mrs. Heaton said. "We had a meeting today. Thanks to word getting out and Elizabeth's and John's articles, several business leaders have heard of our idea and, well, we're getting some good backing. Our initial plan to help Kathleen and her family is going to end up helping many others in the same predicament."

"What's happened?"

"We've begun looking for a house for the first child care arrangement. I'm going to talk to Kathleen and her sister tomorrow about it, but if Colleen thinks she'll be able to run it, she'll get the first one. And we'll have to find another woman who needs to provide for herself or her family to help. It will provide a home for two different families and at the same time provide care for others who must work outside the home. We still have to decide how many children each home will be able to care for."

"What about Kathleen?"

"We have an offer for her, if she'll take it. We need someone who can find out which families have a real need for what we're doing, as well as who can run a child care home."

"But what about her job?"

"Clara says this would be a much better position. The salary will be more than Kathleen is making now or anytime in the future, according to Clara. And we've been asked to come up with someone who can relate to what those living in the tenements are going through in their day-to-day lives. Who better to fill that position than Kathleen?"

"I certainly can't think of anyone," Luke said. Still, he didn't like the idea of her having to be in the tenements on a regular basis. But if she didn't have to live there… "Will Kathleen be living at the home with Colleen?"

Mrs. Heaton shook her head. "No. She'd come back here. We all know how devoted she is to her family and that is all well and good. But it's doubtful there will be enough room. And even if there is, Clara and I believe Kathleen needs to have a life of her own. She'll be able to see her sister and nephews anytime she wants. She just won't have to feel responsible for all their needs."

"When will you be presenting the plan to her?"

"First thing tomorrow."

"Good." For the first time in days Luke felt the heaviness in his chest lift. If his prayers were answered, Kathleen would soon be moving back to Heaton House.

Chapter Ten

After Mrs. Heaton and Violet's visit, Kathleen knew something was in the works to help her family, but she wasn't sure what. When Mrs. Heaton sent word by Luke that she and the ladies would like to bring lunch to her and Colleen on Saturday, Kathleen had a feeling they were about to find out more.

Luke had asked if he could take the boys to Central Park and fly kites with them, since the weather was unseasonably warm, and of course Colleen had agreed. They were all becoming fond of Luke, and the boys loved going on outings with him.

Kathleen kept looking out the window, watching for the ladies' arrival. Finally, a rented hack pulled up and Mrs. Heaton stepped out carrying a huge picnic basket. The other ladies followed her into the building.

Earlier, when she'd told Colleen about the ladies' visit, her sister had hesitated. Kathleen had insisted.

"We can't be rude, Colleen. These women care about us."

"You're right, to be sure. I'm just a little nervous about havin' company here."

Kathleen had understood. She'd felt the same way until she'd come to realize these people genuinely wanted to help her and her family. And just as she knew they would, Mrs. Heaton, Mrs. Driscoll, Elizabeth and Violet all put her sister at ease immediately by showing their concern for her health, for her welfare and the boys', as well as for Kathleen's. They talked to her as if they were lifelong friends and with as much respect as they would give one another.

Kathleen was pleased to see that her sister began to relax as soon as they started to eat the meal Mrs. Heaton had brought over.

"My dears, we've come to tell you some good news. At least we think it is and we're hoping you both do, too."

"What is it, Mrs. Heaton?" Kathleen asked.

"Well, we've found a place for your family to live outside the tenements. It's not overly far from Heaton House and it's—"

Kathleen could see the tension in her sister's face as she sat a little straighter and shook her head and interrupted Mrs. Heaton.

"Aw, now, we can't be taking charity, even though I know your hearts are good and you mean well," Colleen said with a sigh. "We'd never be able to pay for a place the likes of what you're describin' with Kathleen's wages and what I can bring in doing laundry for others."

"Oh, but my dear, please wait until you hear us out. We have a plan for that also."

By the time the ladies finished explaining that Colleen could run one of the child care homes they were establishing around the city, Kathleen could see the hope she felt deep inside reflected in her sister's eyes. Not only did the plan offer a better life for Colleen and the boys, but also the hope of a future for Colleen's children—and her own if she ever had any.

"I assure you, Colleen, you'll be earning every penny you receive," Mrs. Heaton said. "Please don't consider anything we are doing as charity. We've just figured out a way that we can all help you and your family and others to have hope again."

"You say there'll be another woman living there, too. What about Kathleen?" Colleen asked.

"Well, we have an offer to make to Kathleen, too."

"Oh?" Kathleen looked from Mrs. Heaton to Mrs. Driscoll. "And what is that? Do you want me to run another of the homes?"

Mrs. Heaton shook her head. "No, dear. We want you to find others we can hire to run the new homes as we can start them up. And most of all we need you to identify those who are in real need of child care while they work."

"But what about my job at Tiffany Glass? Will I be able to work around it?"

"Kathleen," Mrs. Driscoll said, "I love having you work in my department. You are one of the best workers I have. But this is a much better position. It will pay you more than you are making now—or, for that matter, more than I'm making."

"How can that be?"

"The backers of this project have the money to do it right," Mrs. Heaton said. "And they want someone who has lived in the tenements, who can relate to the women in need. Because it involves talking to women, a man isn't going to be able to do the job as well as you. Many of the women would never even talk to a man."

"And you've expressed a desire to help others," Violet added. "We thought this would be ideal for you to be able to do that in a way we can't."

"But where will she live?" Colleen asked.

"She has a room at Heaton House as long as she wants it," Mrs. Heaton said.

Kathleen felt the sting of tears behind her eyes. She wanted to move back to Heaton House, but— "I'm not sure Colleen is up to this so soon."

"I'll be fine, Kathleen. And now that I know you can go back to Heaton House where you have so many friends, my heart is at ease. You've given up so much over the years to help us and—"

"But, I—"

"Kathleen, it will be a few weeks yet before we get things in place. By then Colleen will feel even better. We don't want you leaving her until you both feel comfortable about it," Mrs. Heaton explained, looking from one to the other. "In the meantime, you could try to find someone with the need of a job who could help run the house and who would be a blessing to your sister. I'm sure you know several people that are friends already who might want this opportunity."

"You know there are, Kathleen," Colleen said. "I can think of several right now."

Mrs. Heaton smiled. "I thought that might be the case. It would be good if it were someone you know and like, Colleen. So, ladies, will you help us?"

Help them? Kathleen looked at her sister and nodded. She saw Colleen's smile before it even reached her mouth and knew she'd agree to the plan. How could she not?

"Oh, yes, ma'am," Colleen answered. "I can't thank you enough for the opportunity you are offering us. I promise you'll never be sorry."

"We're pretty certain of that, dear. Otherwise, we wouldn't be here." Mrs. Heaton smiled and looked at the women who'd come with her. "Well, ladies, I think we can put our plan in motion."

"Thank you." Kathleen hugged the older woman who'd taken her into her home for no other reason than just to help her for a few days or weeks. Now she'd helped her for all time.

Luke enjoyed flying kites with the boys. They loved being at the park, running and playing, letting the kites he'd bought them fly higher and higher in the sky.

They were tuckered out by the time they headed home that afternoon—so much so that Brody had fallen asleep on the trolley ride, and Luke carried him from the trolley stop to their building and up the stairs to their apartment.

Luke had prayed all afternoon that Kathleen and her sister would accept Mrs. Heaton's offer for what it was and not refuse it as charity. He realized they were both proud, but surely they'd see that they would be helping others as well as themselves.

And hopefully Kathleen wanted to move back to Heaton House as badly as he wanted her to. Oh, he knew she loved her family, but she needed a life of her own, too. Clancy was no longer a problem and Luke couldn't bring himself to be anything but glad about that. Kathleen could see her family anytime she wanted without fear of her sister's husband, and she no longer had to fear that her sister or the boys would be hurt.

Collin ran ahead and knocked on the apartment door. When Kathleen opened the door to them and saw her nephew in Luke's arms, she smiled and he tried to read what her decision had been as she reached out and took Brody from him.

"Come on in. Colleen is napping, but I've got some coffee on and Mrs. Heaton left cookies."

"Cookies? May I have one, Aunt Kate?" Collin asked.

"You may. You can keep Luke company while I put Brody down."

Collin led him to the cookie jar in the center of the table. "Mrs. Heaton brings the best cookies." He looked into the jar, reached in and pulled out a huge sugar cookie.

Luke put his hand in and pulled out one for himself. He'd fed the boys lunch on the way to the park, but all the activity had made them hungry.

Kathleen came out of the tiny bedroom the boys shared and poured him a cup of coffee just as a knock came on the door. Collin ran to answer it and found Roger, the neighbor's son, asking if he could come play.

"May I go play with Roger, Aunt Kate?"

"You may." She pulled another cookie out of the jar and handed it to Roger. Then she stood and watched them enter the Walsh apartment before coming back to the kitchen.

"How were they? Did they tire you out?" Kathleen asked as she poured herself a cup of coffee and joined Luke at the table.

"Pretty near. But we had a good time. It didn't take

them long to catch on to the art of kite-flying." He took a sip of coffee and met Kathleen's gaze. "How did the meeting go?"

If the sparkle in her eye was any indication, it went well.

"Did you know of the offer Mrs. Heaton and her group were going to make us?"

"I did. But it wasn't my news to tell and I—"

"I understand. I just didn't know how much to tell you and I'm still not sure I believe it." She smiled and shook her head. "That we're all getting out of the tenements is such a blessing. Colleen couldn't contain her tears once they left. It's a lot to take in."

"You accepted the position they offered you, too?"

"I did. At first I didn't think I'd be qualified for it, but then Mrs. Heaton explained that they want someone who has lived here, who can relate to those who do. I think it's my chance to help others as she's helped us and I'm so grateful for the opportunity."

"I'm a little concerned about you coming and going all the time."

"Luke, I've lived here for a long time. I'll be fine. And Mrs. Heaton has made me promise not to be out and about after dark. I don't do that now, so it was an easy promise to make."

Luke leaned back in his chair, relief washing over him. His prayers had been answered. Kathleen and her family would be out of here before long. And she would be back at Heaton House. It couldn't come soon enough for him.

By the end of the month, things had come together so well that Mrs. Heaton was asking for volunteers to get Kathleen's sister moved into the first home that would serve as both home to her and her boys, along with a friend of Colleen's who'd be helping to run the home and do a lot of the cooking. It would serve as a child care home for one of Kathleen's former coworkers from Tiffany, one from Butterick, and two others who lived in the same tenements as Kathleen and her sister.

Colleen and the other woman they'd hired, Ida, would be watching ten children altogether, and everyone agreed that would be enough at least until they saw how things went. But Colleen would be in charge and with her salary and a furnished home, she'd be able to make a decent living.

"What did Kathleen say when you told her everything was in place?" Elizabeth asked.

Mrs. Heaton had visited her just that afternoon. "She cried. And then she hugged us. Clara and I told her together." Mrs. Heaton clasped her hands together and smiled. "I can't wait to get her family moved in the new home and Kathleen moved back in here."

Luke felt the exact same way. Oh, he'd seen a lot of Kathleen at her and her sister's apartment. But that was nothing like having her in the same house.

"What about furnishings? Will they have enough for the house?" Elizabeth asked.

"We've had wonderful donations of items to furnish it and all of that is already in place. It won't take very long to move the rest of their belongings. There isn't much," Mrs. Heaton said.

"Luke and I are leaving here at nine in the morning. Michael and Violet will meet us at Colleen's. Any of you who wish to help are welcome to come with us."

Julia and Elizabeth immediately offered to help at least part of the day, as did John and Ben.

"I am so eager to get them out of there. The memories they have to live with would be enough reason to find something else, even if it wasn't such an awful place to live," Luke said.

But it was awful, and thinking about all the children living in similar conditions had kept him up late into the night working on his book.

"Once they are out, maybe they can begin to put those awful memories behind them. I pray Collin and Brody can forget that night." Luke had become quite fond of those boys. It was a pity their father hadn't cared enough to throw the bottle out and treat his family the way they deserved.

"I hope so, too," Mrs. Heaton said. "But I'm not sure they can—at least not now. Perhaps, in time, they will."

"Perhaps their mother will remarry one day and hopefully, another man, a good man, will help wipe out those memories," Julia said.

"I have been relieved to know that Officer O'Malley has been checking on them from time to time," Elizabeth said.

What mattered to Luke most right now was getting those children out of that apartment, out of the shadows and into a home where there was sunlight—and hope for their future.

The next morning most of Mrs. Heaton's boarders, all except for Julia, who'd been called in to work at the last minute, showed up to help Kathleen and Colleen get moved.

Kathleen watched her sister. While she would have

been embarrassed at one time, today she was happy to see them and thankful for their help.

There was Mrs. Heaton, Elizabeth and Violet, of course, and Luke. But also Michael, John Talbot and Ben rolled up their sleeves and got to work. Kathleen's heart warmed that they cared enough to give up their Saturday to help her and her family.

"It is so good to see you again and know that you'll be living at Heaton House once more." Elizabeth hugged her. "And your sister will be close enough to visit."

"I know. I'm so thankful for that. Thank you for your help and your friendship," Kathleen said, hugging her back.

Everyone began gathering up boxes or crates to carry down the stairs and it seemed a madhouse for a while. But Luke and Michael had rented a couple of wagons, and soon they were loaded and on their way to the new house by noon.

In short order they pulled up in front of a well-kept, modest two-story home on a nice quiet block not all that far from where Mrs. Heaton lived. It was the first time Kathleen and her family had seen the house Colleen and the boys would be calling home. Kathleen only had to see the expression on Colleen's face to know what her sister was feeling.

"Are we at the right place?" she asked Mrs. Heaton.

The older woman patted her hand. "This is it, dear. Colleen's new home."

Kathleen was speechless. It was...so much more than either she or her sister had imagined when Mrs. Heaton and Elizabeth had told them about it. She felt as if she must still be sleeping and would wake up soon, still in the tenement and finding this was all a dream. It was only when Luke offered his hand to help her and Colleen out of the wagon that she began to believe it was real.

Violet and Mrs. Heaton went in with them while the others began to unload the wagon. Kathleen looked around at the parlor…and put a hand to her mouth as she took in the furnishings. There was a real parlor suite of blue and gold that actually matched. There were paintings on the walls and drapes at the windows. The furnishings were in good condition, if slightly worn. But they made the parlor look homey, comfortable and beautiful in her eyes.

Then she spotted the dining room across the way and saw that it, too, was furnished. The pieces didn't match but they fit each other and all she could do was shake her head as they made their way upstairs and picked out the rooms Colleen and her boys would have. The boys would share a connecting room. There was a room like Colleen's across the hall and she chose it for Ida. "If Ida doesn't like it or wants a different room, she can choose when she arrives."

All the rooms were big, bright and clean, and Kathleen was thrilled. She wouldn't feel so guilty living in Heaton House again, now that Colleen and the boys had such a nice place to live.

The bedrooms were furnished with beds and armoires—the boys would each have their own bed for the first time in their lives. Kathleen turned to Mrs. Heaton. "Oh, we've never had such nice furnishings. Do these come with the house?"

"They do," Mrs. Heaton said. "Many of my friends and I have things in our attics that were in good condition and just sitting there, not being used, Kathleen. It gave everyone who donated something much pleasure to know how it would be used, I can assure you of that."

Colleen looked dazed. "I've never seen such fine things. I don't know how we can ever repay you."

"Just help someone else, dear. And you'll be doing that by keeping the children of others in need."

"But I'll be paid for that. This is all…just too much to take in." Colleen sank into a settee and looked around the parlor. "I've never seen anything so grand and that it will be ours…"

"Yours it is. It will feel like home before long," Violet said. "At least we hope it will."

The group started bringing things in and asking where to put the different boxes, and Colleen stood to take one.

But Mrs. Heaton turned to Colleen as she stood and shook her head. "You just sit here and get used to everything, Colleen. You still don't need to be lifting and all. You'll have your work cut out for you when you start keeping the other children in a few weeks. For now, just tell us where you want certain things put and try to get used to this being your home."

Tears came to Kathleen's eyes as she turned to Elizabeth and Mrs. Heaton. "I truly don't know how to thank you both for all you've done for us. If it weren't for you, we'd have no hope."

"You both have grit, Kathleen. You would have made it. We just wanted to hurry things along."

"You've certainly done that. Thank—"

Mrs. Heaton held her hand up. "You're welcome. And we're glad to have some part in your future. But it is your future and we know that you will both make the best of this new chapter of your lives. You've had a tragedy, to be sure, but you know the Lord can work all manner of things to the good of His people. And He will use you to help others. By understanding what others like you and Colleen have been through, you will be more able to help them."

"I promise you that we will do all we can to be worthy of all of this." Kathleen knew she'd be on her knees for a very long time that night. That the Lord had seen fit to have them helped in such a way was most humbling to her.

"Kathleen, you've always been worthy of help, dear. I'm just glad you came to us. But you know, the Lord has had a plan all along. We've just been a part of it."

"To my way of thinking you've been the best part of it."

"Kathleen, do you know where Colleen might want these things?" Elizabeth asked, a big box of clothing in her arms. Julia had shown up after her half day of work and was right behind her with two smaller boxes.

"I think those go upstairs." Kathleen took the top box from Elizabeth. "Come on and I'll show you where to put them. Or at least where I think Colleen might want them."

"I'll go get some more boxes," Violet said.

"No." Elizabeth turned to her. "Michael said for us just to help put it all up. He and the men will bring the rest of it in."

"All right. It will probably go faster that way."

"Well, I'm going to go get Colleen some tea and help Gretchen get lunch together," Mrs. Heaton said. She'd sent Gretchen over earlier to stock up the kitchen and prepare a lunch for everyone.

Luke came in just then with Kathleen's two nephews right behind him. They each held a couple of items he'd handed them. "The boys think these go in their room. Do you know which one it is?"

"I do. Follow me, boys. I'll show you your new room." Kathleen was glad to get to work on getting her nephews settled in their new room.

"Is this really our new home, Aunt Kathleen?" Collin asked, looking up at the stairs. "Do we have an apartment here?"

"This house is your new home, Collin. The whole house. Do you think you'll like it?"

He looked as dazed as his mother as he followed Kathleen up the stairs. "Oh, yes, I do."

Brody scampered up beside him. "Me, too. I like it lots."

"Well, let's go find your room." Kathleen glanced back to see Luke looking at them. Her chest felt a little funny when he smiled at her and Kathleen turned to hurry up the stairs. As she topped the landing she didn't know if it was the climb or Luke's smile that had her feeling all breathless and fluttery inside.

Chapter Eleven

Luke and Michael had helped Ida get her things upstairs when she arrived later that afternoon. By then nearly everything had at least been put into the rooms they belonged in, and everyone began to go their separate ways.

It'd been a tiring day and once most of the work was done, Michael and Luke took off to return the wagons back to the livery, and brought back a hack to get them home. Michael took his mother and wife home and Luke stayed behind to bring Kathleen back to Heaton House when she was ready.

He didn't rush her, as he knew it wouldn't be easy for her to leave her sister after all they'd been through. Just as he'd figured she wasn't ready to go until she helped Colleen get the boys in bed.

But she came back downstairs with a smile on her face. "Brody fell asleep in the middle of saying his prayers and Collin is barely holding on until he says 'Amen.'"

"I'm sure they're tuckered out. They worked hard today carrying boxes up the stairs and putting things away," Luke said. He'd come to care for her nephews a great deal. "They're good boys."

"They are."

Her tone sounded a little wistful to him. "Are they upset that you're leaving?"

Kathleen shook her head. "Not too much. We've been preparing them for it and they know we can see each other whenever we want now, so they're happy about that. And I promised them I'd see them tomorrow."

But Luke saw a hint of sadness in her eyes. "How about you? Are you wishing you were staying here, too?"

"I have mixed feelings about it all. But I know it's for the best for us all."

"It is," Colleen said as she came up behind them. "The boys are fast asleep."

"I didn't think it would take long. I hope you all sleep well in your new home, Colleen," Kathleen said.

"I believe we will. But what you were saying about things being for the best—they are, you know. You'd only begun to have a life of your own and start to enjoy it when Clancy—" Colleen stopped and took a deep breath. "When I ended up in the hospital. I don't want you feeling you're responsible for me any longer, Kathleen. We've been truly blessed by Mrs. Heaton and the others' efforts. And we're going to make them proud."

"Yes, we are," Kathleen said.

"You go on now. I'm going to lock up, make Ida and me some tea and help her finish getting settled in."

"I know you must be quite exhausted," Kathleen said. "Are you sure—"

"I am. And the tired I feel is the best tired I've ever

been. I know I'll sleep well tonight and I hope you do the same back in Heaton House."

"I think everyone will sleep well tonight," Luke added.

"I believe you're right, Luke. Go on, now, take my sister back to her other home."

"Kathleen?" He nudged her elbow. "Are you ready?"

She turned to him, her eyes filled with an emotion he couldn't name. "I am. Or at least my sister is ready for me to go. She thinks I spoil the boys too much, you know. She's ready to get me out of her hair."

"Now you know that's not so," Colleen said, shaking her head.

Kathleen kissed her sister on the cheek and gave her a hug. "I do. I love you, Colleen. You do have a telephone, you know."

"I didn't. Where is it?"

Kathleen led her to a small table tucked under the staircase. "Right here. And the Heaton House number is right there beside it. If you need anything—"

Colleen turned her around and gave her a little push. "I'll be sure to telephone you if I need you. I promise."

Luke wondered if Kathleen realized her sister was walking her to the door as she spoke.

"Lock up tight," Kathleen said.

"I will. See you tomorrow."

There was nothing more to do but walk outside. The door shut right behind them and they heard the lock turn.

Kathleen turned to Luke. "I think she was ready to get rid of me."

He chuckled. "It did seem that way, but perhaps

she's just wanting to relax and she couldn't do it with me there."

Kathleen laughed and shook her head. "Oh, no, that's not it. I know my sister. I think she's ready to start this new life she's been given without me having to protect her from Clancy."

"And it sounds as if she wants you to be able to start your new life without having to worry about him."

"I'm sure she wants the best for me, just as I do her."

They reached the walk and Luke helped her into the hack he'd called to pick them up, then he got in himself.

"Where to? Are you hungry?"

"A little bit. But you must be starved after all you've done today. I'm sorry, I should have left earlier."

"It's all right. I understood you wanted to see the boys settled down for the night. But I am a little hungry. How about we stop for supper on the way home?" He pulled out his pocket watch and looked at it. "It's getting late and I'm sure they've already eaten at Heaton House."

At Kathleen's hesitation, he added, "Mrs. Heaton will fuss over us if we haven't eaten."

"You're right. She's fussed over others long enough for one day. I'll be glad to have supper with you, Luke."

He leaned toward the driver and gave him directions to a restaurant he liked and then settled back in his seat and looked at Kathleen. "It will do you good to have a time to relax, too, and I know just the place. You've been busy taking care of Colleen and the boys for weeks now, not to mention packing and getting ready for this day, and then getting Colleen and her family settled in. You've got to be exhausted."

"Well, it wasn't only me. You did your part, too. And so many others helped to make it possible."

They arrived at a restaurant that was still quite busy, as Luke knew it would be, but they didn't have to wait and were quickly whisked into the dining room and shown to a table facing a courtyard.

Kathleen ordered only a bowl of clam chowder, but Michael ordered a full meal and shrugged when the waiter left the table. "I suppose it was lugging all those boxes downstairs from the apartment building and then upstairs at the house, but I'm ravenous."

Kathleen's smile made him glad he'd brought her here. "As well you should be after all that work. Thank you for getting the actual moving organized for us, Luke."

"You're welcome. I was glad to do it. Those boys of Colleen's made the day for me. I doubt they'll have trouble sleeping in the new place after all the traipsing up and down stairs they did today."

Kathleen let out a deep breath. "I'm just glad you were there to catch Brody when he slid down the banister."

"So am I. That was too close for comfort. But I think I frightened him enough with what could have happened that he won't be trying it again too soon."

"I certainly hope so." Kathleen put a hand to her heart and shook her head. "I thought for sure he was going to go flying across the room. My, but weren't they happy with their room, though?"

"And that they each had a real bed to sleep in. I think that touched me about as much as anything."

Luke couldn't get the look of wonder in their eyes out of his head.

"I know. It touched me the same way. For so long they've slept together on a mat on the floor. They both looked really happy today. I can't tell you how wonderful it is to see that look rather than the one of worry they usually have," Kathleen said.

"Now I can understand why you didn't want to bring them to the boardinghouse the night Colleen was shot," Luke said.

Kathleen bit her bottom lip and for a moment, Luke wondered if she might cry. But she only said, "You don't know how badly I wanted to. I am just so thankful that they'll never have to live in those conditions again. To see them smile so readily now..." Her expression suddenly darkened. "Still, I'll never forget that night."

"Neither will I." For more reasons than one. Luke's thoughts strayed from the horror of the shooting to a bittersweetness he'd never experienced before when he'd held Kathleen in his arms and she'd sobbed on his shoulder. He'd wanted to kiss her so much that night. And yet he'd been afraid she'd fly right out of his arms had he done so.

Luke's gaze traveled from Kathleen's eyes to her lips and lingered there. When he managed to pull his glance away, it was to see color flooding her cheeks. She ducked her head. Was she remembering, too? He hoped so. He reached across the table and—

The waiter brought their supper just then and Kathleen quickly pulled her gaze from his. Luke sighed. His timing seemed to be atrocious where Kathleen was concerned. Once the man departed, Luke said a blessing, thanking the Lord for letting them be a small part of helping Colleen and her family be able to have a fresh start.

Fearing Kathleen had been embarrassed when the waiter came to the table, Luke tried to keep the conversation on impersonal matters while they ate. This woman had worked her way into his heart and he didn't have the faintest idea what to do about it.

The look in Luke's eyes sent Kathleen's thoughts back to the night he'd held her in his arms and sent her heart pounding like crazy. Something had changed between them since the night her sister had been shot by Clancy. Before then he'd been her hero, her rescuer— the person who'd protected her from Clancy. Then he'd become her friend.

But she wasn't ready for him to become what her heart seemed to want him to be. He was a wonderful man. But she'd seen the dreams of her sister and those of her coworkers disappear when the love they'd felt for the men they'd married turned to fear and insecurity. She couldn't—didn't dare let herself—begin to think of him as anything more than a very good friend. And be thankful to call him that.

She tried to concentrate on her dinner and prayed that the heat she felt in her face was due to the hot soup she'd been served and not the attraction she was fighting toward Luke.

"Are you excited about starting your new position as liaison for the day care homes?" Luke asked.

Kathleen breathed an inward sigh of relief at his change of subject. Did he know how uncomfortable she'd been remembering that night he'd held her in his arms and let her cry? Could he possibly know that she hadn't wanted him to let go? That she'd wanted—

Kathleen squashed the thought and quickly pulled her attention back to his question.

"Excited? I am. I'm also a little nervous about it. I have a meeting on Monday where my duties will be explained more clearly and hopefully, after that, I'll feel better about it all."

"I'm sure you will. And remember I'd like to accompany you to the tenements."

"Luke, there is no need to—"

"We've already had this discussion, Kate. I know you know your way around, but you haven't been in every tenement in your neighborhood. Let me go with you until we know you are safe traveling in and out of the buildings. Please."

"I don't need—" She'd started to insist that she didn't need his protection, but she couldn't bring herself to say the words. She *had* needed his protection several times already. And he knew it as well as she did. "Maybe for the first few times."

Luke grinned across the table at her. "Thank you. That will put Mrs. Heaton's mind at rest, as well as mine. Besides, it's a good place for me to do research."

"What kind of research?"

"For my writing."

Kathleen wasn't sure how she felt about that. "Isn't that taking advantage of those less fortunate?"

"I don't see how it could be, if it's meant to help them, similar to Jacob Riis's book."

The name was vaguely familiar to Kathleen, but she'd never read anything by him…or Luke either, for that matter. Exhausted as she was by the end of the day the only book she managed to read was her Bible.

And she didn't know how writing dime novels could

possibly help the people she knew, but she knew first-hand that Luke's heart was good and he was probably just using his writing as an excuse to get her to think she wasn't wasting his time while he was accompanying her.

This time it was she who changed the subject. "I still can't believe how my and Colleen's lives have changed so suddenly. I'm so happy to be going back to Heaton House. I've missed everyone."

"And we've all missed you. I think we're going to have another boarder or two soon to add to the mix," Luke said.

"Really? Have you met them?"

He shook his head. "No. But I heard from John that Mrs. Heaton said a new man might be moving in next week. Michael's old room is free now that he married Violet. And while you have her room there is still one more on your floor. I did hear that she'd interviewed a young woman yesterday. So we may have a full house again soon."

Kathleen smiled. "Anyone who moves into Heaton House is very fortunate to be there. I don't think all boardinghouses are run the way Mrs. Heaton runs hers."

"I doubt it." Luke leaned back in his chair and smiled. "Mrs. Heaton's house is not just a boarding-house to me. It's home. Has been for several years now. I can't think of anywhere I'd rather live at the moment."

"She has a way of making everyone feel they're part of her family," Kathleen said. "I know I do."

"There've been a couple of boarders who didn't seem to fit in since I've been there, but they're few and far between."

The waiter returned to the table just then and asked if they wanted dessert. Luke looked at Kathleen. "Would you like something?"

She shook her head. "No, I'm fine, thank you."

Luke settled up with the waiter and they started back to Heaton House. "Want to walk or ride?"

They weren't far and Kathleen didn't want him spending more money on her than he already had. It wasn't too cool out and it was a bright starlit night.

"Let's walk."

Luke crooked his arm and she slipped her hand through, resting it on his forearm. His pace was just right. Not too fast or too slow.

"I love the city lights at night," Kathleen said. "Especially in this part of town. But in the tenements, I wish there were more. It's never light enough there at night. Still, it always gave me comfort to look out the windows and see a light on here or there in the apartments across the way."

"I can see how it would. We'll have to go to Gramercy Park one evening. I love it there where you can see lights on in all the homes surrounding it." Luke looked up at the sky. "But it's a nice night out tonight with that full moon and so many stars."

"Yes, it is." Kathleen had heard mention of Gramercy Park and hoped she would get to see it one day, but she was enjoying her time alone with Luke too much to say it to him. She should have told him not to come with her to the tenements. It probably wasn't wise to spend much time with him—it only made her want to see him more.

It didn't take long to get to Heaton House and seeing lights in its windows made her feel happy and warm.

"I can't tell you how glad I am you're back here, Kathleen," Luke said. "It hasn't felt quite the same with you gone."

"Why, thank you, Luke."

"I mean it. You've made a place for yourself here. You do fit in and it's not just me who thinks so."

As they walked up the steps and he opened the door, Kathleen felt as if she had come home. Not to the tenements, not to the house Colleen would be calling home. But here to the place where she'd finally felt safe and cared for.

"Kathleen! You're home at last." Elizabeth came out of the parlor and hugged her. "We've all been waiting up to welcome you back."

Mrs. Heaton and the rest of the boarders all welcomed Kathleen back home as Elizabeth led her and Luke back into the parlor.

They all said how glad they were to have her back and Kathleen had to blink several times to keep her tears at bay. These people had come to mean so much to her in such a short time. She couldn't explain it, but she felt that the Lord had orchestrated it all—from Luke keeping Clancy from hitting her that day in the park, to Mrs. Heaton handing her card to Kathleen before she left. Then to be brought here the night of her beating—she could only believe that the Lord had known all along where she needed to be.

"I can't tell you all how glad I am to be back. And I want to thank each of you for all you've done to help Colleen move into her new home. You've become family to us and we'll be forever grateful to you all."

"That's what family is for, Kathleen, dear," Mrs. Heaton said. "My goal has always been for my boarders to feel they have family here in the city. And I hope that your sister and her boys will soon come to feel as welcome in this house as you are."

Kathleen looked around at all the faces she'd come to care about. They all did feel like family to her. Well, all except for Luke. And he—

She looked over to see Luke smiling at her and the wink he gave her sent her pulse racing. She wasn't sure what Luke was to her—but she knew he owned at least a corner of her heart and always would. And she was determined not to let him claim any more of it.

Thoughts of what Clancy had done to her sister, and to her, clouded the joy of the moment. She wasn't sure she'd ever be able to let any man lay claim to her heart. Not now, and maybe not ever.

Luke watched Kathleen as the others gathered around her. She seemed almost as happy as he was that she was back at Heaton House. And yet, she seemed to be avoiding eye contact with him.

Maybe that wasn't a bad thing. Every time his eyes met hers and she smiled at him, his chest tightened in a way that told him he could care deeply for her if he allowed himself to. But he wasn't going to. He couldn't let himself care that way about anyone again. Couldn't bear the thought of anything happening to her. He still had nightmares about what happened to Beth, holding her in his arms while she took her last breath. Oh, no. He never wanted to experience that kind of pain again. And yet he couldn't deny that he was strongly drawn to Kathleen and very protective of her. But he couldn't fall in love with her.

Gretchen brought in freshly baked cookies and as

everyone gathered around her to grab one, Luke forced his thoughts away from the woman who'd been dominating them lately and onto his writing. Seeing how people who truly cared had been so much a part of helping Kathleen and her sister out of the tenements gave him more confidence that his book could give hope to others facing the same struggles.

Instead of trying to write a book much like Jacob Riis's *How the Other Half Lives,* in which he tried to inspire others to reach out and help, Luke wanted to provide hope to those still living in the tenements. To assure them that their lives could change for the better. And that if offered a helping hand, they needed to be willing to accept it.

He knew that had been difficult for Colleen, but it was easy once she felt she would be helping others as much as she would be helped. Maybe that was the key to it all.

Suddenly he felt a need to get back to work. He waited until the welcome-home party broke up, and was glad it didn't take long. Everyone, Kathleen especially, seemed ready to call it a day.

After good-nights were said and they began to head to their rooms, Kathleen began to follow Elizabeth and Julie and then turned back to him. Luke smiled at her as she approached him.

"Thank you again for all your help today and for dinner," she said.

"You're welcome. I'm glad you've moved back."

"So am I. It feels as if I've come home from a very long trip."

He nodded. It felt that way to him, too. "I'll see you in the morning. Sleep well."

"You, too." She started up the stairs and then turned back. Her lips parted as if she wanted to say something else. But then she gave a little shake of her head and only said, "Good night."

"Good night, Kathleen." Luke watched her up to the landing and then turned to head down to the lower floor. He took the stairs two at a time, wanting to get his thoughts about changes in his manuscript down on paper before he forgot them.

He had a direction for his book, now more so than ever. And once again it was Kathleen and her family who were the inspiration behind it.

Chapter Twelve

The next week passed swiftly for Kathleen. She was in meeting after meeting at the United Charities Building on Fourth Avenue and Twenty-second Street. The building had been set up to assist all the benevolent societies in the city as they tried to help those less fortunate.

The Ladies' Aide Society with their newly formed Child Day Care Program was one such society and it was no surprise to Kathleen that Mrs. Heaton sat on its board. The society had a small office in the building but Kathleen was told she could work from Heaton House where Mrs. Heaton had set up a desk for her in the small back parlor.

She was feeling overwhelmed by the job she'd been hired to do, and as the week progressed she became more and more nervous.

Luke must have sensed her worry, for after dinner on Thursday night he sought her out and asked if she'd like to take a walk.

"Yes, I believe I would, thank you."

They met Mrs. Heaton in the hall and told her they were going for a walk.

"Why don't you take Kathleen to Gramercy Park? I don't believe she's been there yet, has she?"

"No, I haven't," Kathleen answered for herself. "I'd love to see it, though."

"That is a great idea, Mrs. Heaton. I've been meaning to show it to her."

Mrs. Heaton nodded and went to the table in the foyer. She opened the drawer and pulled out a key. "Here you go, Luke. You two enjoy the nice evening."

"Thank you, we will," Luke said.

He swept Kathleen out the door and down the steps and onto the sidewalk. "You'll love the park. It's a great place to go when you need time alone or when you need to talk without worrying about someone walking in on your conversation."

"That might be nice." She loved Heaton House, but it wasn't always easy to have a private conversation with anyone.

Luke tucked her hand in the crook of his arm and they sauntered down the walk until they came to the gated park. Kathleen was a bit surprised when Luke pulled out the key Mrs. Heaton gave him and unlocked the gate.

"I still can't believe this park is private." Kathleen didn't know of another that was.

"It is. And each home only has two keys. It's been that way since the beginning and no one is inclined to change it. It's fairly small and was put in specifically for the residents of the neighborhood."

He led her into the park and Kathleen could see why the residents wanted to keep it to themselves. It was lovely, with trees that'd grown tall through the years and bushes that were sure to be filled with roses or other kinds of flowers as soon as it warmed enough for them to bloom. Luke led her into the middle of the garden and stopped at one of the benches. "Want to sit a little while?"

"Yes, I think I would, thank you." The park seemed an oasis in the middle of the city, much quieter than Central Park and very private. Yet, the lights in the homes surrounding it did make it feel like a safe haven of sorts.

She took a seat and Luke sat down beside her. "Now, tell me what's bothering you. You've become quieter each evening since you started your new position. Are you regretting your decision to work for the Ladies' Aide Society?"

He'd come to read her entirely too well. Kathleen shook her head. "Oh, no, I don't regret it, but I'm afraid they might regret hiring me."

"Now, why would they do that?"

"I don't want to disappoint Mrs. Heaton in any way, Luke, but I fear I'm not educated enough for this position. I—"

"Kathleen, did anyone ask for your credentials?"

"Well, no, but—"

He raised an eyebrow at her. "Did they ask how far you went in school?"

"No, but—"

"Do you know the tenements and relate to those living there?"

"Yes, of course I do. But, Luke, I don't want to fail or disappoint anyone counting on me to hire the right people to run the houses or recommend those that need the day care help. I don't have much experience in that kind of thing."

"I can assure you that none of the women you are working for have the kind of experience you do. They don't understand what it is you and Colleen and your neighbors have gone through. They have good hearts and they want to help, but it's going to take your experiences and your understanding of the people they want to help to be successful. *You* are the person they need, Kathleen."

For the first time that week, the kinks in Kathleen's neck seemed to relax. From the first meeting on Monday until right this minute, she'd begun to doubt her abilities. But Luke made sense.

She did know what it was like to live in the tenements. She knew what it was like to wonder where her next meal was coming from, to worry about physical abuse, to worry about her family. And she could honestly tell the people she talked to that she understood. She could do this job. Everything would be all right.

"My fear was getting the best of me, I'm afraid. I haven't been leaving things in the Lord's hands like I should."

"Oh, maybe not in this instance. But I've watched you, Kathleen. I've seen you pray with your nephews, and I know you put your faith in the Lord to get you through hard times. I believe you trust the Lord more than most people I know."

Kathleen smiled. "I know He's watched over Colleen and the boys, and me." He'd also used Luke to help them, but she wasn't sure Luke realized it.

"That He has. And the Lord is going to use all you've

been through for good. You'll see. You are the right person for this job, Kathleen."

"Thank you, Luke. Your encouragement means a lot to me." It meant more than she could say. No one had ever been there for her in the way Luke had been. But she was going to have to fight the attraction she felt for him. It was simply too easy to be around him.

"That's what friends are for, isn't it?" he asked.

Friends. They could be that, at least. "Yes, but I think you've been a better friend to me than I have been to you."

Luke shook his head. "Not so."

He looked as if he were about to say something more and decided against it. "I'm glad we're friends."

"I am, too." For that's all they could be—at least for now—and maybe for always.

Luke looked up into the star-filled sky and stifled the sigh his chest fought to release. *Friends.* There was no doubt he wanted to be her friend, wanted her to be his. And that was a good thing. And yet, his heart longed for more—in spite of the heartbreak of his past.

First his mother had left him and his father for another man when he was young. From then on, he'd had to live with a bitter man warning him never to trust his heart to a woman. And for years he'd believed him.

But as he'd gotten older he'd realized it was his father's bitterness and not his own, and he'd fallen in love with Beth. He'd been happier than at any time in his life, looking forward to their life together. And then she'd been killed. And he'd vowed never to fall in love again.

Much as he'd begun to care about Kathleen, he

couldn't let his feelings turn to love. He could not go through that kind of heartache again. He was better off living at Heaton House amidst those he considered family.

So why did he suddenly feel...so lonely? He'd been doing just fine, living at Heaton House, enjoying everyone's company. He hadn't wanted more until—

"I suppose we should be getting back," Kathleen said, interrupting his thoughts. "Thank you for bringing me here and helping me feel better about everything."

"You're welcome."

They both stood and sauntered back to the gate. The night was deepening and the stars shone brightly as Luke locked the gate behind them and they started back to Heaton House. "When is it you're going to start visiting buildings in the tenements?"

"I hope to begin Monday morning. I've been mapping out which ones to go to first. I thought I might start with our old neighborhood, with the people I know. They might also be able to suggest someone to run the other houses."

"I think that's a good idea. Might as well start with a familiar area. You'll do fine."

"I think I'll feel better once I get started."

"I'm sure you will. It's the unknown that has you unsettled. After a few weeks you'll have more confidence."

"I hope so. Right now I just want to get to Monday."

"Why don't we see if Colleen and the boys would like to go with our group to the park on Sunday? They love flying kites and I like helping them. I'm sure John and Ben would, too."

"The boys would love it. I'll talk to Colleen about it."

"Good. How are they doing?"

"I stopped by on my way home today and they're doing fine. They're settling in and really looking forward to making new friends, and Colleen and Ida are just ready to get the day care started."

"Much like you wanting to get started in your new position?"

"Exactly." She chuckled. "Now that you mention it, I think we're all a little nervous and excited all at the same time. Kind of silly, I suppose."

The tinkling sound of her laughter lightened Luke's heart. His admiration for her grew even more that she could laugh at herself after all she'd been through.

"Not at all. I think everyone is a bit nervous when they're faced a major change in their lives."

"You're not just trying to make me feel better?"

"No. I know what it's like to start over. It is difficult, but it gets easier with time."

Or it did—until memories surfaced and brought back all the pain of losing a loved one and reminded him why he'd decided never to fall in love again.

They arrived back at Heaton House to find that the new boarder had arrived.

"Kathleen, Luke, come meet Matthew Sterling, our new boarder," Mrs. Heaton said.

They entered the parlor to see a man who appeared to be about Luke's age. But he was a little taller, had almost black hair and blue eyes and was quite tan, as if he worked outside most of the time.

"Matt is the son of one of my childhood friends from Virginia. He's an iron worker come to help finish up the American Surety Company Building and then he'll be helping build the Park Row Building starting in October."

Luke strode across the room and held out his hand. "A pleasure to meet you, Mr.—"

"Oh, please call me Matt. Mrs. Heaton has assured me everyone goes by their first name here."

"All right, Matt. I'm Luke Patterson—just Luke is fine. Welcome to Heaton House. It's always good to have another man in the mix here."

"And this is Kathleen O'Bryan," Mrs. Heaton said as she pulled Kathleen forward. "She's been our newest boarder until you came."

"How do you do…Kathleen?"

"It's nice to meet you, Mr.—ah, Matt. You'll find Heaton House is truly a home, just as the rest of us have."

"I'm already feeling at home here, thank you."

"I've heard the Park Row is going to be one of the tallest buildings in the city," Luke said. "How is it working so high up?"

"Well, I've worked on some tall ones and I love it. But this one is going to be 391 feet. I think it will be the tallest once it's finished. I can't wait to get to work on it."

"Oh, it sounds very dangerous," Kathleen said.

Matt shrugged and grinned at her. "It can be. But we're careful up there."

"Luke, I've given him Michael's old room, of course, but he hasn't had time to get his things downstairs. Everyone had gone to their room when Matt arrived. Would you mind?"

"I'll be glad to help him get settled. Whenever you're ready, Matt." And the sooner the better. Luke could see the interest in the other man's eyes as he looked at Kathleen and he didn't like it at all.

Matt turned his attention to Luke. "I'm ready now. I've got to report in early tomorrow. I didn't bring a lot." He motioned to the two cases on the floor at his feet.

Luke grabbed one of the cases. "Follow me." He barely looked back as he said, "Night, Kathleen, Mrs. Heaton. See you in the morning."

"Good night, Luke. Thank you for showing me Gramercy Park. I enjoyed it very much."

"So did I. We'll have to do it again."

"See you both in the morning," Mrs. Heaton said.

Matt followed Luke out the door, down the hall and then down the stairs.

Even though he had no claim on Kathleen—and was determined not to—Luke didn't mind if this new boarder thought he might. Mrs. Heaton might have known the man's mother a long time ago, but none of them knew the man.

"You've got a nice room. It's next door to mine, and Ben's and John's are across the hall. They're good men. You'll meet them tomorrow."

"How many boarders are there?" Matt asked as he unlocked the room with the key Mrs. Heaton had given him.

"Right now there are four men, including you, and three women. You met Kathleen, and there is Julia and Elizabeth. I believe Mrs. Heaton will be adding one more woman before too long. And then there are the two maids, Gretchen and Maida. They live here, too." He didn't feel the need to explain that Mrs. Heaton sometimes took in temporary boarders. He'd find that out soon enough.

"Mrs. Heaton's son—where is he now?"

Luke grinned. "Not all that far from here. He married one of the lady boarders—an old friend of the family—at Christmas last year and they set up housekeeping a few blocks away. You'll get to know them, too."

"Sounds kind of like one big family."

"It is. And it's quite nice to have it here in this huge city. That's what Mrs. Heaton strives for. It'll be home to you before you know it."

"I hope so."

"If you need anything or have any questions, just knock."

"Thank you."

"See you in the morning. You just go up when you're ready for breakfast and help yourself to whatever is on the sideboard. I'm sure Mrs. Heaton explained it all to you, and she'll be there to introduce you to the others."

"Thanks for your help, Luke."

"You're welcome."

Luke wondered if Kathleen and Mrs. Heaton were still upstairs. He'd wanted to get Matt out of the room so fast he hadn't really had a chance to reassure Kathleen again.

He hurried back upstairs to see if they were around, only to find Gretchen in the kitchen.

"Mr. Patterson, is there anything I can get you? I have some apple pie left from tonight."

"No, I'm fine, Gretchen, thank you. Do you know if Mrs. Heaton and Kathleen are still in the parlor?"

"No, sir. I believe they just went upstairs. Is it important? I can tell them you'd like to talk to them."

"No. That's all right. I'll see them in the morning.

I will take a cup of that coffee with me though, if you don't mind."

"You know I make a fresh pot for you this time of night. Help yourself."

"Thank you, Gretchen."

"You're welcome."

Disappointed he hadn't caught Kathleen before she went upstairs, Luke poured himself a cup of coffee and headed back to his room. He'd see her in the morning and talk to her then. For now, he might as well see if he could get any writing done.

For Kathleen, having a new boarder in the house proved a good distraction from worry over her new position. It was quite entertaining to watch everyone at dinner. Kathleen mostly listened and watched as Elizabeth and Julia engaged Matt in conversation, with all kinds of questions about what it was like to work so high up in the air.

But if the scowl on John Talbot's face was any indication, he wasn't too happy about the attention Elizabeth was giving to the other man. Ben was quieter than usual, but Luke was hard to read. She couldn't tell what he thought of the other man. Still, having someone new at the table made for interesting conversation.

"You're from Boston?" Julia asked. "I'd think there was plenty of building going on there."

Matt chuckled and shrugged. "There is. But it's not New York and I wanted a change. And the buildings are getting taller here."

"You really like working that high up?" Elizabeth asked.

"I love it."

Kathleen couldn't imagine working so high in the sky. The fifth floor she'd lived on in the tenements was plenty high up for her.

"Enough about me. What is it the rest of you do?" His interest picked up when he heard Luke was a writer of dime novels.

"Luke Patterson," Matt said. "I do believe I've read some of your novels. You capture the West quite effectively. I'll have to write my father and let him know that I've met you. He'll be bragging to everyone. He loves your stories."

"Why, thank you, Matt. I appreciate knowing that. I'd be glad to send him a signed copy of my newest one. It comes out next month." Luke smiled at the new boarder.

"I thought you were working on something besides dime novels, Luke," John said.

"I am. But it's not finished yet. I'll have several dime novels out before then."

"Are all your novels set out West?"

"No. I set them here, too. And I've set a few down south."

"And you've been to all the places you've written about?"

"Not all, but most of them. I like traveling."

Somehow that surprised Kathleen. Luke seemed so settled here. Of course, he didn't say he wanted to move—just that he liked to travel. Kathleen had thought she would, too, until she'd come here by ship. That had been a most unpleasant trip and it'd been hard to leave her homeland.

But the thought of traveling now and again, coming back home to the city, might be something she'd enjoy someday. Right now she just needed to concentrate on her new position and getting through the first few weeks until she knew whether or not she was capable of handling the job.

"Are you all right?" Luke whispered to her as the conversation turned to something else.

"I'm fine. Just thinking about my job."

"Please quit worrying about it, Kathleen. You are going to do a great job. If Mrs. Heaton and the others didn't think so, they would never have offered it to you."

"Thank you, Luke."

"I'm not saying it just to make you feel better, although I hope it does have that effect on you. I truly believe it. And I've heard Mrs. Heaton talking about how blessed they were to be able to talk you into taking the position. They don't know the tenements like you do."

"But I'm afraid I don't know them as well as they think I do."

"You know all you need to know. It will all fall into place, you'll see."

Luke's encouragement went a long way in helping Kathleen through the rest of the week. By the weekend she was more excited than nervous to begin her work on Monday.

She spent most of Saturday with her family and was a bit surprised to find that Officer O'Malley had stopped by several times to visit Colleen and the boys in the last week. Before they'd moved, he'd stopped by the apartment a time or two, but Kathleen had put it down to him doing his job, following up on a crime he'd been called in on. But now she wasn't so sure his visits weren't for some other reason. Although if he were attracted to Colleen, he'd better be prepared to wait a good long while for her to be able to even think about remarriage.

As far as Kathleen could tell, except for Collin and Brody, the only thing marriage had brought her sister was heartache. And if witnessing it had made Kathleen leery of giving her heart away, she could only imagine how Colleen felt.

But her sister seemed quite willing to accept the policeman's friendship and it did give Kathleen a measure of comfort to know that he'd be watching out for Colleen and the boys.

Just as she was about to leave, she remembered to ask about going to the park after church the next day. "Luke thought the boys would enjoy flying the kites he bought them. And Mrs. Heaton always has plenty of food for the picnic. She'd love for you to join us."

"Well, now, that is very nice. But I've already asked Officer O'Malley to come for Sunday dinner."

"Oh?"

Colleen shrugged. "The boys seem to like him and—of course they like Luke, too."

"Well, maybe he could come with us. Think about it, okay?"

"I'll think on it. But you have a good time, either way, all right?"

"I will. But Mrs. Heaton meant it when she said she wanted you to feel welcome with all of us."

"I know she did. But, Kathleen, you need a life of your own without worrying about me every minute."

"I'm not worrying all the time anymore. I just want you to begin to enjoy life again."

"I know. And I will. I just have to give it time."

Kathleen nodded. It wasn't easy to put all the sorrows and fears of the past behind. She knew that as well as Colleen did. She could only pray that one day they would.

Chapter Thirteen

Kathleen's first day out in the tenements wasn't as bad as she'd feared. Having Luke along made her feel safer, although it also resulted in having a few doors shut in their faces.

As they left the third building in the neighborhood Kathleen had lived in, she tried to find words that wouldn't offend Luke. But it'd become very obvious as they'd knocked on first one door and then another that he couldn't accompany her on her interviews.

As they walked outside toward the next building, she gnawed her bottom lip before finally saying, "Luke, I'm sorry, but I think you're going to have to let me do this alone or wait downstairs or out of sight in the hallway while I try to talk to these women. They just aren't comfortable talking to both of us."

He rubbed his forehead. "Much as I hate to admit it, I know you're right. I'll wait in the hall and if that doesn't work, I'll wait in the foyer downstairs."

"Thank you." Kathleen was relieved that he'd agreed so readily. Maybe he felt a bit uncomfortable in talking to the harried women holding babes in their arms and other children clinging to their skirts. No. That wasn't fair. It hadn't seemed to bother him that Collin and Brody had clung to her skirts. In fact he'd been very empathetic.

She wondered what kind of childhood he'd had and realized that there was much about Luke she didn't know. How selfish of her—she'd never even asked, letting him see to her and her sister's needs instead of trying to get to know him better.

Where had he come from and what had his life been like before he came to live at Heaton House? It was time she showed some interest in him and his life, after all he'd done for her and her family.

But now wasn't the time. She did have a job to do and she'd like to be able to report that she'd found several people who either could use day care or were interested in helping run one of the homes. Of course, she really couldn't make a decision about anyone from one interview—or without checking them out and getting references. But she'd like to have a few leads at least.

They entered the next building and Kathleen was relieved when Luke said he'd stay out on the stoop and see if he could find anyone to talk to. She supposed it was in connection with his writing and though she still wasn't sure how she felt about his interviewing the less fortunate for a novel, she decided to trust that his intentions were honorable.

"All right," she told him.

"Take your time, but yell if you need me."

"I will." Although Kathleen doubted that he'd be able to hear her, still, she felt better knowing he was near. And she had no doubt that he'd come looking for her if she didn't come back soon enough to satisfy him.

As she began knocking on doors and went from one apartment to another, Kathleen was pleased to find that she actually recognized several of the tenants.

"Well, if it isn't Kathleen O'Bryan! 'Tis good to see you, dear," an older woman named Mrs. Connor said. "Come in and have a cup of tea with me."

Kathleen knew Mrs. Connor wouldn't need day care, as she lived with her daughter and son-in-law who both worked and had no children, but she might know someone who did. "I'd love a cup of tea."

"Good. Take a seat and I'll make us a cup." She motioned to a small table that'd been placed in front of a window looking down upon the street. Mrs. Connor was a widow and Kathleen supposed she spent a lot of her day looking out that window and watching the comings and goings of the other tenants.

Kathleen watched her hostess prepare a pot of tea and bring it and two cups to the table. This apartment was even smaller than the one she and her sister's family had lived in, but Mrs. Connor seemed quite happy in it.

"It's good to have company. I'd heard you all moved out after... How is your sister doing?"

Kathleen quickly assured her, "Colleen is doing well, thank you. We did move. We were both offered wonderful opportunities that we hope will help others as well."

"Oh?" Mrs. Connor poured their tea and settled back in her chair. "Tell me about it."

"Well, Colleen is actually running a day care home the Ladies' Aide Society has started. It's the first of many they hope to start. That's why I'm here. I'm the liaison for them, hoping to find those women who can benefit the most from having somewhere safe for their children to stay while they are at work."

"Really? Why, how much would that cost them?"

"Nothing."

"How can that be?"

"There are people in this city who really want to help. And they try to find ways to do so. Colleen and I have been the recipients of their help and through that, they've enabled us to be able to help others. Do you know anyone who might benefit from the day care?"

Mrs. Connor took a sip of tea and leaned her head to one side. "I might. There's a young mother living upstairs who might be interested. She takes in washing and ironing to support her and her daughter, but I think if she could get a regular job, she might be able to get them both out of here one day."

"Do you know her name?"

"It's Reba…" Mrs. Connor shook her head. "I can't remember her last name. But she lives in 4C. She might be there now, but I don't know."

"Do you think she'd talk to me?"

"I don't know. She's very private. I could tell her you might be coming around in the next few days and find out."

"That would be wonderful, Mrs. Connor. May I check back with you tomorrow?"

"Yes, of course you may. You stop by anytime. I'll try to think of others who might need your help the most. And I'll ask around."

"Thank you. I truly do appreciate that."

"It will give me something to do and if I can help one or two women get out of here, I'll feel I did something good, too."

Kathleen nodded. That was what she was happiest about with her new position—the chance to make a real difference in someone's life. She knew how it felt to look forward to a future in this country she'd come to love. But that had only truly happened because of the help of Mrs. Heaton and Luke and the others.

Oh, her job would bring her back here, but she'd be able to go back to Heaton House at the end of the day. Still it would keep her humble, remembering where she'd come from and counting her blessings.

She took the last sip of tea and stood to leave. Luke was probably thinking she was making her way from one apartment to another by now.

"I'll check back with you tomorrow. Is there any time that is best for you?"

"I'm here most of the day unless I need to run an errand—and I don't have any of those to take care of tomorrow. But should I leave for any reason, I'll leave a note on the door."

"That will be fine. But should you need to talk to me, here is the number of the Ladies' Aide Society's office. They'll let me know to get in touch with you." Kathleen handed Mrs. Connor one of the calling cards the society had made up for her.

"I'll keep it where I can find it. Thanks for sharing a cup of tea with me today."

"Thank you for having me," Kathleen said.

She knocked on a few more doors in the building, but no one answered and she hurried back down the stairs and outside where Luke waited for her on the stoop.

His smile welcomed her back. "You look happy. It must have gone well. Did you find anyone to help?"

"I'm not sure. Possibly." She explained about Mrs. Connor and the young woman she'd told her about. "I should find out more tomorrow."

"Are you ready for some lunch?"

"I'd like to visit one more building. And I really don't want to keep you from your work, Luke. Why don't you go on and—"

"I'm not leaving until you do. Go on to the next building and do whatever you need to do. We can grab something to eat after that."

Kathleen could see from the look on his face that he wasn't going anywhere today until she was through. Hopefully after a few weeks he'd realize she was safe here and that she knew her way around.

In the meantime, she'd count him and his concern as blessings and get on with her work.

Luke watched Kathleen disappear into the next building and then took a seat on one of the steps outside. The air was somewhat fresher out here than inside the buildings—but not much with trash building up outside. Kathleen must have a stronger stomach than he did, for the smells in some of the buildings they'd been in that morning had been nauseating.

He pulled the notepad from his pocket and looked around, watching people come and go on the streets, seeing unsupervised children playing in the middle of them. He wrote down his thoughts and descriptions of different people he saw. There was the older woman who was returning from the grocers or a street vendor. Her bag looked heavy but she shook her head when he offered to carry it home for her.

She kept looking back as she passed him, as if she

expected him to follow her. He couldn't blame her for being suspicious of a man she'd never seen before, but it saddened him he couldn't help her.

He was busy writing down his impressions and questions he'd like to ask, should he get a chance to interview anyone, when Kathleen came outside.

"That didn't take long," he said, stuffing his pencil and pad back into his pocket.

She chuckled. "I was in there nearly an hour. You must have been writing longer than you thought."

"Possibly. But at least that proves you aren't keeping me from working." He pulled her hand through his arm and looked down at her. "Let's go get some lunch. Want to go to a street vendor or…there's a little café a few blocks away that's pretty good."

"Wherever you want to go is fine with me," Kathleen said. "After waiting on me all morning, I think the least I can do is give the choice to you."

"Well, let's go to the café. You could use a break, I'm sure."

As they were a bit later than the normal lunch hour, they were seated right away in the small café over on Third Avenue. While Kathleen looked over the menu, he wondered if she was disappointed in him for not helping out one of the street vendors who possibly lived in the tenements.

"I suppose we could have gotten some clams at one of the vendors. I—"

"No, it's all right, Luke. I don't know many of the vendors and I'd only feel safe buying from one I did know. Not all of the carts are as clean as I'd like and I just talked to a woman who said she got sick from eating oysters at one only last week. I'd have gone had you picked one, but I'm glad you chose someplace you know is good. What do you recommend?"

"Their daily special is usually the freshest and today it's creamed chicken with rolls. I've had it before and it's very good."

"I'll have it, then."

Once they'd given their order Luke smiled across the table at Kathleen. She'd dressed in a plain skirt and shirtwaist, much as she'd worn to work at Tiffany Glass. He'd overheard her and Mrs. Heaton talking about what to wear and Kathleen had wanted to be sure she looked just like she had when she lived there. She didn't want anyone she knew to think she was putting on airs just because she'd moved out of the tenements.

"How did things go this time? Did you find anyone you could recommend?"

"I found several, but either their husbands don't want them to work outside the home even though they might need for her to, or they are too prideful to accept free and reliable child care. I think that could be one of the biggest problems and I'll have to be careful on how I present the offer. I can understand the pride. I've had my share of it, too, and wrongfully so. *Proverbs* talks about pride coming before destruction and having a haughty spirit comes before a fall. I don't want either of those things happening to me, so I must be watchful always to be neither haughty or prideful."

"I suppose we all have trouble with those two feelings."

"Yes, but we can't quit fighting against them."

"True." He admired this woman more all the time. She had such high morals and love for the Lord—more so than any other woman he knew.

"I'm sorry. I don't mean to sound preachy. I—" She leaned back in her chair and sighed. "I've been so blessed that coming back here makes me feel kind of bad, almost guilty that I've moved out and so many are still there. Will always be there."

Luke nodded. "I understand. I felt somewhat that way as I waited for you. Knowing I didn't have to live there and so glad that you don't either. But don't feel guilty, Kathleen. You are going to be able to help many people over the years."

"I suppose I might feel better when I know that I've been able to do so. Hopefully Mrs. Connor will talk to the young woman she thinks needs child care. Of course we don't have another home up and running just yet—I have to find someone for that soon. But perhaps, if the need is great enough, Colleen and Ida could take one more child. But it's made me realize that my first priority is to find people to get the new homes started."

Their meal came just then and they spent the next half hour talking about where to look for someone who could run one of the homes. "I'm trying to think. Maybe... Mrs. Walsh is wonderful with children. Her husband does work, but I'm sure they could use the extra money and—"

"You know, if he's handy, it's possible that Mrs. Heaton and the others would want someone who could take care of the homes and—"

"Oh, Luke, that is a wonderful idea! I need to run it by Mrs. Heaton before I even think about talking to Rose about it. I'm not even sure how handy her husband is, but maybe—" She broke off and looked at Luke, her expression one of hope. "Maybe he can learn what he needs to—if he needs to?"

"There are all kinds of trade schools around. I'm sure he could learn anything he needs to."

"The homes will be in good shape when they are moved into and by the time something goes wrong perhaps he will know what to do." She gave a little laugh. "I'm getting way too excited about this, but it could help them get out of the tenements and, well, I know Rose would be wonderful at running one of the homes."

"I think Mrs. Heaton will like the idea."

Kathleen nodded. "Yes. So do I. And although this was started to help working women, I don't think anyone would object if it helped a man out of the tenements, either. He could keep the job he has now, I would think."

"I'm sure he could. And you knowing the couple would probably make the ladies feel better about hiring them."

By the time they left the restaurant, Luke wasn't sure who was more excited about his idea—him or Kathleen.

When Kathleen and Luke returned to Heaton House and presented Mrs. Heaton with the proposal to hire Rose and her husband to run the next child care home, she was almost as excited as they were.

"Oh, my dears, I love the idea. I will have to run it by the others, of course, but I don't think there will be one objection to it."

Kathleen leaned back in the chair in Mrs. Heaton's study and released a pleased sigh and smiled at Luke. "I told Luke it was a wonderful idea."

Mrs. Heaton looked from one to the other. "Well,

you're right. I'll get on the telephone and try to have an answer for you by dinnertime."

"Thank you, Mrs. Heaton. I suppose I should go write up notes on what I did today and about the young woman Mrs. Connor told me about. I'll fill you in on that at dinner. But right now, I'll leave you to make your call."

"Oh, and we have a new boarder. She'll be joining us for dinner tonight. Her name is Millicent Faircloud and she's a photographer. I think you'll both like her."

"I'm sure we will. I'll be sure to welcome her, if I see her before dinner," Kathleen said.

"Thank you, dear. I appreciate that. And please tell the others."

"Yes, ma'am," Luke said. He followed Kathleen out of Mrs. Heaton's study and into the hall.

Kathleen turned to him. "I think Mrs. Heaton likes your idea as much as we do, Luke."

He smiled at her. "I told you it was going to be all right, Kathleen."

"Thanks to you—you're the one who came up with the idea that might get us our next home up and running."

"You probably would have thought of it on your own, but I'm glad to help in any way." They reached the staircase and Kathleen turned to Luke. "I do appreciate you going with me today and for lunch. But—"

"If you are going to tell me I don't need to come tomorrow, don't. Please. I actually got some good ideas from people-watching while waiting for you. You are not hindering my writing in any way. I've always worked better late at night."

"But you aren't going to get enough sleep."

"I don't require a lot."

"I'm not going to convince you, am I?"

"No, ma'am. You aren't. I'll either be going along with you or following you—at least for a while." He smiled. "But I'll go get some work done now so you don't have to worry about keeping me from it. See you at dinnertime."

Kathleen watched him hurry downstairs before she headed upstairs to get her notes in order. She couldn't honestly say she was disappointed in Luke's response. She had felt safer with him along, but he couldn't shadow her everywhere all the time. She was going to have to become more comfortable coming and going in the area she'd lived in for so long.

She'd never really thought about her safety as much as her sister's before now, but going in and out some of the buildings today, she'd realized she'd have to be very aware of her surroundings. And there would be some buildings she might not enter. Once she got the word out to those she trusted, eventually people would end up contacting her for the day care opportunity. Then maybe Luke wouldn't feel quite so responsible for her. And she wouldn't feel quite so—

"Kathleen, wait up!" Elizabeth hurried up the steps to join her at the landing. "How did your day go?"

"It went very well. I have a lead on someone who might really need to put her child in the day care home and Luke gave me an idea on who I might talk to about running the next one."

"That is wonderful! I heard we have a new boarder. Have you met her yet?"

"No, not yet. But I'm looking forward to it."

"So am I. I do hope she's easy to get along with," Elizabeth said.

"I'm sure she will be. I can't imagine anyone Mrs. Heaton has accepted as a boarder wouldn't be."

"Oh, you'd be surprised. There have been one or two. But thankfully, they're no longer with us."

"Well, I look forward to meeting Miss Faircloud."

"It's always interesting to find out more about our boarders. Matt has been a nice addition."

"Yes, he has. I don't think John likes the attention you give him, though."

The smile on Elizabeth's face told Kathleen that was not bad news for her.

"Really? I didn't think he noticed."

"Oh, he's noticed."

"Hmm," Elizabeth said.

She'd never mentioned being interested in John, but anyone who sat at the dinner table with the two of them would have to be blind not to know they cared about each other.

The two women parted at the top of the stairs to get ready for dinner and Kathleen found she was looking forward to it a great deal. She was excited to hear what Mrs. Heaton had found out about taking an offer to the Walshes—and to see how everyone took to the newest boarder. Living at Heaton House was never boring.

Chapter Fourteen

Dinner was every bit as entertaining as Kathleen thought it might be. Millicent Faircloud was petite with light blond hair and blue eyes, and she captured the attention of most everyone at the table the moment she took her seat.

"A photographer, you say?" John asked. "And you're going to start up your own business?"

That fact seemed to take everyone a little by surprise. It certainly wasn't normal to see a woman going into business on her own, but to the women at the table it was quite an admirable thing to try.

"It's what I want." Millicent gave a little shrug. "But it might be a while before I get a name big enough to actually make it work. I truly would like to photograph weddings and families, capturing just the right shot to show people at their best for years to come. But in the meantime, I've set up appointments with several magazines and newspapers this week, to show them my work and try to get on their list of photographers."

"Did you put *The Delineator* on your list? I'm sure

they'd be interested," Elizabeth said. "If you didn't, I'd be glad to talk to my supervisor and—"

"You work there?" Millicent leaned across the table toward her.

"I do."

"I love that magazine and I definitely have them on my list. I'm supposed to meet with them on Friday."

"Good." Elizabeth nodded. "I hope you're successful in starting your own business and I will mention that I know you."

"Thank you, Elizabeth."

"It's refreshing to see women taking advantage of all the opportunities available to them today," Mrs. Heaton said. "I hope you all know how blessed you are."

"We truly are," Kathleen added. She still couldn't quite believe the changes in her life.

"Well, I wouldn't have this opportunity had my grandmother not left me enough to live on until I can get started," Millicent said. "But I need work so I don't have to dip into my little nest egg too much. And of course, had Mother not known you, Mrs. Heaton, I know I wouldn't have been able to come to New York City."

"I'm glad she sent you to Heaton House, Millicent."

"I am, too."

Kathleen knew firsthand how blessed the young woman was to be here and she'd soon know it, too.

As dinner progressed and conversation flowed around the table, Kathleen noticed that Elizabeth didn't look any happier about the attention John was giving Millicent than he'd been about the attention she'd given Matt a few evenings earlier.

"Do you think those two will ever admit their feelings for one another?" Luke whispered to her.

"Maybe they're trying to deny how they feel." She could understand if they were. She'd been trying to ignore a few feelings lately herself.

Luke shrugged. "I suppose they might be. But they seem made for each other. She works for a magazine and he works for a newspaper. They even cover some of the same stories."

Kathleen had been at Heaton House long enough now to know that John covered much of the social goings-on in the city. He entertained them with stories often. And Elizabeth occasionally covered some of the same things for *The Delineator*. Yet they sometimes seemed in competition with each other—maybe that was the way they fought their attraction to each other. But hard as they might try to ignore their feelings for each other, Kathleen didn't think there was anyone at the table who didn't believe they cared for each other.

Her heart suddenly skipped a beat, and then another. Could everyone at the table tell how she struggled with her growing feelings for Luke? Oh, she hoped not. She—

"Kathleen, dear, I have news for you." Mrs. Heaton broke into her thoughts. "You've been given permission—no, actually you've been greatly encouraged to see if the Walshes might be interested in running the next home. Everyone thinks it a wonderful idea just as I did."

"Oh, that is fantastic news, Mrs. Heaton! I'll be sure to go see Mrs. Walsh first thing tomorrow."

"We don't have a home ready yet, but all should be

in place within the next few months. So that would give them time to prepare."

"I will let them know."

"Might I ask what these homes are?" Millicent asked.

Mrs. Heaton explained about the day care homes and how Kathleen was working to identify the families in need.

"Aren't you a little frightened going to the tenements?" Millicent asked Kathleen.

She shook her head. Even if she were at times, she wasn't going to admit it—not with Luke listening to her every word. Still, she didn't want to lie. "So far I've mostly been visiting the area I lived in and—"

"You lived there? Oh, I would love for someone to show me around."

"I've heard it's not a place for anyone to go alone, unless they are very familiar with the area," Matt said from across the table. "So don't be taking off by yourself, Millie."

"I do not like being called Millie, Mr. Sterling. And furthermore I don't like being told what to do by someone I've just met. I said I'd like someone to show me around. I have no intention of going by myself."

"Oh, I'm sorry if I overstepped, Miss—"

"You may call me Millicent and I'll call you Matt. I've been told everyone is on first-name basis here."

"Yes, that's what I've been told, Millicent."

Mrs. Heaton cleared her throat as she passed a basket of rolls down the table. "It's so nice to have a full table again."

Luke nudged Kathleen's elbow and leaned a little

nearer to whisper, "Seems like those two might have lit a spark of some kind between them."

It certainly seemed like it. She could almost feel the electricity in the air. Or was it her reaction to Luke's nearness she was feeling?

Tired from her first day out in the tenements, Kathleen didn't want to linger in the parlor for too long after dinner. But she wanted to stay long enough to make Millicent and Matt feel welcome. She knew how much it'd meant to her to have everyone try to make her feel at home in Heaton House.

Julia played the piano and they gathered round to sing along with her. Kathleen liked all the songs— "After the Ball," and "Daisy Bell," but her favorite and that of most of the boarders was "The Sidewalks of New York." When Julia played it, everyone knew it would be the last song of the evening.

The group put their all into it and Kathleen loved hearing Luke's rich baritone from right behind her. It gave her goose bumps and made her shiver, while her heart turned kind of mushy at the same time.

If he ever quit writing, he could probably make a good living singing.

The last note died away and everyone began to go their separate ways. Luke touched her elbow before she headed out the parlor door, sending tingles up her arm. "I'll see you in the morning. I'm eager to find out what the Walshes say about your offer."

"Yes, so am I." She almost told him once more that he didn't have to accompany her, but she knew it would fall on deaf ears and besides, it was his idea to include Mr. Walsh. He deserved to know what their reaction was. "See you tomorrow."

* * *

The next day Kathleen and Luke set out for Mrs. Connor's first. They took the trolley as far as Third Avenue and then walked by foot amid the hustle and bustle of the city streets.

The days were getting warmer and the street vendors began hawking their goods earlier.

"We'll go to visit Rose a little later. But right now, I really want to find out if Mrs. Connor had a chance to speak to the young woman she told me about. And I believe it will be fine for you to come with me to both places. I think Mrs. Connor gets lonely while her family is at work and of course you've met Rose. I don't think either of them will mind talking to me with you there."

"Are you sure? I don't want to get in the way of you doing your job."

Kathleen grinned at him. "Don't worry. I won't let you hinder my work. If I have a chance to speak to this woman, I'll ask you to wait for me. Or better yet, if she comes to Mrs. Connor's you can just tell me you'll wait outside for me."

Luke seemed to appreciate that she didn't want to appear to be telling him what to do in front of other women. He gave a little nod. "That will work well."

Luke followed her up the stairs in a building much like the one she'd lived in. There wasn't much difference in the apartment buildings in this neighborhood— only whether or not the buildings were kept up by the owners and how well the tenants took care of their own apartments.

She'd felt quite comfortable in Mrs. Connor's and was sure that Luke would, too. The apartment was as clean as one could make it and the older woman was happy to welcome them into it.

Kathleen lightly touched Luke's arm. "This is a friend of mine, Mrs. Connor. His name is Luke Patterson."

"How do you do, ma'am. I'm pleased to meet you." Luke gave her a smile that Kathleen was sure would melt the older woman's heart—it always did funny things to hers.

"Thank you. If you are a friend of Kathleen's, you're as welcome here as she is. Please, take a seat and I'll make some tea—or would you prefer coffee, Mr. Patterson?"

"I'll have whatever you ladies are having, thank you."

She'd obviously been expecting Kathleen, for she had a small plate of cookies ready and the kettle was steaming on a back burner. "Won't take but a minute to steep the tea."

"Were you able to speak to the young woman you told me about, Mrs. Connor?" Kathleen got right to the point.

"Reba? Yes, I did. And she's very interested, but said she'd have to meet you and anyone she'd be leaving her little girl with before she'll commit to anything."

"Oh, I understand completely. I'd want to do the very same thing," Kathleen assured her.

Mrs. Connor brought a tray of cups and the teapot to the table and poured them each a cup before taking her own seat. "She lives on the fourth floor and I believe she's home. She's in 4C, if you want to go up. Mr. Patterson can stay and keep me company."

"I'd like to talk to her. I—" She looked at Luke.

"It's fine with me, Kathleen. If Mrs. Connor doesn't mind I'd really like another one of her cookies."

The older woman smiled at the compliment and Kathleen had no doubt that both of them would get along just fine while she was away. "Will Reba be expecting me?"

"I told her I'd send you up if you came by today. Oh, and her last name is Dickerson."

Kathleen took a last sip of tea and stood. "I'll be back in a bit then."

Mrs. Connor showed her to the door and Kathleen took the stairs to the fourth floor. The stuffiness in the hallway seemed to make the breakfast smells, along with every other aroma in the building, linger longer. She was careful not to breathe deeply as she knocked on apartment 4C.

"Yes? Who is it?"

"Mrs. Dickerson? It's Kathleen O'Bryan. Mrs. Connor told me she talked to you about me and—"

The door cracked open ever so slightly and all she could see was one blue eye and some reddish-blond hair. Kathleen smiled and the woman opened the door wider. "Come in."

A little girl of about three or four peeked around her mother's skirts. She had her mother's blue eyes but her hair was blonder and had no red in it. She had a finger stuck in her mouth and as Kathleen smiled down at her, she ducked behind her mother.

There was something familiar about the young woman, but Kathleen couldn't place her. She stood straight and proud as Kathleen entered and looked around, and she recognized the stance well. There was a time when she would have reacted the same way. And not long at all since her sister had. She hurried to put Mrs. Dickerson at ease.

"This apartment is much like the one I used to live in down the street."

"You're from the tenements?"

"I am, yes. I've only recently moved out."

Kathleen could see the young woman's stiff stance begin to relax. She picked her child up and motioned to the worn sofa. "Please, have a seat while I get Jenny occupied with her toys."

Kathleen looked around the two rooms she could see—the small parlor and tiny kitchen. They were both clean with only a bowl at the table where the child had most probably been eating.

The young mother was back in only a few minutes. "Would you like some coffee or tea?"

"I'm fine, thank you. Unless you'd like something and in that case I'll join you."

"Come, take a seat at the kitchen table and tell me more about this child care home Mrs. Connor mentioned."

Kathleen wasted no time in doing just that as Mrs. Dickerson poured them both a cup of coffee. She pulled a few flyers from her bag that explained the day care homes and other things the Ladies' Aide Society wanted to do.

"And it doesn't cost anything?"

"Not a cent. There are people in the city who have money and truly do want to help others."

"I sure would love to have some regular income. I take in laundry, but it doesn't go near far enough."

"With child care, you'd be able to take a job that

pays better. I think you're a perfect candidate for the service, Mrs. Dickerson."

"Please, just call me Reba. It does sound wonderful. I've thought of applying at Macy's for a position, but—"

"You could do that now. Please, think about it. Pray about it. If you let me know soon I can get you on the top of the list for the next home."

"There isn't an opening now?"

"Well, I could see if there is room for one more, if you should find employment before the other home is up and running."

"I think I'd like that. I'll see if Mrs. Connor can watch Jenny so that I can go apply at a few places."

"I'm sure she'll be happy to. She's a very nice woman. I'll check back with you in a few days or you can leave a message for me at the Ladies' Aide Society." She handed Reba one of her cards.

Reba took it. "Thank you."

"You're welcome. I'll be praying you find the right job. You do that, and we'll find a place for your little girl."

Kathleen left the apartment with a light heart. It felt wonderful to see the expression in the woman's eyes change from resignation to hope. Kathleen sent up a silent prayer that she would be able to help her.

As soon as Kathleen returned to Mrs. Connor's apartment, Luke could tell from the expression on her face that things went well. So, apparently, could Mrs. Connor.

"She said yes, didn't she?" the older woman said.

"Well, she seemed very interested," Kathleen replied. "She said she's going to see if you will watch her daughter while she puts in applications."

"Of course I will. I want that young woman to have a better life."

Kathleen nodded and Luke knew she wanted the same thing.

"Thank you for telling me about her, Mrs. Connor. Seeing her with her little girl, knowing that making their living is up to her…well, I'll pray she finds something quickly."

"We'll leave it in the Lord's hands. It's for sure He will work it all out in the best way."

Luke had a feeling the woman prayed often. Something he needed to do more.

"We all need to be praying about it," Kathleen said. "I told Reba to pray about it also. I'm sure the Lord will guide her. You know, there is something about her—I feel I've seen her before."

"That's possible. She lives in the same neighborhood that you did. More than likely you've passed her on the street."

"That's true. We probably passed each other numerous times." She seemed to be in deep thought and then gave her head a shake. "I suppose we should go now. I have a few more people to see today."

"Thank you for putting up with me, Mrs. Connor," Luke said. He'd had quite an enjoyable time talking to the woman. She'd given him all kinds of insight into the kind of people he wanted to help.

"Thank you for keeping me company, Mr. Patterson. It was a pleasure to meet a real author. You come back anytime and I'll see if I can come up with any more memories for you. Or just come by for coffee when you're in the neighborhood."

"Thank you, ma'am. I may very well take you up on your offer."

"I hope you do." She turned to Kathleen. "Thank you for bringing him with you, Kathleen. Something about this young man reminds me of my son."

"You're quite welcome. I'm sure we'll be seeing you again."

"I'm counting on it."

She let Kathleen and Luke out and then locked the door behind them. Kathleen sighed as they began to walk away. "I wish I could get her and her family out of here, too."

"I know. But you know she's much better off than some. She's not dreaming of getting out as much as she's trying to help others."

"We can learn a lot from Mrs. Connor. She reminds me of Mrs. Heaton in many ways."

"Yes, she does me, too."

They made their way up the street to Kathleen's old building. It looked the same to Luke, and he was surprised when she said, "It doesn't feel the same now that we don't live here. And we haven't been out very long. How can that be?"

"I don't know. It seems the same to me."

They climbed the stairs and Kathleen wrinkled her nose and began to chuckle. "It smells about the same."

"It does."

They passed an apartment where loud arguing was heard. "And it sounds much the same."

"Like I said. Only difference is that you don't live here any longer."

They reached the Walshes' apartment and Kathleen knocked on the door. For a moment Luke thought everyone must be gone, but then the door opened a crack and Mrs. Walsh peeked out.

"Kathleen! Mr. Patterson! My, but it's good to see you. Come in, come in." She opened the door wide and Luke followed Kathleen inside.

"Please take a seat and tell me what brings you here. Colleen and the boys are all right, aren't they?"

"They are wonderful. She'd very much like you to come see her, and the boys would love to see Roger."

"I've been meaning to visit but I thought perhaps she's been so busy getting everything set up. I think it is such a fine thing the Ladies' Aide Society is doing, Kathleen. And I'm so glad it's provided you and Colleen a better life."

"So are we. And, well, Rose…would you like to… what would you say if you were offered the same kind of chance?"

"What do you mean?"

"The city is in need of more day care homes and the Ladies' Aide Society is wanting to get the next one going as soon as possible."

"But I have no need of it, Kathleen. My husband doesn't want me to leave Roger to go to work."

"What if you didn't have to leave him? And what if your husband could continue to work at his job but earn a little more?"

"What are you talking about, Kathleen? Do tell me."

Kathleen explained the offer to her and Luke could tell Rose was trying to contain her excitement about it. "You mean we'd be running another house? We'd be able to move out of here?"

"If your husband agrees to it, yes."

Rose put a hand over her heart and tears gathered in the corners of her eyes. "I don't know what to say. I—"

"You don't have to say anything just yet. Talk to your husband and let me know as soon as possible. And if you have any other questions, you are welcome to come talk to me and Mrs. Heaton."

"Oh, I'm sure there'll be questions. But it sounds too good to be true."

"Have no worries, Rose. You'll be working, probably harder than you ever have, taking care of a passel of children—but it's a chance to have a life out of here. You'll have a nice home, make good money and have a future—not to mention that you'll be helping others at the same time."

Luke watched Kathleen's former neighbor as she put a hand over her mouth and nodded. "I don't know what to say. Thank you for thinking of this."

"It wasn't just me. Luke actually came up with the idea that your husband could be hired to help keep up the houses—if it's something he'd like to do."

"I think he'd love it. I can't wait for him to get home so that I can talk to him about it. But I can't see how he'd even think of turning it down."

Luke was glad to hear it. He had a soft spot for this family. After all, it was Rose's husband who'd brought Kathleen to Heaton House. He deserved some kind of reward in Luke's eyes for that very reason.

The two women chatted for a few minutes and then Kathleen looked at Luke. "I suppose we should be going now."

Rose saw them out. "Thank you. I'll be getting in touch with you as soon as I can."

"I look forward to hearing from you, Rose. And you know, you and your husband can always ask Colleen about the position and how she's liking it."

"I might just pay her a visit today."

"I'm sure she'll be very glad to see you."

The two women hugged and he and Kathleen left the apartment.

"Another good day for you," he said to her as they made their way down the flights of stairs.

"Oh, yes, I think so. Now all I have to do is wait for answers."

"You'll get them soon, I'm sure. I can't imagine anyone turning down the offers you've made today."

"Neither can I." They reached the bottom floor and Luke wondered if Kathleen realized they both took a cleansing, deep breath at the same time.

The grin on her face and the gleam in her eye told him she did. "You were so right. It hasn't changed a bit. I don't think I really knew how bad it was until I moved away. Oh, I knew, but it didn't matter as much because most of the people I worked with and knew lived in the same conditions. But there is so much more out there—so many opportunities if only…"

"I know. But we can't help everyone at once, Kathleen. Just a few at a time. And we can get the word out about how much more help is needed and what opportunities there are. And then we have to leave things in the Lord's hands."

"I know. I'm not always very good at that, though."

"None of us are. But I believe you are better at it than you think you are. I think it comes naturally to you." She was a wonderful example of being there for her sister, of doing what she could to protect her and the boys, to help support them when her brother-in-law either couldn't or wouldn't. And she'd even gone back to help once she'd gotten out of this place. She'd given up living at Heaton House to come back and help her sister. And she'd have kept doing it as long as she had to.

"No, Luke, I—"

"Kathleen." Luke stopped in the middle of the walk and turned to her. "Anyone can see you look to the Lord to guide you. And you do what you believe He wants you to do—even if it might be the last thing you want."

"Luke, I only wish I was like that. I know deep down that I'm not. I'm not brave and I'm not willing to go out on a limb in many ways. I have a hard time trusting others and—"

"Do you trust the Lord?"

"Of course I do. But—"

"Then just trust that the Lord will bring people into your life whom you can trust. Like Mrs. Heaton." *And me.*

He wished she knew that she could trust him to be her friend, to be there to protect her, but, because of all she'd been through, he understood why she found it extremely difficult to trust men—including him. He'd like to change that, but it might mean making a commitment that he couldn't make now—and wasn't sure he ever could.

And yet who did he think he was telling Kathleen that she should trust the Lord when he needed to do the very same thing?

Chapter Fifteen

Kathleen had visited both Reba and Mrs. Connor later in the week and the younger woman was busy putting in applications for work but hadn't found anything yet. Rose and her husband had visited with Colleen to find out more about what to expect and promised to have an answer by the coming Monday. Kathleen had no choice but to wait for their decisions and as frustrating as that was for her, Mrs. Heaton and the other ladies were hopeful and encouraged by her first real week out in the tenements.

At dinner on Friday evening everyone began talking about the weekend.

"We should have a group outing. We haven't done that in a while," Elizabeth suggested.

"You know what? It's getting warmer out. Maybe we should go to Coney Island this weekend? It's still much too cool for a swim, but we could enjoy the amusement parks and perhaps have lunch there."

"I've never been to Coney Island," Kathleen said. "But I heard a lot about it when I worked at Tiffany. The group went once in a while, but I…" Her voice trailed off, thinking about the outings she'd been asked to go on but always refused because of money or just not feeling right about enjoying her weekend when Colleen and the boys were stuck with Clancy. But she didn't have that worry now. "I'd love to go."

"So would I," Millicent and Elizabeth said at the same time.

"We'd need to get an early start. We can take the El partway and then use the trolley," Luke said. "Does everyone want to go?"

"Yes, let's." Julia grinned. "I'm off this Saturday and I haven't been in ages."

It appeared everyone would be able to go—even Mrs. Heaton.

"I'd like to join you all, and I'm sure Michael and Violet might like to go, too."

"The more the merrier," Luke said.

"May I ask Colleen if she'd like to take the boys?" Kathleen asked. For now her sister and Ida had decided to take turns watching the children on Saturdays as only a few were left there on that day. And they were both off on Sundays. She thought Ida would be in charge this Saturday. "They've never been, either."

"Of course!" Elizabeth said. "They'll love it."

"I'll walk over with you after dinner so you can ask, if you'd like," Luke offered. "Or you can telephone her."

"Thank you, Luke. I'd love to go visit them for a bit." Mrs. Heaton didn't have many rules but she was firm about not letting the women go out alone after dark. One of the male boarders would escort them where they wanted to go and back to Heaton House.

Once dinner was over, Luke said, "Are you ready?"

"Let me run up and get my wrap and I'll be right back," Kathleen said.

He nodded. "I'll be in the parlor. Just call me when you're ready."

Kathleen met up with Elizabeth, Julia and Millicent at the landing. They were talking about what to wear the next day.

"Oh, I need some advice for that, too. But I don't want to keep Luke waiting and I'd like to see the boys before Colleen puts them to bed."

"Just come to my room when you get back," Elizabeth said. "I'll tell you what we're wearing and we can choose something for you."

"Thank you, Elizabeth. I'll do that. See you all later."

Kathleen hurried to her room and grabbed a lightweight shawl before heading back down to the parlor.

Evidently Luke had been waiting for the sound of her footsteps, for he joined her just outside the parlor door.

"I'm ready if you are," Kathleen said.

"At your service, ma'am." Luke opened the front door and they headed to her sister's.

Luke offered her his arm and she took it, knowing by now that he was only being gentlemanly. Still it brought her into closer contact with him and her heart fluttered. But she didn't want to appear rude by not taking his arm. Thankfully, he never overstepped the bounds of being a gentleman and she was sure he never would.

"Are you looking forward to tomorrow?"

"I am. What's it like?"

"Oh, it's very interesting and there are a lot of rides I'm sure the boys will love. Have you ever been on a roller coaster?"

"No, I never have and of course neither have they. But we've seen pictures of them."

"What about a carousel? Have they ever ridden one of those?"

"No."

"Well, then, I'm getting more excited by the minute about showing it to you and them. It's going to be a fun day."

"But what if Colleen doesn't go?"

"I'll look forward to showing it to you and then again to them at another time."

The evening was quite nice and Kathleen enjoyed the walk to her sister's. They were welcomed in as if they hadn't seen them in a very long time. The boys hugged Kathleen and then gave their attention to Luke.

"I'm not sure whether to be insulted or not."

Her sister looked at her. "Oh, Kathleen, you know they love you. But they haven't seen Luke in a while and he found a place in their hearts when I was so sick and he took them to fly kites."

"I know. I was only teasing."

"Well, come out to the kitchen with me and I'll get some refreshment while they are playing with Luke. What brings you over tonight? Have you heard from Rose?"

She shook her head. "She said they'd have a decision by Monday."

"I'm sure they are going to say yes. They'd be plumb crazy not to and I told them so when they came over this afternoon."

Kathleen took a seat at the kitchen table and watched her sister pour glasses of lemonade—a treat they'd rarely been able to afford.

"I made some cookies today. The boys will be happy to have another before bedtime."

"Well, before we go in, I'll let you know one of the reasons we came this evening."

"You have a reason other than you miss us?" Colleen grinned at her and Kathleen smiled back. It was so good to see her sister the way she used to be—long ago before Clancy.

"I do. We're all going to Coney Island tomorrow and wondered if you and the boys might want to join us."

"Oh, my, they would love to go. And Ida is in charge tomorrow. So, yes! We will go." The smile left her face but joy was in her eyes. "Oh, Kathleen, do you know how good that felt? To say 'yes, we will go'?"

"I have an idea." Kathleen crossed the room and hugged her sister. They rocked back and forth for a few moments and then Colleen brushed at her eyes.

"The good Lord has seen us through, hasn't He?" she asked.

"Oh, yes, He has."

Colleen let out a big sigh and smiled. "Let's get these things on a tray and go tell the boys they are going to Coney Island tomorrow. I don't think they'll believe me."

Kathleen laughed as she took in the tray of cookies while her sister took in the lemonade she'd made earlier. "If they don't now, they will tomorrow."

"You know, I don't think I will tell them tonight. They'll never get to sleep if I do. I'll wait until the morning."

"Good idea."

And it was. The boys were already wound up, playing with Luke. Kathleen smiled as she watched them arm wrestle. He won once and then let the boys each win once. He was so good with them. He should have children of his own to play with. Her heart skittered at the very thought. He'd have to be married first and— She didn't want to think about that. If he found someone and got married, she knew their friendship would never be the same. At that thought her heart twisted. No. She couldn't think about it. Wouldn't let herself.

She lifted the plate of cookies high. "Cookie, anyone?"

The boys hurried over and Luke followed. She gave the boys theirs and then handed him a cookie, leaning forward to whisper, "Colleen said they'll go but she doesn't want the boys to know. Said they'd never sleep if she did."

Luke chuckled. "She's probably right. They're pretty wound up. She might not let me come see them at night anymore."

"I shouldn't." Colleen came up behind them. "But I wouldn't deprive any of you from having such a good time."

"Thanks, Colleen." Luke took the glass she handed him. "I'll try not to get them quite so wound up next time."

They didn't stay much longer so that Colleen could get the boys settled down and into bed. Luke promised Collin and Brody he'd see them soon and that made both boys happy. Kathleen couldn't wait to see their faces the next day when they realized they'd spend the day with him.

They headed back home under a moonlit, star-filled sky. Kathleen loved the quiet of the evening.

"Those nephews of yours have changed so much

since they moved. They seem full of life and happy. Has your sister said anything about the boys missing their father?"

Kathleen shook her head. "No, not really. We don't talk about Clancy much. She'll talk when she's ready."

"And you? How are you feeling?"

"I still don't remember what happened the night I came to Heaton House. Only vague images and, well, I don't try to remember any more. And I don't want to ask Colleen—she has enough awful memories to live with. I survived that night and he's gone. And my sister and the boys are safe. I've got a lot of blessings to count."

"Perhaps I should do some of the same."

"What's that?" Kathleen turned her head to look at him.

"Try not to remember the past and count my blessings."

"You have memories you'd like to forget?"

"I do."

Of course he did. Didn't everyone? But he always seemed so strong and sure of himself, Kathleen had never asked much about him. She recalled her vow to start. "Would you like to talk about it?"

"I don't want to burden you with—"

Kathleen stopped in the middle of the walk and turned to him, hands on her hips. "Luke Patterson, I can't believe you said that. You have watched over me and protected me from the first day we met. You've even let me cry on your shoulder." She let out a sigh. "How could you possibly think that listening to you could ever be a burden to me?"

* * *

Luke raised his hands in surrender. "I'm sorry. It's not that I've tried to keep any of my life secret—not really. I just haven't wanted to talk about it. It hurt too much for a long time and then, well, you've had a lot to deal with on your own, Kate."

"I'm sorry, Luke. I shouldn't pressure you to talk. It's none of my business anyway. I just want you to know that I am here for you, too."

Luke's heart slammed against his chest and he wasn't sure how to reply. Her words made him want to pull her into his arms and hold her, pour out his heart to her. But she wasn't ready for that—nor was he. What was he thinking? She hadn't declared love for him. She'd only made the offer of a good friend and here he was letting his thoughts run away from him.

"Thank you, Kathleen." Luke took a step forward and began to speak, Kathleen keeping pace beside him. "I haven't told anyone at Heaton House—haven't really seen the need to, but your words about not trying to remember made me realize that I haven't let go of the memories I can't do anything about. Perhaps I need to sort through them and keep the good ones and say goodbye to the bad ones once and for all."

"Perhaps it would help to tell someone—it doesn't have to be me if you aren't comfortable talking to me about it. But maybe Mrs. Heaton?"

"I have no problem telling you." He took a deep breath and forged ahead. "Before I came to Heaton House, back home in Texas, I was engaged to be married. My fiancée was a bank teller." Memories came flooding back and Luke swallowed around the lump in his throat.

"There was a robbery and my Beth was shot. I arrived only moments after, and—" His voice broke and he cleared his throat. "She died in my arms. If only I could have gotten there earlier. I—"

Kathleen stopped and both hands grasped his arm. Luke could never remember her touching him at all other than when they were walking. But now she was grasping his arm and looking at him with tears in her eyes.

"Luke, I'm so sorry. I didn't mean to bring you pain. I'm sorry about your Beth, but you must know by now that what happened wasn't your fault."

Her words soothed his aching heart and he let out a cleansing breath. "I do now. But it's been a long time coming. And then there's been guilt when the memory of her face began to fade. I did love her…with all my heart. But she's no longer here and—"

"Luke, I believe that is normal. I think anyone would feel the same way. If not for the pictures I have of my parents, I wouldn't remember what they looked like, either. But you have the memories, even if her face isn't clear to you."

"Those are fading now, too, Kate."

"Maybe it's the Lord's way of easing the pain?"

Luke had never thought of it that way.

"Maybe He's paving the way for you to find someone else?"

He shook his head. The Lord above knew better than anyone that Luke didn't plan on ever falling in love again. "I don't think so. But thank you for your thoughts and for listening. It has helped to talk about it."

"I'm glad. Anytime you want to talk about it, remember I'm here."

"I'll remember." He did feel better. "Now maybe I can put the bad memories to rest and concentrate on my blessings."

"I hope so."

Her smile lightened his heart even more. He was blessed to have this woman as a friend. "So do I."

They walked back to Heaton House then and they entered the foyer. A peek into the parlor told them everyone had gone their separate ways.

"They probably want a good night's sleep before tomorrow. I am so looking forward to it!" Kathleen said. "I suppose I should see if Elizabeth is still up. She promised to help me pick out something to wear. Thank you for escorting me to Colleen's—and for sharing with me."

"Thank you for listening, Kathleen." He wanted to pull her into his arms but he settled for looking deep into her eyes, seeing the compassion there. "You are one of the blessings I'll be counting tonight."

He could hear the quick intake of her breath and his own breath caught in his throat. He watched her chew her bottom lip as if she didn't know what to say next. Had he overstepped?

"Thank you, Luke. You're high on my list, too. I suppose the Lord knew we both needed a good friend. Good night. See you in the morning." With that she turned to hurry up the stairs, leaving Luke to watch.

She disappeared around the landing and suddenly Luke realized Kathleen was much more than just a friend to him—and that his feelings for her seemed to grow with each passing day. And he didn't have the faintest idea what to do about it. So, he did the only thing he knew to do. He prayed.

There was a holiday feel to the day the next morning at breakfast when Kathleen came downstairs dressed in the lightweight beige skirt and shirtwaist that Elizabeth had loaned her.

"It will reflect the heat off you. Being outside most of the day, you'll need it," she'd said.

Kathleen was pleased to find she was dressed similarly to the other women in the house. And even Colleen had seemed to know what to wear as she showed up in a light-colored dress. The boys both had on light brown knickers and white shirts.

Instead of taking the trolley, Michael had hired an omnibus to take them out to Coney Island. As they all piled in, it was Brody and Collin who had everyone's attention. There was nothing quite like seeing things through a child's eyes.

"Where we goin', Luke?" Brody asked.

"We're going to Coney Island."

"Is there pirates there?" Collin asked.

"No. Well, maybe, but not real ones. There are lots of amusements."

"What's amusements?"

"Amusements are places that are for entertainment—to have fun at."

"Oh!" Brody said. "I like to have fun. Is it like arm wrestlin' with you?"

"Oh, I think you'll like it better," Luke said.

"Okay." Brody grinned and looked out the window. "Is it a long ways?"

"It's farther than you've been before, Brody," Colleen said. "And we're going to go over a bridge to get there."

"The Brooklyn Bridge?" Collin's eyes flashed with excitement.

"Yes, that's the one," Kathleen said as she brushed his hair out of his eyes.

"Oh, boy! I can't wait to go over it." He turned around and got on his knees to join Brody in looking at the passing scenery.

"I can't wait to see the look on their faces when they actually see the Elephant Colossus!" Luke grinned. "They are going to love everything."

"I think I am, too. What's the Elephant Colossus?"

"You'll see."

The boys' excitement was contagious and Kathleen couldn't wait to see the sights any more than they could. Going over the Brooklyn Bridge was quite breathtaking as they left Manhattan behind and headed toward Brooklyn and then Coney Island. It was quite the ride and Kathleen understood why they wanted to get off early.

It was midmorning before they arrived at Coney Island and Luke didn't have to point out the Elephant Colossus. The boys were overwhelmed at the sight.

"Look, Aunt Kate! Look at the Elephant!" Brody yelled.

"How big is it?" Collin asked.

"It's 150 feet tall and has all kinds of amusements inside. There are even telescopes inside where you can look out his eyes."

"I don't know if I want to get that close to him," Brody said.

"He won't hurt you, Brody. It's not a real elephant after all," Collin assured him.

Everyone piled out of the omnibus and Kathleen found herself looking to Luke for direction. "Where do we go first?"

"Doesn't matter. We can just take off in any direction, stop when something interests you or the boys. We've got all day and can backtrack if we need to. Just stick with me and we'll see it all—well, most of it. What we miss now, we'll see another time. I'm sure the boys would love to go swimming when it warms up."

"Yes, they would love it," Colleen said.

"I thought you might ask Officer O'Malley to come with us," Kathleen said to her sister as they walked along.

"Actually, I did telephone him after you left last night. He's on duty today and couldn't come. He was excited for the boys, though. He's pretty taken with them."

"Who isn't?" Luke nodded his head toward Michael, Violet and Mrs. Heaton, who were carrying on a conversation with the boys in front of them. "They're pretty hard to resist."

Kathleen's heart warmed as it always did when Luke talked about Brody and Collin. He was very taken with them himself.

"They don't get sick easily, do they?" Luke asked Colleen.

"Not that I know of, but they've never been on rides like this."

"Well, we'll try some of the tamer ones and see how they do. If they make it through those, maybe we'll go on the Switchback Railway and then the Serpentine

Railway roller coasters. I haven't been on any of these in a while."

After the first few tamer rides, Colleen said they'd be fine and for the next few hours they rode roller coasters, carousels and anything else that struck the boys' fancy. By noontime everyone was starved and they all picnicked on hot dogs and lemonade.

Afterward everyone separated into groups to go their own way with an agreement to meet back up by four o'clock. The Heatons wanted to see the Sea Lion Park that had opened the year before.

Some of the others hadn't had their fill of rides and took off in search of more.

"I think we'll just walk around for a bit," Colleen said once they'd finished eating. "I'm not sure it'd be a good idea to go on a ride so soon after eating. But you two go on. We'll catch up with you later or see you at four."

Luke looked at Kathleen and grinned. "Want to ride something else, or do you want to stroll for a bit, too?"

"I think I'll opt for strolling. That last ride had my stomach taking a dive." She pointed across the way. "What's that long building out there?"

"That's the Brighton Beach Hotel. There's a boardwalk right on the water and benches to sit on. Would you like to see it?"

"I'd love to." She turned to her sister. "Colleen? Do you and the boys want to go?"

"We'll walk with you as far as the first bench, then I think the boys and I will just enjoy watching the people and the water while you two take your stroll."

They made their way to the boardwalk and true to her word, Colleen settled herself and her boys on the first empty bench they came to. "Now you two go along and enjoy your walk."

"Are you sure?"

"I'm sure, Kathleen." Brody leaned against his mother and yawned. "I think the boys might enjoy a bit of a nap with the sound of the water and the light breeze. I might nod off myself."

"All right, then. We'll be back this way soon."

Luke offered his arm and Kathleen slipped her hand through, resting it on his sleeve as they sauntered down the walk.

It'd been late into the night before she'd fallen asleep the night before—she couldn't get her mind off what Luke had told her about his fiancée. How heartbreaking that must have been for him. That he shared it with her, when he hadn't told anyone else, meant a great deal to Kathleen. In the past it was only her worries and problems they'd shared. Now that she'd seen a glimpse of his, she felt they were on more even footing than ever before.

"Kathleen," Luke said, breaking into her thoughts as he led her over to the railing overlooking the water, "I wanted to thank you again for listening to me last night. I didn't realize how much better I would feel just telling someone about Beth."

"You don't need to thank me, Luke. You've been there for me on numerous occasions. And I was glad to listen. I'm so very sorry you had to go through that kind of heartbreak."

He broke his gaze from hers and looked out to sea. "It's gotten easier over the years, but I still needed to talk about it. I slept better than I have in years last night."

"I'm glad. You know you can talk to me anytime."

She didn't tell him that she'd had a hard time going to sleep. Or that along with hurting for him, she had another ache inside of her—one she couldn't name, but it felt a little like jealousy.

She had no right to be jealous, especially of someone who'd passed away. So why should she feel so disturbed that Luke had been in love before? Could it be that her growing feelings for him were more than friendship? Was it possible Luke was the one man she could ever trust with her heart? And what was she going to do about it?

Chapter Sixteen

Luke had enjoyed the weekend immensely—spending time with Kathleen and her family, having time with her alone and sitting by her in church on Sunday. They'd shared a hymnal and he'd loved the sound of her alto mixed with his baritone.

He could spend hours singing with her. After church, she spent most of the day with her sister and as daylight waned, he debated going to escort her home. However, she arrived just before dark and in time for dinner. But she seemed quieter than she had the past few days and he wondered if something had happened to upset her.

As soon as dinner was over and she made to leave, he quickly pulled back her chair and spoke quietly, "Are you all right? Would you like to talk?"

She bit her bottom lip and nodded to him.

"Let's go to Mrs. Heaton's garden. No one else will be out there now."

"All right."

They waited until everyone had either entered the parlor or gone to their rooms and then headed out to the small garden Mrs. Heaton tended to so lovingly.

There were a couple of small benches set in the garden and Luke led her to one that couldn't be seen from the house. He waited for her to sit down and then sat down beside her, taking care to put some distance between them.

"What's happened to upset you, Kathleen?"

"Nothing, really. It's just that Colleen told me she'd asked Officer O'Malley to dinner and, well, I'm afraid he's sweet on her and I'm not sure how she feels about him."

"Did you ask?"

"Yes. And she got upset. Said she was a grown woman and I didn't have to be looking out for her anymore. That it was time I—"

"Time you what?"

Kathleen let out a deep breath and shook her head. "I just don't understand how she can trust another man after all Clancy put her through. And it seems much too soon for her to…"

"Do you think she's fallen in love with Officer O'Malley?"

"I don't know. She says she cares a lot for him and that she trusts him and…" Kathleen closed her eyes. "He seems a very good man, I'll give him that. But she has only known him a short while and I don't want her doing something rash like marrying him just because she's lonely or wants someone to take care of her. She should only marry for love."

"I agree."

Kathleen let out a shaky breath. "But then she did that the first time and look where it got her."

She seemed so confused and upset, Luke wanted to ease her mind. "Kathleen, maybe Colleen's love for

Clancy died a long time ago—after he changed and put her through so much. Maybe she knows what it is she's looking for this time—before she gives her heart away. And maybe, because of that love dying, she's ready to love again."

"I hadn't thought of it that way. I guess I was just thinking about how hard it is for me to trust after the way I saw her treated."

It was plain to Luke that Kathleen was finding it more difficult to trust men than her sister was. His heart constricted at the very thought that she might never get past it.

"I'm sorry, Luke. I want her to be happy, to find true love if that's what she wants. I just don't want her to rush into another marriage."

"I understand. The best thing you can do is pray for the Lord to guide her. For Him to keep her from doing anything rash but also for her to know if the time and the person are right."

"That's true. And I will."

"Did she say anything about marriage? Or if Officer O'Malley has asked her to marry him?"

"No. Not really. I suppose I could be jumping to conclusions."

"You might be. And Kathleen, remember that Officer O'Malley was there that night. He was at the hospital and knows what shape she was in. He's the one who might have shot Clancy. I don't think he's going to rush her into anything."

"I hope not. And I hope he's not…just trying to get past the guilt he might feel over Clancy's death."

"You and your sister are beautiful women, Kathleen. It's highly unlikely that Officer O'Malley is keeping

Colleen company because of guilt. Besides, whichever officer shot Clancy, he saved Colleen's life. There's no need for him to feel guilty over it."

Luke had leaned closer as he talked and he could almost feel Kathleen's shoulders relax as she sighed. "That's true. Thank you for reminding me, Luke."

"You're welcome. It was my turn after the other night."

"Oh, Luke, after all the encouragement you've given me, all the times you've been there for me, you have a lot of catching up to do."

He chuckled. "As long as I don't have to do it all at once."

"No, you don't. Thanks for listening again and for your thoughts. You gave me a lot to think about and I think I owe it to my sister to let her make the decisions that are important to her. I have been overprotective of her and sometimes I forget that Clancy is no longer here to hurt her."

"Or you." Luke regretted his words the moment they left his lips.

Just as he opened his mouth to say he was sorry, he heard Kathleen whisper, "Or me."

Her fingers covered her mouth and she looked up at him. He could see her eyes shimmer with unshed tears in the moonlight. But she swallowed hard and blinked them back. Luke wished he could cry for her.

He reached out his hand to touch her cheek and she stilled but didn't flinch. He could see the wariness in her eyes, and something else that pulled him nearer. His fingers grazed her cheek. "You are the strongest woman I've ever met, Kate. Clancy is gone. He'll never hurt you again."

"Never again." She closed her eyes and nodded. She reached up and covered his hand with hers. "Thank you, Luke."

"You're welcome." He turned his hand over and captured hers. His glance lowered to her lips and back to her eyes. He'd never wanted to kiss anyone more, and it was all he could do to keep from pulling her into his arms. But the wariness lingered in her eyes and he leaned his forehead against hers. If-onlys whirled through his mind. If only she could trust again. If only he could, too.

He glanced at her lips once more and cleared his throat. "We'd better go in before—"

"Someone wonders where we are?"

No. Before he threw caution to the wind, pulled her into his arms and kissed her.

Kathleen punched her pillow one more time. She'd tossed and turned for hours, it seemed, thinking about Luke and their time in the garden.

She didn't know what to do. The more time she spent with Luke the more time she wanted to be with him. He'd become her confidant and if she wasn't mistaken, she'd become his. One minute she thought she should distance herself from Luke in order to keep her feelings for him from deepening. The next she told herself that she couldn't desert him just as he'd begun to confide in her.

If she made him feel she didn't want to listen to him, what might that do to him? After all Luke had done for her, all the times he'd been there for her, there was no way she could not be there for him.

Still, she had to find a way to guard her heart, to

keep from letting her growing feelings show. If there were one man in the world she could trust, it would be Luke. But he'd lost the love of his life and she didn't want to come in second to the memories of another woman. If she ever gave her heart to a man, she wanted to be first in his life, after the Lord. Always.

Besides, he'd given no indication that they were any more than friends. Except, there was a look in his eyes tonight that made her wonder what it would be like to be kissed by him.

"Arrgh!" She turned her pillow over and punched it once again. She needed to get to sleep. Tomorrow promised to be a busy day and she wanted to be fresh. She had to quit thinking of Luke. Still, she wondered, had he wanted to kiss her as much as she'd wanted him to? For one short moment she'd thought he would. And then he'd said they should go in.

It was for the best. She knew it was. She closed her eyes and prayed. *Dear Lord, please help me to quit thinking of Luke in a romantic way, please help me to quit longing for the impossible. Or please show me if it is possible for me to trust my heart to—*

The only man she could imagine trusting her heart to was Luke. And she didn't even know if he wanted it. Tears sprung to her eyes.

I don't know what to do, Lord. Please help me to know Your will for my life and guide me to do it. In Jesus's name, Amen.

Only then was she able to drift off to sleep.

"No!" Luke yanked himself out of the nightmare, breathing deep and hard. His brow damp with sweat, he flung off his covers and sat up on the side of the bed, trying to get his bearings. He was awake; it wasn't real. None of it was real. He took one deep, cleansing breath after another until he quit shaking.

He got up, crossed over to the small window that looked out at street level and rubbed the back of his neck. Dawn was breaking and he was more than ready for the night to end and day to begin. He'd tossed and turned all night, moving from one nightmare to another.

First he'd relived Beth's death as he still did from time to time. But somehow as he'd held her lifeless body and bent down to kiss her brow, the woman he'd been holding in his arms had turned into Kathleen.

He'd barely roused himself out of that nightmare when he'd begun to dream of the day in the park when he'd first seen Kathleen being badgered by her brother-in-law and come to her aid.

The ache in his heart as she left the park, wondering if she would be all right, was as real as it had been that day. Just as it was when the dream moved to him carrying her up the stairs when she'd arrived at Heaton House. He kept waking himself, thinking it wasn't real. Kathleen was here now and she was safe. Only then did he fall into a deeper sleep.

But the dreams of the past turned into his fear of the present. He watched Kathleen go in one tenement building after another, only he wasn't with her. No one was with her.

Luke went to the bathroom and splashed cold water in his face, fighting the memory of what happened next. But his breathing became shallow as the last nightmare came back to him full force.

He was in the tenements looking for Kathleen when

he heard a moan in an alleyway. He rushed in and his heart stopped as he saw a woman, with hair the color of Kathleen's, lying there, motionless.

He'd gathered her up in his arms. Somehow, the nightmare switched to the day Beth died, and then back to him holding Kathleen in the alleyway, trying to assess her injuries. But he felt something wet and warm at her side. She'd been shot and he'd prayed, *Dear Lord, please don't let me lose Kathleen, too.* Her head lolled to the side and that was when he'd yanked himself out of the nightmare and jumped out of bed.

He'd failed Beth. He couldn't fail Kathleen.

When Kathleen joined the others at the breakfast table she noticed Luke looked as if he hadn't slept any better than she had. Much as she'd like to think it was because he was thinking about her as much as she'd thought about him, she figured he'd probably stayed up too late writing. She'd been taking up way too much of his time. And she had to put a stop to it. It wasn't fair to him.

"You ready?" he asked as they finished breakfast and she laid her napkin on the table.

"I am, but really, Luke, I don't need you to go with me today. I'm just going to the Walshes' and to see Reba. I know the way and I will be fine."

He slid her chair out from the table. "I'm going to see you there safely, Kathleen."

"Luke, I can't keep taking up your time. You have your own work to do and I'm feeling bad that you're staying up late to catch up."

"I told you, that's when I write best. Come on, at least let me see you there safely and—" He sighed deeply. "I really wish they'd find a safer way for you to do your job."

"I'm safe, Luke. I went in and out of those tenements for years. I know my way around and I'll be fine."

Mrs. Heaton walked into the dining room. "Excuse me, but you have a phone call, Luke. I think it's your publisher."

Luke turned to Kathleen. "Wait for me. I'm sure this won't take long."

When he had left the room, Mrs. Heaton sat down next to her. "I couldn't help but overhear part of your conversation with Luke, Kathleen. You know he has a point and I'm going to take it up with the ladies. Perhaps we need to hire someone to go along with you, or find a way to get the word out and have the interested parties come to you."

"But you wanted someone who knows their way around the tenements and who can relate to those living there."

"Yes, and you fill that qualification perfectly. But we don't want you in any kind of danger. Let me see what we can come up with. And in the meantime, please let Luke go with you when he can. If anything happened to you, I'd blame myself."

"Oh, Mrs. Heaton, you mustn't take that burden on yourself."

"Please let Luke accompany you until we can come up with a plan, Kathleen."

After all the woman had done for her and all she'd been through, Kathleen couldn't bring herself to refuse. "Yes, ma'am, I will."

"Will what?" Luke asked, coming back into the room.

"Let you accompany me to the tenements."

Mrs. Heaton turned to him. "I'm going to talk to the board. We're going to come up with a way to make sure Kathleen is safe going in and out of the tenements."

"I'll see that she is."

"Yes, but you have your own work to do at times and you won't always be able to accompany her. But I appreciate you taking care of it now, Luke."

"It's not a problem at all." Luke turned to Kathleen. "I'm ready whenever you are."

There was nothing to do but go with him and try not to let Mrs. Heaton see how frustrated she was at Luke for starting all this. It hurt that they didn't feel she could do the job by herself. "Let's go. See you this afternoon, Mrs. Heaton."

"You two have a good day," the older woman said as they headed toward the front door.

Once they were on the trolley, Luke turned to her. "What was that all about?"

"Mrs. Heaton overheard you talking about my safety and decided you were right. But, Luke, it's the job they hired me to do. I can't always have someone with me."

"Maybe it is a job for two people."

Kathleen sighed. "I don't want them thinking I can't handle it."

"They aren't going to think that for a moment. But they aren't going to want you in danger any more than I do."

Her pulse skittered at his words. How was she going to distance herself from him when he turned her heart to mush?

Chapter Seventeen

Luke went with Kathleen to the Walshes' and was welcomed into their apartment right along with her. Mrs. Walsh had the kettle on, along with a pot of coffee.

"Which do you prefer, Mr. Patterson?"

"Coffee, please."

She set a cup in front of him and brought a teapot and two cups to the table for her and Kathleen.

"Well, what is your decision?" Kathleen asked once the woman joined them at the table.

She let out a huge sigh and grinned. "We would very much like to run the home if the Ladies' Aide Society wants us to."

"Oh, Rose, I'm so glad. With Colleen running the first one, I don't know anyone I'd trust more to run another than you and your husband."

"And Harold is as happy about it as I am. To think we'll be able to get out of here for good. I can't thank you enough for thinking of us, Kathleen."

"Well, I have to give Luke credit for suggesting that Harold might be able to have work, too."

"Thank you, Mr. Patterson."

The sheen of tears in her eyes was hard to ignore. "You're welcome, Mrs. Walsh."

"I'll let you know when your interview will be with the board," Kathleen told the woman, "but I know they are going to be very pleased to have you and Harold in charge of the next home."

"I certainly hope they are. I'll be waiting anxiously to hear from you."

The two women hugged and then he and Kathleen were on their way to see Reba and find out if she'd landed a job yet.

Kathleen seemed to be in better spirits after the news Rose gave her and he was glad. He knew she was upset with him over bringing up her safety in Mrs. Heaton's hearing.

Luke hadn't meant to make her feel incompetent in any way. He just didn't want anything happening to her. Maybe he'd talk to Michael and get some ideas from him on how to protect her without her knowing it. There had to be a way for her to do her job, be protected and not feel smothered.

When they arrived at Reba's building she turned to him. "I think I need to go by myself to visit Reba, Luke. I'm barely getting to know her and I want her to trust me. I'm afraid she might feel uncomfortable with you along."

"I understand. Do you want me to wait outside or visit with Mrs. Connor?"

"It's your choice."

Her tone was a little cool and Luke really didn't know what to do about it other than to let her do her job. "Well, Mrs. Connor isn't expecting us, so I'll wait for you out here on the stoop. I brought my notepad, and I'll stay busy. Take all the time you need."

"I will, thank you." She started up the steps and then turned back. "I'm sorry I've been grouchy today. I do appreciate that you want to protect me, and—"

"It's all right, Kate. The last thing I want is for you to feel suffocated while you work. And you won't always be coming here so often. For now—"

"For now, we'll do it your and Mrs. Heaton's way. But only for a while."

Kathleen hurried up the stairs. She didn't know whether to be relieved or disappointed Luke wasn't with her. Much as she protested and felt bad that he was giving up writing time to go with her, she did appreciate it and she liked his company.

But that was the problem. She liked his company too much for her own good and she was dangerously close to falling in love with him.

Reba opened the door slightly and after recognizing Kathleen, she smiled and let her in. "Good morning. I was hoping you would come today. Would you like some tea?"

Though Kathleen had already drunk two cups at breakfast, she didn't want to offend Reba. "Yes, please."

Reba's daughter was at the kitchen table and gave Kathleen a shy smile when she sat down opposite her.

"Good morning, Jenny. You look very pretty today."

The child didn't speak but her smile grew.

"Tell Miss O'Bryan thank-you, Jenny."

The little girl ducked her head. "Thank you."

"You're welcome."

Reba brought the tea to the table along with some

gingersnaps that reminded Kathleen of the ones Mrs. Heaton made. "Well, have you any news for me? Did you hear back from any of the places you applied for?"

"I did. In fact I'm to go back for an interview at Macy's this afternoon. Mrs. Connor is going to watch Jenny for me and I'll let you know as soon as I know. I do hope I get to work there. But if so, I'll need someone to keep Jenny on a regular basis soon. Mrs. Connor has said she'd help, but I don't want to impose on her for long."

"I think I can get Jenny in the child care home my sister is running. I'll check and see. Otherwise, my old neighbor is going to be running the next home but I'm not sure how long it will take to get it going. I'll check on it as well."

"This is such an answer to prayer, Kathleen. I can't tell you how blessed I feel that you came by to see me."

"Well, Mrs. Connor gets the credit for that. But she didn't tell me a lot about you other than you are raising your daughter alone. My sister is raising her sons alone since her husband…" Kathleen didn't want to go into all the details just yet. "Since he died. Are you a widow, too?"

She felt horrible at the look on Reba's face. "I'm sorry. That is certainly none of my business."

Reba took a sip of her tea and looked at her daughter. "All done with breakfast?"

Jenny nodded. "Can I go play now?"

"Yes, you may play in our bedroom."

The little girl scooted out of her chair and ran to the bedroom. The door was open and they could see her pull out a small cloth doll.

"Mrs. Connor made that for her. She doesn't have a lot of toys like I—"

Kathleen felt sure that Reba hadn't always lived this way. She seemed to be educated and there was a manner about her that bespoke of better times in the past. Of course, a lot of the immigrants in the tenements had had better lives before coming to America—at least at one time. However, Kathleen didn't think Reba was an immigrant. But she'd already pried when she shouldn't have. She wasn't going to ask.

"Do you mind if I iron while we talk?" She put her iron on the stove to heat up and pulled out her ironing board.

"No, of course not." There was no way Kathleen would object—this was how the woman made her living after all. But the fact that she hadn't just asked her to leave made Kathleen think she might want to talk.

Reba took a shirtwaist, sprinkled water on it and began to iron. "I—I actually ran away from home with the man I loved—or thought I loved. He promised a great life if we came to the city and it all sounded so wonderful. My mama didn't approve of him and, well, we ran off."

She looked over to where Jenny was playing in her room and smiled, then she looked at Kathleen. "Jenny is the blessing that came out of it all, but I never thought I'd be raising her alone."

"She's very pretty and quite sweet." She'd never answered whether or not she was a widow, but it didn't matter. What did matter was that Reba appeared to have been duped by the man she loved—the man she thought she could trust. More than ever Kathleen wanted to help her be able to raise her child and get out of the tenements one day.

"Thank you. I just want a better life for her. I'm not an immigrant—I'm actually from Virginia."

"Did you ever think about going back? Do you have family there?" There she went again, asking questions she had no right to ask. "I'm sorry, Reba. I'm being quite nosy today."

"It's all right. I expected some questions. I won't go back to Virginia."

Kathleen nodded. There were things she'd decided she wouldn't do, too.

They talked a bit more and she saw Reba's hope and optimism for the future.

"I was beginning to think it'd never be possible to leave here," she said, "but thanks to Mrs. Connor and you, I believe it is."

"So do I." Kathleen took the last sip of tea. She knew a little more about Reba than before and she liked the young woman. Still, she couldn't shake the niggling feeling that she'd seen her somewhere before. But if she was from Virginia, then it must have been just passing in the street or the grocer, as Luke and Mrs. Connor had suggested.

She got up to leave. "No need to see me out. You keep working. I'll be back in the office this afternoon, so just let me know how your interview turns out. I'll be praying all goes well and you have a job when I hear from you."

"Thank you, Kathleen. I need all the prayers I can get."

Kathleen let herself out, and headed back downstairs, praying all the way that Reba got the job today, and that Colleen would make room for Jenny.

Kathleen opened the door to the outside to see that Luke was observing the people around him and making notes. She supposed that all writers enjoyed watching people. He'd explained to her that he might hear a snippet of conversation that might make it into one of his stories, or see a particularly interesting person whose looks might fit a character he was writing about.

Now her heart did a little twist and dive as he looked up at her and smiled. "Well, how'd it go?"

"Good. She's going for an interview this afternoon, so say a prayer she gets the job. She really wants it."

"I'll certainly do that. Where to next?"

"I've got to stop by Colleen's and see if she has room for one more child before I go to the office. I want to be there in case Reba calls me later."

Luke pulled his watch out of his pocket. "Want to grab something for lunch from one of the street vendors?"

"Why don't we see if Colleen has something? No need spending money when we can get something better for free."

"Now, that's a better idea. Let's go." He stuffed his notepad and pencil stub in the inside pocket of his jacket and held out his arm.

Kathleen took it and they were on their way. They caught a trolley on Second Avenue and got off on Twenty-fourth. From there it was a short walk to Colleen's.

"Why and what brings you two here just in time to eat today?" Colleen asked, motioning them into the dining room where the children were seated around the table. "The children are almost finished, but we've plenty of stew for the two of you. Come into the kitchen."

"I was hoping you'd say that. Can you keep us company for a few minutes? I've something to ask of you," Kathleen said.

Colleen ladled up the stew and set it down before them. "Take a seat and I'll let Ida know."

Luke said a blessing and they'd just begun to eat when Colleen came back into the room. She ladled a bowl for herself and sat down with them.

"Now, what is it you want to ask?"

"Well, first I've got a bit of good news for you. The Walshes are going to run the next home."

"Oh, but that is good news, isn't it?"

"It is, for sure. And the other news is that Reba Dickerson, the young woman I told you about, is close to getting a job at Macy's. But she'll need care for her little girl quickly if she gets it."

"Ah, and I know what the questions is, then. Of course we'll make room for one more child."

"It might only be until the other home is up and running, but I'd like to be able to tell her that Jenny can be taken care of as soon as she gets the job."

"Tell her, then. Actually, Ida and I have been thinking we could take a few more on."

"Thank you, Colleen. I knew you'd agree. And if you can take on several more children, I know that will be good news for Mrs. Heaton and the others."

"Now that you've got someone to run the next home I'm sure it won't take long to fill it up—at least according to what the parents of our children tell me."

"An idea just came to me," Luke said. "Colleen could ask for referrals from the women who are bringing their children here. Perhaps that would make it easier on you, Kathleen."

"That is a good idea, Luke," Colleen said.

Kathleen smiled and gave Luke a little shake of her head. She had a feeling his motive came from trying to keep her out of the tenements as much as possible but how could she be upset at him for caring enough to try to keep her safe? "It is a very good idea. You seem to be full of them lately."

"Let me know when you're ready for me to start gettin' a list of names together."

"I will. I'll try to find out how long it will take to get the other home up and running first. I don't want to get anyone's hopes up too fast."

"I understand that, I do. I am so glad Rose and Harold want to do this. It is such an opportunity for them. For so many people. When I think of all the people the Ladies' Aide Society will end up helping because of the child care homes, it makes me want to cry. Every day I see the mothers of these children relieved that they can help their families and it's only because they have someone to look after their children. I am so happy to be part of it."

"I know that feeling," Kathleen said. She'd never thought to see her sister as happy as she was now. She took her and Luke's bowls to the sink and washed them out, laying them on the drain board. "Thank you for lunch. I need to get back to the office now, but I'll telephone you and let you know what I find out from Reba."

"Good. In the meantime, I'll let Ida know we'll be getting at least one more child soon."

Kathleen and Luke said goodbye to Ida and the children as they went back through the dining room on their way out. With the exception of her grouchiness to Luke that morning, it'd been a good day. Now if only Reba got her job, it'd be a great start to the week.

Chapter Eighteen

Kathleen was the last one in the office when Reba telephoned to let her know she got the position at Macy's and that she was to start the next Monday. Kathleen promised to return the next day to have her fill out the paperwork needed for Jenny to be accepted for the day care and to take her to meet Colleen and Ida and see the home herself.

She had convinced Luke that she could get to her office without him accompanying her there and back, only now she missed him as she took the trolley back to the stop nearest Heaton House. She couldn't wait to share the news of the day with everyone.

But Mrs. Heaton wasn't in her study and Luke was nowhere to be seen. Maybe he was working. Kathleen hoped so. She headed upstairs to get ready for dinner. Her news would just have to wait until then.

She freshened up and redid her hair, pulling it up in the newest style she and Elizabeth had been trying out. As it was a Monday, she kept on the brown skirt and beige shirtwaist she'd started the day out in.

She was the first to get to the parlor, which was unusual, but she used the time to look at some of the pictures around the room. She'd been told that Mrs. Heaton changed them every so often, adding newer ones and putting older pictures in a box. She walked around the room, picking up first one and then another. There was one of Michael and Violet at their wedding and another of the group of boarders on an outing at Central Park, before she became part of the group. She grinned as she spotted one Elizabeth had taken the day they went to Coney Island. It was nice to feel she truly was one of the family of boarders now.

She moved to another table and caught her breath. Her heart began to pound as she picked up the frame and looked closer at the photo.

The woman in the photograph looked very much like Reba. Only younger by several years at least, and her hair was done much differently. She was dressed much nicer but she so resembled Reba that Kathleen had to wonder if they could be the same woman. But that was impossible. Or was it? Perhaps she'd been a boarder at one time? No, if she was important enough for Mrs. Heaton to have a photo of her in the parlor, Kathleen was sure she'd never have ended up in the tenements. Still, she looked so much like Reba—

"Kathleen, you're down early," Luke said as he crossed the room and came to stand beside her. "How did things go? Did you hear from Reba?"

"I did. She got the job!"

"That's wonderful news."

"It is. But, Luke, who is this young woman? Do you know?"

"I do. It's Mrs. Heaton's daughter, the one who is missing. Do you know about her?"

"Yes. Elizabeth mentioned her to me."

"Well, for a long time, she couldn't bring herself to put Rebecca's photo up, but then there was a letter or something that gave her and Michael hope that she is still alive and I believe she finally felt able to have her photo up where she could see it."

Tears burned the back of Kathleen's eyelids. Could Reba be Mrs. Heaton's daughter?

"Luke, I—"

"Good evening, you two," Elizabeth said as she entered the parlor.

"Good evening, Elizabeth."

The room quickly began to fill up as Julia and Millicent, John, Ben and Matt entered.

"You were going to tell me something?" Luke asked as the others greeted each other.

"Yes but not now. Maybe after dinner if you have time?"

"Yes, of course. Is it something— Would you like to go to the park?"

The man read her entirely too well. She didn't want to talk about her suspicions where she could be overheard. "That would work well, thank you."

"Thank you."

"Whatever for?"

He smiled and leaned closer, sending her heart galloping. "For—"

"Dinner is served," Mrs. Heaton said from the doorway.

"Later." Luke held out his arm and Kathleen took it with no hesitation at all, knowing she trusted him more with each passing day. Trusted him to keep her safe, to be ready to listen to anything she had to say, to be there for her. Her heart longed for her to trust him with it as well, but could she? After hearing how Jenny's father had treated Reba she wasn't sure she ever would.

. Luke thought Kathleen had never looked lovelier as she told Mrs. Heaton and the boarders about her day. She was so animated there was no doubt that she was as happy to be helping others get out of the tenements as she'd been herself.

He wanted to know what it was she'd been about to tell him when the others came into the parlor, but as Mrs. Heaton asked them both to her study after dinner, he knew it was going to have to wait.

They settled in the chairs across from her desk and she clasped her hands together and grinned. "I am so happy about your news, Kathleen. We've got things going on the purchase of the next house and it won't be long before you'll be needing to fill it up."

And that meant more visits to the tenements for Kathleen. Only she would be protected whether she liked it or not.

"I can't tell you how happy I am."

Kathleen's smile warmed his heart.

"You don't have to, dear. It shows," Mrs. Heaton said. "I know we have the right person as our liaison in you. But we are going to come up with some ways to assure your safety as you go in and out of the tenements."

"What are you thinking?" Kathleen asked.

Luke knew, for he'd talked to Michael Heaton about it after leaving Kathleen that afternoon. But he thought Kathleen would take it better if it came from Mrs. Heaton instead of him.

"I'm getting Michael's advice on it and of course we

want to hear what you think, Luke. But the Society is thinking of hiring someone to accompany—"

"Oh, Mrs. Heaton, please don't—"

Mrs. Heaton held up her hand and waved it once in a way that everyone came to know meant "say no more."

"Kathleen, dear, I know you are a strong woman and not afraid to come and go in the tenements. But we are afraid for you to. I'm not sure you've been told about my daughter?"

"Yes, ma'am. Elizabeth told me when I first came here. I'm so sorry. I…"

Mrs. Heaton nodded. "Well, we have recently learned that she is still alive, but we have no idea where she is. I can only pray that she is safe."

Luke saw Kathleen swallow hard. It was heartbreaking to think of all Mrs. Heaton had been through.

"I must ask that you allow us to make sure you are safe in your work for the Ladies' Aide Society. The fact that you lived in the tenements once might keep you safe—or the fact that you've made it out might cause someone to—" She took a deep breath and shook her head as if she couldn't bear to continue.

"You must let us do what we feel is in your and our best interests. It wouldn't do us any good to have something happen to our liaison, now, would it?"

"No, ma'am, I suppose not."

Luke breathed a silent sigh of relief at Kathleen's response. She might not like having an escort while she worked, but she would no longer fight it.

"Thank you. Now, you did say that Colleen has room for more children and that she had an idea on how to go about finding others who need our services?"

"Actually, it was Luke's idea. I'll let him explain it to you."

Luke did, and when he was finished, Mrs. Heaton smiled. "I love it! Who better to get names from than neighbors and friends of those in need? Eventually, it will cut down on having to knock on so many doors and actually make it safer for you, too, Kathleen." She nodded. "We'll meet again soon and see what Michael and Luke come up with."

"Yes, ma'am."

"And in the meantime, you'll be seeing this young mother, Reba, and getting her daughter enrolled?"

"First thing tomorrow."

"Good. I'm glad we can help her. Thank you for the report. I've got to telephone the others now. I know they'll be as happy as I am with your news."

"I hope so."

Kathleen stood and Luke did the same. He wondered if she still wanted to go to the park or if she was too upset about having to be escorted from now on. He didn't have to wait long as she turned to him almost as soon as they walked out the door.

"May we go to the park now, or is it too late? We can go to Mrs. Heaton's garden if need be, but I must talk to you."

The urgency in her voice had him going to the table where the park keys were kept and he grabbed one and held it up. "Let's go."

They managed to get out the door without anyone noticing and once they were out of sight of the house he turned to her. "What is it? What's so important?"

"I think I may know where Mrs. Heaton's daughter is."

* * *

Luke seemed to be at a loss for words as he hurried Kathleen to the park, unlocked the gate and led her to a bench.

"What are you talking about? How could you know where Rebecca Heaton is? No one has heard anything from her except for a letter she'd sent to Violet's mother months ago letting them know that she was alive at that time."

"I think Reba Dickerson may be Rebecca Heaton."

"What?" Luke jumped up from the seat. "Why would you think that?"

"She looks almost exactly like the photo in Mrs. Heaton's parlor, only a little older and more mature. It's uncanny, Luke."

"This is what you were about to tell me before dinner?"

"Yes. I wanted to tell Mrs. Heaton, but I can't get her hopes up if Reba is not Rebecca."

"No, you can't do that. She's been through way too much already. But surely, Kathleen, if it were Mrs. Heaton's daughter, why would she be living in the tenements?"

"I don't know. I think it's possible she might feel she's shamed her family, but I'm not sure. When I go back tomorrow I need you to come with me at least long enough to get a good look at her."

Luke nodded and sat back down beside her. "All right, I will. It would be wonderful if she is Mrs. Heaton's daughter and they could be reunited."

"I know. But I'm not sure it will be easy. If it is her, there's got to be a reason she didn't feel she could go home and it might bring more heartbreak for everyone."

"It could, yes. We must pray it doesn't."

"But first, I need to know if you think it could be her. And then, could you help me to find out for sure?"

"I'll do all I can, surely you know that by now, Kate."

And she did. Luke was indeed the trustworthy person she knew and— She stopped, amazed at her own thoughts. Yes, in spite of Reba's story, and Colleen's, she knew Luke could be trusted. She felt it in her heart.

"Kate? Are you all right? You look a little bemused."

Bemused, bewildered, that she was. "I'm all right. I just…" Her heart began to pound as she looked at him, and she jumped up from the seat. "I suppose we should be getting back to the house. We left late and—" She turned and looked at Luke.

He had a slight smile on his face as if he were trying to figure her out. They needed to go—now—before he read her thoughts as he'd become quite good at. "Are you coming?"

"Yes, I'm coming." He lightly grasped her elbow and turned her toward him. "Kathleen, we'll find out if Reba is Mrs. Heaton's daughter. And as soon as possible. Trust me."

"I do." There, she'd said it out loud and to him.

He smiled and his eyes crinkled. "Thank you."

"You're welcome."

Luke leaned a little nearer and for a moment she thought he might kiss her. Was sure he would. Wanted him to. She stood still and held her breath. And then he closed his eyes and gave a little tug to her elbow, propelling her out of the park and up the street.

They walked back to Heaton House in quiet. Kathleen wasn't sure what to think. She was almost certain he'd been about to kiss her, but he hadn't. Why? She knew she was falling in love with Luke. And that she trusted him…to keep her safe, to help her find out who Reba really was. But could she truly trust her heart to him? And did he even want her to?

She trusted him. She'd said so. Luke's heart slammed against his ribs. But did she really? Just because she trusted him to help her find out who Reba really was didn't mean she trusted him in everything.

And yet, something was different. He hadn't seen the wariness in her eyes when he'd leaned nearer. But he'd heard her quick intake of breath. What had it meant— that she was afraid he would kiss her or wishing that he might?

Oh, how he'd wanted to pull her into his arms and kiss her. And yet, once he did, he'd be committing to… loving her. And he did. There. He admitted it to himself. Kathleen had come into his life that day in Central Park and he hadn't quit thinking about her since. She had his insides twisted up in all kinds of ways.

She'd replaced Beth—first in his thoughts, then his dreams, and finally in his heart. He loved her. Plain and simple. But to admit it to her, to woo her, to commit to her? To put himself in the position of possibly losing the person he loved most in life as he had Beth?

Luke wasn't sure he could do it. And even if he declared his love for Kathleen, could she trust her heart to him completely?

Maybe all they both needed was time. And helping her find out about Reba would give them some. Instead of just escorting her in and out of the tenements, they'd need to spend some time together, alone, to talk it over. Maybe then he could get a sense of how she felt about him.

It was when they arrived at Heaton House that he realized they hadn't spoken on the way back. He paused at the steps. "I'm sorry, Kathleen. I was lost in my thoughts."

"It's all right, so was I."

Had they been thinking along the same lines? "Kathleen, I—"

"I hope Mrs. Heaton won't be able to sense I'm keeping something from her. She reads me well."

Evidently not. "I don't think she sensed anything earlier."

Kathleen nodded. "No, I don't either. I'll just have to be careful, but oh, I hope we can find out for sure, and soon."

Much as Luke wanted Reba Dickerson to be Rebecca Heaton, he wouldn't mind it taking a few weeks to give him more time to spend with Kathleen. More time to figure out what he was going to do now that he could no longer deny how he felt about her.

Chapter Nineteen

Kathleen and Luke didn't tarry long at the breakfast table the next morning. In fact they were the first ones to leave the house.

"Oh," Kathleen breathed as they headed for the trolley stop. "I thought for sure Mrs. Heaton was going to ask me what I was hiding. I hope we find out something soon. I don't like not being open with her."

"You don't have to worry," he told her. "She really doesn't think you're hiding anything from her. Of course if we keep leaving earlier than everyone else, she might begin to wonder."

"Oh, no! Do you think?"

The trolley came to a stop just then and Luke chuckled as he followed Kathleen on and sat down beside her. This was a side of her he'd never seen. "Do you just find things to worry about?"

"Normally, no. Life gives us enough of that on its own. But I do hate to feel like I'm lying—although I'm not. I don't know who Reba really is, but still…"

"We can't say anything about it until we know for sure. It will be much better for Mrs. Heaton to know nothing than to think she's found her daughter and it turn out not to be her."

Kathleen leaned back in her seat and expelled a huge sigh. "Of course."

"So please quit worrying."

"I'll try. I don't want to hurt Reba, either, so I'll have to be careful on how I question her."

"That's true. But the forms you help her with should ask for some of the information we need."

"I'm glad I saw the photograph yesterday. Otherwise, I would just turn in the paperwork and not be able to get it back without explaining why or telling a lie."

It came as no surprise to Luke that she didn't want to lie—he'd known from the first she was a woman of integrity. It was one of the reasons he was so attracted to her. He'd tossed and turned most of the night again, flitting from one dream—one nightmare—to another. There was no doubt in his mind that this woman had replaced Beth in his heart.

When he'd awakened this morning realizing that it was only Kathleen who was on his mind all night, he'd felt almost guilty that it wasn't Beth who occupied his thoughts day and night. And then, he'd felt hopeful. He was moving on.

Maybe this was the Lord's way of telling him to put his heart on the line again. To give it to Kathleen, holding nothing back, and trusting in the Lord to help him keep her safe. In truth, he hoped so. Because denying he cared that deeply about her would be lying.

"Now, how do I introduce you to Reba? I don't quite know what she's going to think of my bringing you with me."

"Hmm. And we don't want to lie to her." He thought

for a moment. "How about you just say that I'm your friend. We are friends, right?"

Kathleen nodded. "Yes, we are."

"And that I'm accompanying you today because you want to go to lunch with me when you're through and I needed to know where to pick you up."

"Oh! Yes, that will probably work."

"How long will it take to fill out the papers and have your talk?"

"A few hours," she replied.

The trolley stopped and they got out on Second Avenue and walked the rest of the way to the building. Luke was eager to meet Reba Dickerson and see for himself if she looked like Rebecca Heaton.

When they reached her floor, Kathleen turned to him. "Are you sure this will work?"

"No. But I don't have any other ideas, and we're here."

"That we are." She reached out and knocked on the door, making sure that she was the one Reba would see when she cracked it open.

The young woman gave Kathleen a smile, but it quickly disappeared when she saw him.

"Reba, this is my friend Luke Patterson. Luke, this is Reba Dickerson. Luke came with me because we're having lunch together later and I wanted him to know where to meet me. Will it be all right if he calls for me around noon?"

Reba looked from one to the other and then smiled. Suddenly she did resemble the woman in Mrs. Heaton's photograph—a little older and more mature as Kathleen had said. Still, he wasn't certain she was Rebecca.

"Of course Mr. Patterson may pick you up."

"Thank you, Mrs. Dickerson." Luke turned to Kathleen. "I'll see you later. You two have a nice visit."

"Thank you, we will." Kathleen turned back to Reba, and Luke turned to leave. He'd have to look at the photograph of Rebecca again. He tried to commit Mrs. Dickerson's face to memory so that he could compare the two. And he'd see her again when he came to get Kathleen. He wondered how they could get a photograph of Mrs. Dickerson. Suddenly an idea came to him and he hurried back to the woman's apartment and knocked on the door.

Once again, Mrs. Dickerson cracked it open only far enough to see who was there. She smiled this time. "Mr. Patterson, you're a bit early, aren't you?"

Luke chuckled. "I'm sorry but I need to speak to Kathleen for a moment, if possible."

She must have heard her name, for she came to the door just then. "Luke? Is something wrong?"

"No, I just—" He hoped he wasn't overstepping, but it was the only way he knew to get his idea across to her. "I wondered—you didn't have your camera with you to take the pictures for your records—would you like me to bring it when I come back?"

He could see that she caught on quickly as she nodded and smiled. "Oh, yes, please. Thank you for thinking of it."

"You're welcome. I'll bring it back with me." He hurried down the stairs this time, feeling quite proud of himself for coming up with the idea. It could never hurt to have pictures of the people applying to the day care homes, or to run one. He'd tell Mrs. Heaton about the idea—if she saw him with the camera and asked about it. Then, once the film was developed, he and Kathleen could compare the photographs side by side. Then they'd know if Reba was who they thought she was.

Kathleen followed Reba back to the kitchen table where they'd just begun to chat while the tea steeped.

Luke came up with some of the best ideas. She'd never even thought of bringing a camera—not that she had one anyway—but it was a wonderful idea to include photographs with the application records. Not to mention it'd help in trying to find out who Reba really was.

"I didn't know you'd be needing a photograph. I'm not much on having mine taken."

Kathleen wondered if she were going to refuse to have her picture taken. "Neither am I, so I understand. But—"

Reba's hand came up and sliced the air—in almost the exact same way Kathleen had seen Mrs. Heaton do on numerous occasions. The breath caught in her throat as she waited to hear what Reba had to say.

"But since it's necessary... I'll have time to freshen up a bit before you take it."

Kathleen released a silent sigh of relief as Reba poured them both a cup of tea. "I'll need one of you and Jenny, if it's all right."

"I guess so, if you must have them for the record, I suppose I don't really have a choice. I'll go get her from Mrs. Connor's when you're ready."

"You know it never hurts to have a picture or two of yourself and your loved ones. We never know what might happen that we might need it."

The color drained from Reba's face and Kathleen quickly tried to explain. "My parents passed away before my sister and I came here. If not for their photographs, I think I would have forgotten what they looked like."

Kathleen was almost sure that there were tears in Reba's eyes as she quickly turned to get a plate of cookies and bring them to the table.

"I'm sorry for your loss, Kathleen. And you are right. Photographs would be good to have."

Glad that was settled, Kathleen pulled out the forms she needed filled out and they began to go over them. She let Reba fill them out, hoping that it would give her and Luke the information they needed to find out if she was Mrs. Heaton's daughter. She wasn't familiar with feeling deceitful to anyone and didn't like it, but they had to find out the truth.

Reba was from Virginia and she was twenty-one—younger than Kathleen—and on her own with a child to raise alone. "Does your family still live in Virginia?"

"As far as I know." Reba's head was bent over the paper as she filled it out.

Evidently she hadn't kept contact with them after she left. Kathleen opened her mouth to ask why, but that question was not on the form and she really didn't know Reba well enough to ask something that personal. At least not now. But her heart went out to the younger woman and she prayed that she might be Mrs. Heaton's daughter—and that if she were, it would bring joy and not heartache to both women.

Reba had finished filling out the paperwork and they were enjoying another cup of tea and getting to know each other a little better when Luke came back.

"Oh, my, time went by fast," Reba said. "I'd best run down to Mrs. Connor's and get Jenny so we can get ready for that picture-taking. Please, Mr. Patterson, have a seat and some tea. I'm sure Kathleen will be glad to fix you a cup. I'll be right back." With that she hurried out the door, leaving Luke and Kathleen waiting for her.

"We get to take a picture of her daughter, too?"

"Yes. I came up with that one on my own, thank you." Kathleen grinned at him.

"It's a good idea." He crossed the room in a hurry and pulled out his camera from its bag. "Have you used one of these before?"

"No."

"Well, this is a Number 2 Bulls-Eye Kodak and it's easy to use." He pointed out the features to her. "This is where you look through the lens and this is the key you use to advance the film. And this is the shutter to take the picture."

"And I just slide this to take the picture?" She touched the small slide.

"That's all you have to do." He handed it to her. "Here, get the feel of it before she gets back." He handed it to her and she looked through the lens at him, and he smiled. She quickly slid the slide and heard a click. "I think I got you."

"I think you did, too." He smiled and the look in his eyes had her pulse racing as he approached her. "Now just turn the key to advance the film. And now it's my turn."

He took the camera from her and stood back a ways. "You can't exactly refuse to let me take your picture when you took mine without even asking."

"I'm sorry, Luke." She laughed as he took aim

through the lens. "But please don't take—" Kathleen heard the click.

He grinned. "Looks like I got you, too."

"Yes. And probably with my eyes closed and my mouth wide open."

"Nope. I don't take those kinds of pictures."

"Humph." She sighed. "But I suppose I really don't have the right to complain."

"You're right about—"

The door opened and Reba and Jenny entered. "It won't take but a minute for us to freshen up. We'll be right back." She smiled as she hurried her daughter into their bedroom.

"So, what do you think?" Kathleen whispered. "Do you think she could be Rebecca?"

"I think it's a good possibility, but I'm just not sure." He leaned close to her ear. "The photos will help. I'll have them developed as soon as I can. But what do you think?"

"Oh, I think it is a real possibility. She has this hand movement that is just like Mrs. Heaton's. You know the one. Like this." Kathleen mimicked the movement and Luke nodded. "I know it could just be coincidence, but I think it might be her. I really do."

The bedroom door opened and out came Reba and Jenny. "Well, I suppose we'd best get to this. I hope you take good pictures."

"You know, Luke is really better at taking them than I am. Let's let him do it. He says he doesn't take bad ones."

"If that's the case, then all right. I'd like it to be a good one."

Luke took several photos, near the windows where there was light, and Reba and Jenny posed for each shot.

"We'll make sure you get the extra photos for your own album."

"Thank you, that's very nice, Kathleen."

"It's the least we can do." And maybe she wouldn't feel so bad for taking them when as yet, they really weren't part of the application. She grabbed her bag and the papers Reba had filled out. "Tomorrow I'll take you to meet Colleen and the other children she's watching, if you'd like."

"Oh, yes, I would. That way Jenny will feel better when I drop her off. Thank you for thinking of it."

"Would around ten in the morning be all right?"

"It will be fine."

"I'll see you then."

Jenny smiled shyly at Luke and he tweaked her nose on the way out. She giggled and rubbed her nose. She was a delightful child. After Reba shut the door behind them and they were down the hall, Kathleen turned to Luke. "If Reba turns out to be Mrs. Heaton's daughter, can you imagine how she's going to feel finding out she not only has her daughter back but a granddaughter, too?"

After dropping the film off to a developer, Luke took Kathleen to lunch at a small café not too far from her office. After the waiter took their order they began to discuss the magnitude of what they might be on the brink of discovering.

"I really feel we should tell Michael about our suspicions, but I don't want to see him or Mrs. Heaton heartbroken if it's not her," he said.

"I know. Neither do I. But aren't they from Virginia?"

"Yes. Is Reba from there, too?"

Kathleen nodded and pulled out some papers from her bag. "She's from Ashland."

Luke blew out a huge sigh. "Mrs. Heaton is from Ashland."

"It's got to be her, Luke."

"Not necessarily, Kathleen. There are a lot of people who live in Ashland. We can't jump to conclusions. I'll get the photos late this afternoon and we'll look at them. If we are sure, then we'll have to at least tell Michael."

Kathleen nodded. "I agree."

"You know he's thought for a while that there might be a possibility that Reba might be living in the tenements."

"Why would he think that?"

"He thinks she might have—" How did he say it delicately? "—gotten into trouble…and was too ashamed to come home."

Kathleen blushed and Luke felt sure she knew what he was talking about. He shrugged.

"It's possible, I suppose. And it would explain why she wouldn't go home. When I asked if her family still lived in Virginia, she said 'as far as I know.' I thought that an odd answer at the time, but…" Kathleen's voice faded away and neither of them seemed to know what to say next.

Luke was relieved when the waiter brought their lunch. "Don't worry about it now. We don't know much more than we did this morning. Let's just pray for the Lord to guide us the rest of the way."

At Kathleen's nod, they bowed their heads and Luke did just that.

Chapter Twenty

Kathleen could barely look at Mrs. Heaton at dinnertime for fear of giving away what she and Luke now believed to be true.

When she'd arrived back at Heaton House after work, it was to find Luke waiting for her in the parlor. He'd motioned to her to come in and after making sure no one else was around, she hurried to his side. He had several photographs he'd taken of Reba and Jenny and quickly held them up to the photo of Rebecca.

To Kathleen's eye, they had to be one and the same person. She was almost positive that they were. "What do you think?"

He'd taken another look at the photos before slipping them back into his jacket pocket. "I think Reba is indeed Rebecca. But now we have to prove it. Maybe we should go to Michael's after dinner and let him know?"

Kathleen had nodded. "I don't think we should put it off."

"No, neither do I. We'll go for a walk and end up at Michael and Violet's."

"All right."

And now she made herself take a bite of the roast chicken on her plate when she really wasn't hungry— too afraid Mrs. Heaton would ask what was wrong with her if she didn't eat.

"Kathleen, dear," Mrs. Heaton called from the head of the table.

Her heart jumped. "Yes, ma'am?"

"I just wanted to tell you that I think it's a wonderful idea to take photographs of the mothers and children who will be using the day care homes. If anything should happen to one of the children while in our care or even out of it, there would be a photo to help identify them."

Kathleen breathed a sigh of relief that she hadn't asked what she was hiding. "I'm glad you think it is a good idea."

But she could see the pain in her sweet landlady's eyes and was sure she was thinking of her own daughter. *Oh, dear Lord, please let Reba be her, if for no other reason than that Mrs. Heaton will know she is alive and well. But if it is her, please let it bring joy and not heartache.*

"Oh, and Luke, did you get the letter from your publisher that came today?"

"I did." Luke's eyes lit with excitement. "He wants to see the complete manuscript as soon as I have it done and I'm not that far from it. But he liked what I'd sent him."

"I knew he would."

"That is wonderful, Luke." Kathleen was glad that he at least seemed to be getting his writing done even with all the time he'd been spending with her. He must require much less sleep than she did.

Once the meal was over and everyone began leaving the dining room, Luke turned to her. "Want to go for that walk?"

"I'd like that, yes."

"It's nice out tonight," Mrs. Heaton said. "You two enjoy yourselves."

"Thank you." Again Kathleen felt bad for keeping so much from Mrs. Heaton, but they simply couldn't tell her until they were certain about her daughter.

She didn't know whose sigh of relief was the loudest when they got outside—hers or Luke's.

Luke took hold of her elbow as they started down the walk. "I hope we get this settled soon. It is one thing to investigate for people you barely know, but this involves so many people I care about. I pray it turns out well for all of them."

"I know. That is my biggest fear—that if Reba is Rebecca, she might not want her mother and brother to know where she is."

"Let's don't even think that way."

"No. Let's don't." But she knew it was there in the back of both their minds as they made their way over to Michael and Violet's.

Hilda answered the door and showed them into the parlor where Violet sat reading a book. She jumped up when she saw them and hurried to greet them.

"Luke, Kathleen, how wonderful to see you. What brings you out tonight?"

"Well, we came to see you and Michael," Kathleen said, "but I suppose I should have telephoned first."

"Oh, nonsense, you know we don't hold to social protocol with you all. But Michael is out of town, so I hope it isn't a wasted trip for you." She motioned to the couch. "Please have a seat and I'll have Hilda bring us some refreshment."

"Oh, please, don't trouble yourself. We just got up from the dinner table."

Violet laughed. "Say no more. I know Mother Heaton takes care of her boarders very well." She took her seat on the couch and Luke and Kathleen sat down across from her. "Now, is there anything I can help you with?"

Kathleen and Luke exchanged glances and Luke nodded. "Actually, it might be best that we talk to you, first."

"Now you have my curiosity up. Whatever is it?"

Luke nodded to Kathleen. "It's your story."

She took a deep breath. There was no easy way to say it. "I think I may have found Mrs. Heaton's daughter."

Violet gasped, stood up and sat back down. "Rebecca? You know where she is?"

"I believe so." Kathleen explained about Reba and how she'd come to think she might be Mrs. Heaton's daughter.

"And her last name?"

"Is Dickerson."

Violet's face paled. "Mother Heaton's maiden name is Dickerson. What does she look like?"

Kathleen turned to Luke, and he pulled the photographs out of his pocket and handed them to her. Kathleen looked down at them, more certain than ever that this was Mrs. Heaton's daughter and granddaughter. She handed the photos to Violet. "She has a little girl."

Violet reached out and took the photos with trembling fingers. She looked at each one, placed a hand over her mouth and looked at Kathleen with tears in her eyes. "I think it might be. But I'd need to see her, hear her voice to know for sure. And I'm glad Michael isn't here. He'll be home tomorrow, but I don't want him to know anything until we are positive. Is there any way I can see her for myself?"

"I'm taking her and Jenny—"

"That's the little girl's name?" Violet released a little sob. "Rebecca always said if she had a little girl, she wanted to name her Jennifer."

Kathleen wiped at her own tears as she went to sit beside Violet and gave her a hug. "I know this must be so much to take in and I don't in any way want to bring pain to Mrs. Heaton or Michael and you, but I do believe this is Rebecca. I am taking them to meet Colleen and the other children tomorrow around ten. If you could be there visiting Colleen—"

"I'll arrange to take some time off. I'll be there. Oh, I pray this is her. But what if she still doesn't want Michael or his mother to know where she is?"

"I don't know what we'll do then. But if it is Rebecca, I will do all I can to bring them together unless you tell me different."

"All right. Thank you so much for coming to me with this. And I know it's hard, but I think it's wise not to let Michael and his mother know just yet. They've been through so much heartache with Rebecca—and I'm sure she's gone through her own. I know she was close to both of them and loves them. Oh, please pray that it turns out good for all of them."

By the time they left Violet's they had a plan in place. Violet was sure she would know if Reba was

Rebecca once she saw her, and if she was, she'd let Michael know.

If that was the case, Kathleen would talk to Reba and tell her she had a mother and brother right here in the city. And they all prayed they'd be able to get them together again where their love for each other would be obvious.

But Kathleen was awfully quiet as they left Violet, and Luke was pretty sure he knew why. He remembered the small park in Michael's neighborhood right around the corner from their house.

He took hold of Kathleen's arm and led her there. It wasn't gated and just as he thought, no one was there this time of night. It would be the perfect place to talk.

"We need to talk where no one will overhear anything about this. Want to sit for a few minutes?"

"Yes, that would be nice. I feel anyone who sees me will know something is going on. I need to get my thoughts together."

They found a bench that was just far enough inside that no one walking by would hear what they were saying. Once they were both seated he turned to Kathleen.

"You know, if this doesn't turn out well, it's not going to be your fault. No one is going to blame you."

"Oh, Luke, I don't want to bring heartache to any of them, especially after all they've done for me and my family."

"I know and I understand. I feel the same way. And remember you aren't in this alone."

"Oh, no. I probably shouldn't have dragged you into all this. I don't want them upset with you, either. I'll take all the blame—"

Luke stopped her words by lightly touching her lips

with his fingertips. "Kathleen, shush. This is not your doing. The Lord brought Reba into your life through Mrs. Connor, who wanted to help her. You want to help her and Mrs. Heaton. Perhaps this is all the Lord's will and His timing." He moved his hand to her cheek.

"I've never thought of it that way. I just don't want any of you who have helped me so much to be hurt by my actions."

"Has it never dawned on you that you've helped all of us in your own way, too?"

"Oh, Luke, no, I—" She shook her head.

"Kate." He looked into her eyes. Oh, how he wanted to kiss her, to let her know of his growing feelings for her. Of how much she meant to him. But this wasn't the time or the place. "Don't you know the Lord is as capable of using you to help others as anyone else?"

Finally he saw her lips turn up in a smile. "Thank you. Again. For reminding me of what I already know."

"You're welcome." He cupped her cheek in his hand and tipped her face up—thankful that she no longer flinched if he touched her. "It's going to all work out, Kate. You'll see."

"I hope so."

Then he was no longer able to resist the temptation. He lowered his head and heard Kathleen's quick intake of breath. But she didn't move. He lowered his lips to hers. And she responded. Her lips were soft and sweet and— She broke it off and stood.

"I— We'd better be going, Luke."

"Yes, of course." She hadn't slapped him. Surely that meant something?

The rest of the walk home was in silence, but Luke didn't know if it was a good or a bad one. Was she upset about the kiss? And if so, was it because he'd kissed her, or that she'd kissed him back?

Once they arrived at the house, she started up the steps. "Kate?"

She stopped and turned to him.

"I'm sorry—" they both said at the exact same time.

"I should have—" again together. Finally they both chuckled and broke the tension between them.

"Let's leave this for another time—after all this with Reba is taken care of. But then we need to talk about us. Agreed?" He held out his hand and his heart hammered as he waited.

Kathleen slipped her hand in his. "Agreed."

Luke escorted Kathleen to Reba's apartment building as usual the next morning, but they didn't discuss anything other than their plans in regard to Reba.

They'd made a deal and taken it seriously. But Kathleen knew they would have a talk about what had happened between them the night before. Luke was a man of his word, and she was a woman of hers.

"I'll not be far away at any time, but you might not see me. If you need me, just call my name and I'll be there," Luke said just before she entered the building.

"All right. See you later." Kathleen hurried up the stairs, buoyed by just knowing that he would be near. And that she trusted that he would be.

She'd slept better than she'd expected the night before. The Lord must have known she needed to sleep instead of reliving Luke's kiss. But it'd been on her mind as soon as she'd awakened. She still couldn't believe she'd responded the way she had and deep in her heart she knew she could no longer deny that she was falling in love with him.

But for now she put it all out of her mind. Today was about Reba and the Heatons and she needed a clear mind to handle whatever came of it once Violet saw the young woman.

Reba and Jenny were ready as soon as she knocked on the door and they both seemed to be in high spirits. Kathleen paid for the trolley for all of them and they were soon on their way. She could tell they rarely road the trolley from Jenny's excitement. She was such a pretty little girl and there was no way around the fact that she resembled Mrs. Heaton enough to be her granddaughter.

She'd telephoned Colleen that morning and she knew to expect Violet first and then her and Reba and Jenny. Her sister opened the door wide and welcomed them inside as Kathleen made the introductions.

"Many of the children come before breakfast," Colleen explained, "so that is available to Jenny if you need to leave for work early. And of course we serve them lunch, too. You're welcome to stay for that today, if you'd like."

After they dropped Jenny off in the playroom and introduced her to the other children, Colleen took them on a tour. Kathleen wondered where Violet was. Would she make herself known or surreptitiously get a look at Reba?

Reba seemed quite pleased with the home as Colleen led her through one room and then the other, including the kitchen and the small garden out back where the children sometimes played.

"Oh, this is even nicer than I imagined," Reba said

as they headed back into the house. "I know Jenny is going to love being here."

Colleen opened the door and the hallway seemed dim after the bright sunshine outside. Kathleen heard Violet's voice say, "Oh, I'm sorry."

"It's all righ—" Reba took a quick breath and seemed to hold it.

"Ida said you were outside, Colleen. I was just coming to find you." Violet turned back to Reba. "I— You look so familiar, do I know y—"

"No, I don't think we've met before."

"Oh, I'm sorry. I truly thought—"

"No. I need to get Jenny now." Her voice seemed shaky.

"Oh, you don't want to stay for lunch?" Colleen asked.

"We can't—I—" She seemed to be getting more agitated by the minute.

"Come with me. I'll get her," Colleen said.

"I'll meet you by the front door, Reba," Kathleen said. But once they were out of sight she turned to Violet and whispered, "Well, could you tell?"

Violet's eyes were filled with tears. "It's Rebecca. I know it is."

Kathleen nodded. "I'll see what I can do."

"Thank you."

Kathleen hurried to the front door and waited for Reba to come with Jenny. Jenny hated to leave, but Colleen assured her she'd be back soon and calmed her down.

But the look on Reba's face as they walked to the trolley stop unsettled Kathleen and she prayed that she wouldn't change her mind about using the day care.

On the way to the apartment Jenny chattered about the day care and the children she'd met and how much she wanted to go back. Finally Reba assured her she'd get to go back and Kathleen was sure she was as relieved as Jenny was at that news.

"But now be a good girl and go change into your everyday clothes and play for a bit while I talk to Kathleen and make your lunch."

"Yes, ma'am." Jenny skipped off to the bedroom with a smile on her face.

She'd no more than left the room when Reba turned to Kathleen. "Who was that woman who thought she knew me?"

"She's a friend of Colleen's. She's not usually there—she works at Butterick."

"You're sure she's not always there?"

"I'm certain of it. She must have had the day off and stopped by for a visit."

Reba went to the kitchen and Kathleen followed her. She could tell the young woman was still upset by the way her hands shook as she filled her teakettle and put it on the stove.

"Are you all right, Reba? You seem upset."

Reba turned from the stove, tears flowing down her cheeks and Kathleen hurried over to her. "What is it? Is it Violet?"

Reba nodded and began to sob. Kathleen wrapped an arm around her. "It's all right, come sit down and tell me about it."

Reba let her lead her to the table and sat down. She pulled a handkerchief out of her pocket and blew her nose as Kathleen sat down opposite her. "Violet Burton was our neighbor in Virginia. I'm not sure why she's here."

Kathleen had to tell her what she knew. "She's Violet Heaton now."

Reba began to cry all over again. "She's my sister-in-law, then. I didn't know Michael had moved here."

"I'm sorry, I—"

"My name isn't Dickerson. It's Heaton and I've never been married. Dickerson is my mother's maiden name." Reba stood up and began to pace as the floodgates opened and she talked. "I left home and came here with a man I thought loved me, wanted to marry me. But it was all a lie and when he left me here, I was pregnant with Jenny and too ashamed to go home and face my family. I didn't want to bring shame on them and I—" She sat back down and began to sob in earnest. Kathleen grasped her hands until she was spent and sniffing.

"You are Rebecca Heaton?"

Reba nodded.

"I must be truthful with you. Your mother came here shortly after you went missing and she and Michael both have spent years trying to find you. They aren't worried about you bringing shame on them, Reba. They just want you back, to know you are alive and well and to be part of their lives again."

"Did they send you here?"

"No! They know nothing about you yet. But, oh, Reba, you have a family who loves you with all their hearts right here in the city. Please consider letting them know you're here."

"My mother is here? In New York City? She didn't go back after they couldn't find me?"

"No. She's always believed that they would find

you—or you would find them when you were ready. And she's made it her life's work to help other young women who might need a place to stay. She runs Heaton House where I live."

"Please tell me more about her and Michael."

The kettle began to blow steam and Kathleen took it on herself to make them both a cup of tea as she told Reba all Mrs. Heaton had done for her and her family, how wonderful a couple Michael and Violet were and how she came to think Reba was Mrs. Heaton's daughter.

That Reba wanted to see them was as apparent as her fear of doing so. She was clearly at war with herself.

"I love your mother, Reba, and I don't want to see her go through any more heartbreak."

"But I'm afraid they won't want—"

"Reba, surely you remember the story of the prodigal son? And how his father welcomed him home? You must know deep down that your mother and brother will do the same with you."

"I know the Lord has forgiven me, but I don't want Jenny to suffer for my sins."

"There is no way that will happen and you know it. Your mother and brother and Violet, too, are going to dote upon her. Jenny deserves to know her grandmother and uncle, Reba. Please let me tell them about you."

Finally, Reba nodded. "Yes. You can tell them. But if they don't want to see me—"

"That's not going to be the case. I can promise you that."

Chapter Twenty-One

Kathleen no more than got out the door of Reba's apartment before Luke was there. She didn't even know where he'd come from but suddenly he was walking toward her.

"I didn't have to call you."

"No, you didn't. I was here all along. What happened?"

They walked and talked at the same time. "Reba is Rebecca and she's agreed to meet with Michael and Violet. But I don't want her to change her mind so the quicker we can make it happen the better."

"Let's go see Michael. He should be home by now."

Kathleen filled in Luke on what had happened with Reba on the way to Michael and Violet's. Once they got there, her heart went out to Michael.

His voice was filled with emotion as he asked, "Is this woman really my sister, Kathleen?"

"She is. She recognized Violet this morning even though she denied knowing her and when we got back to her apartment, she broke down and told me everything."

Michael turned away for a few moments and gathered his wife in his arms. Kathleen's eyes were full of tears as she looked at Luke and saw his were filled also.

Finally Michael was able to compose himself. "After all these years of looking for her it's hard to believe she's been found. Can you tell me more?"

Kathleen filled him in on everything, including the fact that Reba—Rebecca—was afraid they'd want nothing to do with her once they found she had a child out of wedlock. "I assured her that wasn't the case and finally talked her into letting me tell you about her. She's agreed to see you and Mrs. Heaton."

"When?"

"As soon as you can. I don't think she'll run away—I told her Jenny deserved to know her grandmother and uncle—but I'd say the sooner the better."

"I'll go get Mother and bring her over. Violet and I will prepare her. Can you and Luke bring Rebecca and Jenny back here?"

Kathleen looked at Luke and he nodded. "We can. We'll go now."

They headed back to the tenements immediately, and Kathleen prayed all the while that Reba would be home and that she hadn't changed her mind about seeing her mother and brother.

Luke went with her this time and Reba let them both in. She told the woman who Luke really was, that he lived at Heaton House, too. Then she relayed Michael's request to meet. "You haven't changed your mind, have you?"

"No. I haven't changed my mind. It wouldn't be fair to anyone after I told you I would. And you're right. My daughter deserves to know her grandmother and uncle. I've even told Jenny she was going to get to meet them. I can't go back now."

Only then did Kathleen begin to relax. It was going to be all right. She and Luke waited while Reba and her daughter got ready.

"I can't even imagine what Mrs. Heaton must be feeling right now. I'm so glad Michael went to get her and will explain it all to her. I'm not sure I could do it again."

Luke agreed. "We'll get to see the reunion. I can't wait for that."

"Me, either. But then I think we should leave them alone, don't you?"

"Yes, I do. How about you let me take you to dinner? So we don't have to answer the boarders' questions just yet?"

His smile had Kathleen's heart doing a funny little twist. "I'd like that, thank you."

Reba and Jenny came out of their room, excitement on the face of the child, and a bit of apprehension on her mother's. They walked out to Second Avenue where Luke procured a hack to get them there as quickly as possible.

When they arrived at Michael's, Violet let them in and immediately hugged Reba. "I knew it was you. I'm so glad…" She stopped and took a deep breath, then looked down at Jenny. "Hello, Jenny. I'm your aunt Violet and I'm very glad to meet you."

"I'm glad, too," Jenny said.

Just then the doors to the parlor opened and Mrs. Heaton and Michael came out. In spite of the fact that the older woman had been crying, her eyes were filled with joy for anyone to see.

"Mama." Reba ran to her mother who wrapped her in her arms and sobbed. "I'm so sorry, Mama. I never wanted to hurt you so."

"Shh, child. You're here. My prayers have been answered. These are tears of joy, not sadness." Mrs. Heaton wiped her eyes on the handkerchief she held in her hand. Then she looked at Jenny, who had a grip on her mother's skirt. "And you must be Jenny, my granddaughter?"

Reba picked her up and held her in her arms. Jenny nodded. "I think so."

"Oh, I know so. You look just like your mama did at your age. I'm very happy to meet you." She leaned over and kissed Jenny's cheek.

"Me too, Granma."

One could hear Reba swallow her sob as she turned toward Michael. "And this is your uncle Michael, Jenny."

Jenny gave him a smile and a little wave as Michael crossed the foyer and hugged them both. "I've always wanted to be an uncle, Jenny."

He held out his arms and the child fairly jumped into them.

Kathleen took the handkerchief Luke handed her to wipe the flow of tears before she turned and found herself in his arms.

"I told you it would be all right, didn't I?"

Kathleen nodded but before she could step out of Luke's arms, Mrs. Heaton was there, crying, hugging and kissing them both. "Kathleen, Luke, thank you, thank you."

"Oh, Mrs. Heaton, you are so welcome. We're just thankful it's turned out this way."

"You'll stay for supper?" Violet asked.

"No," Luke said. "Thank you, but Kathleen and I want this time to be yours. I'm going to take her to dinner and we'll celebrate with you all—"

"This weekend. At Heaton House," Mrs. Heaton said. "We'll all celebrate then."

Luke took Kathleen to a small Italian café where one didn't have to dress up and the lighting wasn't good enough to tell if one had been crying all afternoon.

Now as they each enjoyed the rich lasagna they'd ordered, Luke was relieved to see Kathleen smiling.

"I don't think I've ever seen anything quite so touching." Her eyes shone with unshed tears.

"Oh, it was that. I had a hard time there for a while. But I have also been witness to something just as touching. The night you went to your sister's side and then to get your nephews." He'd never forget that night, or this one either for that matter.

"Oh, Luke, did I ever thank you for being there for me?"

"Many times." He took a bite of the rich pasta dish and leaned back in his seat.

"This is wonderful. I don't think I've ever eaten any Italian food. I love it."

"It's a favorite of mine. And we can come here again anytime you'd like to." He hoped she'd want to come back with him.

"That would be nice."

She looked exhausted by the time they'd finished their meal and he got a cab to take them back to Heaton House. "Want to take the long way home so that maybe we don't have to run into anyone at home?"

"Yes, I think I would. I just…"

"No need to explain to me. I know it's been a long, grueling, wonderful day for you." He leaned forward and spoke to the driver and then sat back. "Were going to drive through Central Park. Have you ever done that at night?"

"No, I never have."

As they drove down the streets of the city, Luke knew there was no one he'd rather be with—now or forever. He loved this woman with all his heart and he wanted to tell her. But tonight wasn't the night to declare his love. She was worn out. He needed to wait until she'd had a good night's sleep and was rested. But he could tell her how proud he was of her.

"You know, you worried all for nothing. The Lord did have it under control and He used you in a huge way to get the Heaton family back together again. I can't tell you how much I admire what you've done and what you want to do to help those still in the tenements, Kate."

"Oh, Luke. Thank you. But you had just as big a part in helping the Heatons as I did. And I know you are as happy as I am at the outcome."

"I am. I do hope that my book will help people in the tenements as much as your work with the Ladies' Aide Society is going to."

"I'm sorry. I'm not sure how a dime novel could help, unless you give all the proceeds from it to—"

Luke laughed. "No, Kathleen. I thought you knew—that you realized I've been writing a different kind of book, one that I hope will give the people in the tenements hope that they can get out of there and make new lives for themselves like you and your sister have."

"Like us?" Kathleen sat up straight and he could

see she was angry. "You used my family as examples? Luke, how could you?"

"How could I what? I'm trying to help, to—"

"You wrote about me and Colleen and our family? You used us to write your book?"

"No! Kathleen, I'd never—"

"Have the driver take us home. Now, please."

"Kathleen, listen to me."

"I've heard enough. That you could use our situation to your gain!"

Luke felt the blood rush to his face. How dare she accuse him of something like that?

"Driver," she called out, "there's been a change in plans. Take us to Heaton House now, please."

"Kathleen—"

"I have nothing more to say to you." She turned away and shut him out. There was nothing to do but pray that he'd find a way to make her see how wrong she was.

The driver had barely stopped the hack at Heaton House and she was out of it like a flash and in the house before Luke could pay the man.

"She's not very happy with you, mate."

"No. Nor am I with her." Luke handed the man his money and rushed up the steps to the house. He opened the door and resisted the urge to slam it. Kathleen was nowhere to be seen, but thankfully, neither were any of the other boarders. He took the stairs down to his floor and to his room.

What was she thinking? She had to know him better than to think he would do her or her family any harm! He slammed his fist down on top of the manuscript pages he had ready to send his publisher. That she could believe something like that left him with a knot in his gut and feeling as if a sharp knife had just pierced his heart.

Kathleen paced the floor of her room. How could Luke have used her and her family for research for his book? Just as she'd begun to trust him, he'd betrayed that trust. But what was worse, she could no longer deny she loved him. And it hurt unbearably that he'd done something like this.

There was a knock on her door and she went to answer, thinking it might be Mrs. Heaton back from Michael's. Maybe Reba was with her. She opened the door to find Gretchen there.

"Miss Kathleen. Mr. Luke wanted me to ask you to come to Mrs. Heaton's study. Said he needs to speak with you—"

"I don't want to talk to Luke right now, Gretchen."

"Oh, please, Miss Kathleen. He said if you don't come down he's coming up to get you and you know how that will upset Mrs. Heaton." She began wringing her hands.

Kathleen heaved a huge sigh. "All right. He's in Mrs. Heaton's study?"

"Yes, ma'am."

Kathleen marched down the stairs, indignant that he would use Gretchen in that way. He could get her into all kinds of trouble. She didn't bother to knock on the study door.

"Luke Patterson, what are you thinking? We have nothing more to discuss! And I don't feel like talking."

"You don't have to talk!" His eyes flashed. "But there are a few things I have to say, and you're going to listen. I understand how hard it might be for you to trust a man after all you've been through, but there's one thing you need to know."

Kathleen held her breath, waiting for his next words. "I love you with all my heart, even though I know you'll never trust me with yours. And I don't know what to do about it except give you this." He handed her a box.

"Take it." He thrust it at her and she had no choice but to take it. "It's my manuscript, but it's yours to do with as you will. Burn it, tear it up—I don't care."

With that, he turned and left her speechless as he walked out the door.

Kathleen hurried up the stairs with it, ready to do just as he suggested. Before she'd let her family become a laughingstock she'd— Kathleen stopped in her steps. Would he really have given it to her if he'd done what she accused him of? Luke?

Kathleen sat down on the settee in front of the fireplace and held the box in her lap. She'd have to light a fire to burn it and it was really too warm for that now. She lifted the top off the box and took the pages out with trembling fingers. She could tear them up. She took the first page, held it in her hands and began to read.

Six hours later at the crack of dawn she was crying. Again. How could she ever have accused Luke the way she did? She'd come to trust him, so why did she light into him the way she had?

Maybe it had been hearing how Reba had been treated by Jenny's father—one more example of a woman trusting a man and being betrayed—that had brought up all of her trust issues again. But that wasn't

Luke and she knew it. When the woman he'd loved died, he was by her side; he hadn't betrayed her.

And he'd been there for Kathleen, every time she'd needed him. To the point that she finally knew she had no reason not to give her heart to him. And that scared her with every fiber of her being. What if it didn't work out?

She blew her nose and wiped her eyes. Yes, she was afraid of giving her heart to Luke, but not doing so frightened her even more. She had to decide if she was going to be brave enough to do what her heart begged her to do, or if she was going to live the rest of her life in regret.

She slid to her knees and prayed. "Dear Lord, please forgive me for treating Luke so badly, for not having faith in You to help me trust my heart to him. For not letting go of my fear when I know I have nothing to fear with You by my side. I don't know if Luke can forgive me, but please give me the courage to ask him to. And show me Your will for us. In Jesus's name, Amen."

Kathleen dried her eyes, put the manuscript pages back in the box and ran back downstairs to the kitchen where she knew she'd find Gretchen even though no one else would be up by now.

"Gretchen, can you ask Luke to come to the little parlor? I need to speak to him."

She must think the two of them were crazy, but if so, she didn't say. "Of course. Actually he came up for coffee just a few minutes ago and asked if I'd seen you. I'll let him know."

"Thank you."

Kathleen hurried to the back parlor and paced back

and forth, waiting to see if Luke would give her another chance, if he could forgive—

"Kathleen? Gretchen said you wanted to speak to me?"

He looked as if he'd lost his best friend and she was afraid she'd lost hers. *Oh, dear Lord, please help me here.*

"I did. I…" She swallowed around the knot of tears in her throat and picked up his boxed manuscript. "I wanted to give this back to you so that you can send it off to your publisher as quickly as possible."

He took it from her but his gaze never left hers. "You read it?"

"Yes. I'm so sorry for hurting you, Luke. I don't know what got into me. Yes, I do. It was fear, plain and simple. Fear of giving my complete trust to you, even though you and the Lord have been showing me how very trustworthy you are for weeks now. I've asked for His forgiveness—now I ask for yours although I know I don't deserve it." She took a deep breath and continued. "I've known that I love you for a while now, but I've been afraid to admit it and trust that you might love me, too."

Luke dropped the box on the nearest table and pulled her into his arms. "You love me?"

"I love you. And I know I can trust your love for me. Will you forgive me for accusing you so wrongly? Can you still love me after hurting you the way I have?"

"Kate, I've had my own fears about loving you. I can't bear the thought of losing you the way I lost Beth. But the thought of living without you is too painful to contemplate and I'm going to trust that the Lord will see us through everything together. My love for you isn't fleeting, it's for a lifetime, if you want it."

Kathleen's heart filled with so much love for this man she thought it might burst with happiness. "Oh, yes, that's exactly what I want—today, tomorrow and always."

"Will you trust me to love you for the rest of our lives and become my wife, Kate?"

"I will trust my heart to you, Luke, and I'll be honored to become your wife."

Luke bent his head and she stood on tiptoe as his lips claimed hers in a kiss that assured her heart a lifetime of happiness and love. Kate kissed him back and sent up a prayer of thanksgiving to the Lord for bringing this trustworthy man into her life.

* * * * *

Dear Reader,

While writing my previous Love Inspired Historical book *Somewhere to Call Home,* I wondered what it would be like to live in the tenements, striving to make a living, just merely getting by. And then I thought about the family dynamics of being crowded into a tiny apartment, the tensions and the stress of dealing with it all. Out of all that, a new character came to mind named Kathleen O'Bryan.

But Kathleen became such a strong secondary character that she very nearly took away from Michael and Violet's romance. And they deserved their own story. So Kathleen's part in *Somewhere to Call Home* became a short scene that took place in Central Park when her brother-in-law threatened her and her sister, and Luke Patterson came to her aid. I think Luke fell a little bit in love with her that day, for he never stopped thinking of her. Thankfully, I was given a chance to write another Heaton House book and this time it's Kathleen and Luke's story.

I hope you've enjoyed reading about how they fell in love—in spite of their vows to never give their hearts to another. Kathleen because she doesn't trust men at all, after all she's seen and been through, and Luke because he fears losing someone he loves once again. This couple longs for lasting love, but must decide to trust the Lord to guide them to each other and trust their future together to Him.

I hope you enjoyed reading Kathleen's story as much as I loved writing it.

Blessings,
Janet Lee Barton

Questions for Discussion

1. When Kathleen is delivered to Heaton House, how does Luke feel about what's happened to this woman who has changed the direction of his writing? What does he decide to do?

2. After all that her brother-in-law put her sister and her through, Kathleen finds it hard to trust any man. Have you ever felt that way? How did you get past it? Did you trust in the Lord to help you?

3. Kathleen is amazed at how everyone at Heaton House accepts her. Do you think she would be accepted that way today? Why or why not?

4. If the things that happened in Kathleen's and Luke's pasts happened to you, would you have felt the same way they did? Would you find it hard to trust the Lord or would you turn to Him to help you get through it?

5. When Kathleen's sister is shot and she goes back to the tenements to help, do you think she made the right decision by not taking her nephews to Heaton House? Would you have made the same decision?

6. Were Luke's fears over Kathleen going in and out of the tenements understandable after what had happened to his fiancée? Or was he being overly protective of her?

7. Luke's fiancée died in his arms and he blamed himself for not being there to keep her from being shot. Do you think that is a normal reaction? How would you have advised him to deal with his guilt and go on with his life? Did talking to Kathleen help him?

8. When Kathleen suspects that Reba might be Mrs. Heaton's daughter, she turns to Luke for advice. They decide not to tell Mrs. Heaton until they are sure Reba is Rebecca. Do you think they did the right thing? Would you have made the same decision? Why or why not?

9. When Luke tells Kathleen about the book he has written, she accuses him of using her and her family. How do you think that made Luke feel? Who did he turn to? Was he right in giving her the manuscript to do whatever she wanted with? Have you ever felt the Lord's guidance after you've asked for His help?

10. Once Kathleen reads the manuscript and realizes how wrong she was, how do you think she felt? Whose forgiveness and help did she ask for first? And did the Lord answer her prayer?

COMING NEXT MONTH
from Love Inspired® Historical
AVAILABLE OCTOBER 1, 2013

A FAMILY FOR CHRISTMAS
Texas Grooms
Winnie Griggs

Stranded in a small town after defending an orphan stowaway on the train, Eve Pickering decides Turnabout, Texas, may be just the place to start over with her new charge. Especially when a smooth-talking Texan rides to their rescue....

THE SECRET PRINCESS
Protecting the Crown
Rachelle McCalla

When Prince Luke rescued Evelyn from a life of servitude he never suspected she was the daughter of his greatest enemy. But this Cinderella must keep her royal blood secret lest she lose her heart—and her life.

TAMING THE TEXAS RANCHER
Rhonda Gibson

In a race to the altar to claim his inheritance, Daniel Westland thinks love is a luxury. But things change when he meets his beautiful mail-order bride....

AN UNLIKELY UNION
Shannon Farrington

Union doctor Evan Mackay has no tolerance for Southern sympathizers—no matter how lovely. As they work together to heal Baltimore's wounded soldiers, can Southern nurse Emily Davis soften his Yankee heart?

LIHCNM0913

REQUEST YOUR FREE BOOKS!

2 FREE INSPIRATIONAL NOVELS
PLUS 2
FREE
MYSTERY GIFTS

Love Inspired
HISTORICAL
INSPIRATIONAL HISTORICAL ROMANCE

YES! Please send me 2 FREE Love Inspired® Historical novels and my 2 FREE mystery gifts (gifts are worth about $10). After receiving them, if I don't wish to receive any more books, I can return the shipping statement marked "cancel." If I don't cancel, I will receive 4 brand-new novels every month and be billed just $4.74 per book in the U.S. or $5.24 per book in Canada. That's a saving of at least 21% off the cover price. It's quite a bargain! Shipping and handling is just 50¢ per book in the U.S. and 75¢ per book in Canada.* I understand that accepting the 2 free books and gifts places me under no obligation to buy anything. I can always return a shipment and cancel at any time. Even if I never buy another book, the two free books and gifts are mine to keep forever.

102/302 IDN F5CN

Name	(PLEASE PRINT)	
Address		Apt. #
City	State/Prov.	Zip/Postal Code

Signature (if under 18, a parent or guardian must sign)

Mail to the **Harlequin® Reader Service:**
IN U.S.A.: P.O. Box 1867, Buffalo, NY 14240-1867
IN CANADA: P.O. Box 609, Fort Erie, Ontario L2A 5X3

Want to try two free books from another series?
Call 1-800-873-8635 or visit www.ReaderService.com.

* Terms and prices subject to change without notice. Prices do not include applicable taxes. Sales tax applicable in N.Y. Canadian residents will be charged applicable taxes. Offer not valid in Quebec. This offer is limited to one order per household. Not valid for current subscribers to Love Inspired Historical books. All orders subject to credit approval. Credit or debit balances in a customer's account(s) may be offset by any other outstanding balance owed by or to the customer. Please allow 4 to 6 weeks for delivery. Offer available while quantities last.

Your Privacy—The Harlequin® Reader Service is committed to protecting your privacy. Our Privacy Policy is available online at www.ReaderService.com or upon request from the Harlequin Reader Service.

We make a portion of our mailing list available to reputable third parties that offer products we believe may interest you. If you prefer that we not exchange your name with third parties, or if you wish to clarify or modify your communication preferences, please visit us at www.ReaderService.com/consumerchoice or write to us at Harlequin Reader Service Preference Service, P.O. Box 9062, Buffalo, NY 14269. Include your complete name and address.

LIHI3R

SPECIAL EXCERPT FROM

Love Inspired

He was her high school crush, and now he's a single father of twins. Allison True just got a second chance at love.

Read on for a sneak preview of
STORYBOOK ROMANCE by Lissa Manley,
the exciting fifth book in
THE HEART OF MAIN STREET *series,*
available October 2013.

Something clunked from the back of the bookstore, drawing Allison True's ever-vigilant attention. Her ears perking up, she rounded the end of the front counter. Another clunk sounded, and then another. Allison decided the noise was coming from the Kids' Korner, so she picked up the pace and veered toward the back right part of the store, creasing her brow.

She arrived in the area set up for kids. Her gaze zeroed in on a dark-haired toddler dressed in jeans and a red shirt, slowly yet methodically yanking books off a shelf, one after the other. Each book fell to the floor with a heavy clunk, and in between each sound, the little guy laughed, clearly enjoying the sound of his relatively harmless yet messy play.

Allison rushed over, noting there was no adult in sight. "Hey, there, bud," she said. "Whatcha doing?"

He turned big brown eyes fringed with long, dark eyelashes toward her. He looked vaguely familiar even though she was certain she'd never met this little boy.

"Fun!" A chubby hand sent another book crashing to the floor. He giggled and stomped his feet on the floor in a little happy dance. "See?"

LIEXP0913

Carefully she reached out and stilled his marauding hands. "Whoa, there, little guy." She gently pulled him away. "The books are supposed to stay on the shelf." Holding on to him, she cast her gaze about the enclosed area set aside for kids, but her view was limited by the tall bookshelves lined up from the edge of the Kids' Korner to the front of the store. "Are you here with your mommy or daddy?"

The boy tugged. "Daddy!" he squealed.

"Nicky!" a deep masculine voice replied behind her. "Oh, man. Looks like you've been making a mess."

A nebulous sense of familiarity swept through her at the sound of that voice. Not breathing, still holding the boy's hand, Allison slowly turned around. Her whole body froze and her heart gave a little spasm then fell to her toes as she looked into deep brown eyes that matched Nicky's.

Sam Franklin. The only man Allison had ever loved.

Pick up STORYBOOK ROMANCE
in October 2013 wherever Love Inspired® Books are sold.

Love Inspired HISTORICAL

Eve Pickering knows what it's like to be judged because of your past. So she's not about to leave the orphaned boy she's befriended alone and unprotected in this unfamiliar Texas town. And if Chance Dawson's offer of shelter is the only way she can look after Leo, Eve will turn it into a warm, welcoming home for the holidays. No matter how temporary it may be—or how much she's really longing to stay for good....

Chance came all the way from the big city to make it on his own in spite of his secret...and his overbearing rich family. But Eve's bravery and caring is giving him a confidence he never expected—and a new direction for his dream. And with a little Christmas luck, he'll dare to win her heart as well as her trust—and make their family one for a lifetime.

Texas Grooms

A Family for Christmas

by

WINNIE GRIGGS

Available October 2013 wherever
Love Inspired Historical books are sold.

Find us on Facebook at
www.Facebook.com/LoveInspiredBooks

LIH82983

Love Inspired®
SUSPENSE
RIVETING INSPIRATIONAL ROMANCE

FALL FROM GRACE by **MARTA PERRY**

Teacher Sara Esch helps widower Caleb King comfort his daughter who witnessed a crime. But then Sara gets too close to the truth and Caleb must risk it all for the woman who's taught him to love again.

DANGEROUS HOMECOMING by **DIANE BURKE**

Katie Lapp needs her childhood friend Joshua Miller more than ever when someone threatens her late husband's farm. Katie wants it settled the Amish way...but not everyone can be trusted. Can Joshua protect her...even if it endangers his heart?

RETURN TO WILLOW TRACE by **KIT WILKINSON**

Lydia Stoltz wants to avoid the man who courted her years ago. But a series of accidents startles their Plain community...and leads her straight to Joseph Yoder. At every turn, it seems their shared past holds the key to their future.

DANGER IN AMISH COUNTRY,
a 3-in-1 anthology including novellas by
MARTA PERRY, DIANE BURKE and
KIT WILKINSON

Available October 2013 wherever
Love Inspired Suspense books are sold.

Find us on Facebook at
www.Facebook.com/LoveInspiredBooks

LIS44558